Accidental Arrival

BOOK ONE OF THE
WATER STONE TRILOGY

Lutricia H. Barnett

Book design by Lutricia H. Barnett

Lutricia H. Barnett Books are available for
order through Ingram Press Catalogues

Lutricia H. Barnett
Visit my website at www.lutriciahbarnett.com

Printed in the United States of America
First Printing: December 2015
Published by Sojourn Publishing, LLC

ISBN: 978-1-62747-186-2
Ebook ISBN: 978-1-62747-187-9

First and foremost, a huge thanks to Ewing and Trey. I could not have finished the story without your constant support and encouragement. Ewing, I do not even want to remember how many times I asked you to read, reread, and then read again. Trey, the website is amazing. Pat Smith, thank you for supporting the book signing and for your boundless enthusiasm. Melinda and Dan, thank you for hosting the best book signing party a girl could ever imagine. Chris and Whitney, thank you for the perfect picture. And to my writing buddy, Alyssa, you're next.

This story is written for my sister, Debra, who always had a book in her hand, on the bedside table, in her bag, reserved at the library, and in the passenger seat of the car. She loved to read.

If there is magic on this planet, it is contained in the water.
-Loren Eisley

Jokull wrapped his knee-length midnight blue coat against the suspended concrete dust as he walked across the cracked and frayed rubble of destroyed buildings toward the elderly man standing next to a swarm of erratic flashing lights. If Grier, head of The Accordance, is on the planet and is the person delivering the news, then it... "Why are they here?" Jokull asked, swatting the back of his hand through the darting lights.

Grier turned toward the frantic swarm, and said with a half-bow, "Alert the others." Turning back to Jokull, he waited until the Seren were out of sight before saying, "They found her body here, beneath the rubble. I wanted to inform you in person."

"Pesky interfering life form," Jokull said, his jaw clenching, amplifying his angular features. "You were the one who gave her permission to assist with this mission even though you knew the danger."

"Orlaith understood. She accepted the risks. Her oath to The Accordance was always steadfast and selfless," Grier said, his voice cracking on the last word.

"Ah, yes," Jokull sneered, balling his hands into fists. "The Accordance and their antiquated policies and procedures."

"Those policies and procedures were put in place for exactly this type of situation," Grier said, looking around at the destroyed city. "Something was smoldering in the background, stalling the reveal at every step. We have no idea why this happened or what group is responsible. Rest assured–I will find out."

"Did she tell you she was pregnant?" Jokull asked, almost shaking now. "This was our chance to make a new life for ourselves."

"I loved her too," Grier whispered. "We all loved her."

Jokull began to evanesce; a deep, bluish-red color wavering down the full-length of his incorporeal body.

Grier's back stiffened. "Jokull, if you take this path then you can never..."

In a snap of rage, Jokull hurled his vaporous body directly at his former mentor, stopping just before passing all the way through Grier's solid form, and then stepping backward.

Grier's lifeless body dropped into a jumble of arms and legs on the top of the rubble, an acrid smell of singed hair saturating the air.

δ^+

Wait! This makes no sense. How did I get here? I ran up the four or five rough-hewn, broad granite steps flanked on both sides by grassy knolls to catch the person who'd stepped out from the water next to me, carefully avoiding the slimy patches on the uneven surface. I'd left my flip-flops next to the creek at the lake house. "Excuse me," I said, tapping his shoulder. He turned, and a pair of steady green eyes met mine. I felt a flush in my chest.

Crap! I didn't expect him to be my age. Earlier this morning, knowing I wouldn't see anyone that I cared about, I'd skipped the usual morning shower. The downside: lifeless, mousy-brown hair hung flat against my face. "Sorry to bother you," I said, running a hand through the long strands. "I guess I zigged when I should've zagged. I have no idea where I landed."

"Arden," he said. He had a look on his face. A look that said he was about to deliver unwelcome news. I knew because I'd seen that look more than once this past year.

"Arden, with an A," I said, keeping my voice level. "Never heard of it. What country?"

"Country?" he said, sounding confused.

"Lachlan!"

We both turned in the direction of that determined voice. The guy on the top landing wore a crisp military-style uniform and had his hair tied back with a leather cord just like the guy I'd stopped. Standing in a sunny spot, the fabric of his uniform appeared to pixelate. "Everyone awaits your arrival," he said, waving his hand in the universal 'get a move on' gesture.

"Never mind," I said, blinking to try and bring the fabric into focus. "You've obviously got something more important to do. I'll go ask someone else." Before he could speak, I turned and ran up the remaining granite steps in the opposite direction, stopping on the grassy knoll. "One, two, three," I whispered before glancing over my shoulder. I watched as they disappeared into the crowd of shoppers, relieved that I'd never see him again.

The quaint little village before me spread out into a fan of sunlit lanes nestled between the cottage-style shops draped in lush foliage from the surrounding trees. The pattern and stonework in the plaza felt European to me as did a grouping of three immense standing stones at this end of the village; the visual weight of the capstones outlined against the bright blue sky was impressive. This was the kind of place you could wander around and lose track of time. But time was not a luxury I had right now. I needed to know my precise location before stepping back into the water if I was going to make it to the lake house in time for supper.

I walked past the elongated, diamond-paned, windowed storefront filled with furniture, carpets, and glassware. Veering left, I scooted around the overgrown tree roots shifting the neatly laid bricks in the stonework, catching a spray of cool mist from a nearby water fountain. I made my way to the open-air marketplace, the air loud with lively conversation. Unlike the more traditional style of the shops bordering the plaza periphery, the marketplace had a Renaissance festival feel in design, color, and theme. I approached a pudgy, matronly woman wrapping a bouquet of lime green flowers in brightly colored, thick wax paper. I'd never seen flowers in that shade of green before.

"Hello," I said, extending a hand, deciding to take a more formal approach. "Emily Harrison."

The woman placed the flowers on the tabletop next to several bundles of flowers tied with twine and wiped her hands on her muslin work apron. "Good day, Emily," she said, taking both of my hands into hers. "I am Metta, which means *pearl*."

How very strange that she said her name meant, *pearl*. Maybe she's in character for the festival. "Ah…I must've taken a wrong turn. I ended up here. Not exactly sure where here is. I left my cell phone at the lake house. Do you have a phone I can borrow?"

"I am sorry. I do not own one of those cell phones you speak of."

"GPS locator?" I asked. "I know this is Arden. What I don't know is what country or what continent. Did I land somewhere in Europe?"

"Oh, dearie," she said with a smile. "Arden is not a country, it is a planet."

I was at a loss for words. That rarely happens. "Hmm. What! Planet…?"

"Yes. What planet are you from?" she asked like it was a perfectly normal question to ask a stranger.

"Earth," I whispered, leaning forward. "Are you in character for the festival?"

She looked a bit confused. "And in what galaxy is Earth located?"

"Well…as we both know, Earth is located in the Milky Way Galaxy."

"If this is true," she said, wringing her hands as if she was looking for assistance. "Then perhaps you should come inside the flower shop with me."

"I just need to know where I landed so that I can get my bearings before stepping back into the water. I don't want to be late for supper." Not exactly sure why I said that. It was a funny thing really. Maybe it was because I wanted her to know that at some point I'd be missed.

"Let me think," Metta said. "You traveled to Arden with the water?"

"Yes. I traveled with the water," I said, keeping my voice steady. "How else would I get here?"

"Earth is familiar with water travel," she continued. "On Arden, we travel with the water to planets in our galaxy and also to planets in other galaxies."

I exhaled sharply. "Other planets…other galaxies." This festival thing was getting old.

"Yes," she said. "Please step inside the flower shop. Together we will get to the bottom of your predicament."

"Can't you just whisper in my ear what continent I'm on?" Maybe it was old-fashioned fear kicking into gear, not the self-created insecure kind I'm prone to. No, this was the necessary fear that keeps you alive by alerting you to danger. "Hmm, never mind," I said, wondering why I was even bothering being polite to a crazy person. "Thank you."

I turned, and headed back to the large pool of water at the bottom of the broad granite steps, focusing intently on the creek behind the lake house in Rabun County, Georgia, on the North American continent. I'd been taught from a young age that the most important step in water travel is determination.

"Rabun County…Georgia…North America," I muttered, quickening my pace.

As I passed the diamond-paned, windowed storefront, a familiar something caught my eye; a symbol pounded into a copper circle in the top left-hand corner of the sign in front of the shop. It was the exact symbol chiseled into the flat surface of Pop's crazy singing stone. I stopped walking, my heart pounding in sync with the wildly flapping banners sprinkled up and down the plaza periphery.

That was odd for a dozen different reasons.

Metta appeared by my side.

"What does that symbol mean?" I asked, pointing a finger at the hanging wooden sign. "The one inside of that copper circle."

"That is the symbol for Arden," she said, looking relieved to have a reference point. "Each planet in The Accordance is assigned a unique symbol."

I reached around and pulled Pop's stone from the back pocket of my denim cut-offs. "You mean like this?" I said, opening my hand.

Even Metta couldn't hide the shocked look in her eyes. "Emily, I think it is very important for you to come to the flower shop with me. I will contact those who will assist us."

I couldn't have agreed more.

δ^+

I sat on the wooden stool at the marred wooden counter inside the flower shop, staring out through the wavy, leaded glass window at the distorted shoppers milling around the village. I'm not going to say that I wasn't petrified. I was petrified, but pushed aside those thoughts the moment they entered my mind. Metta had poured me a mug of sweet-smelling tea. She was right; it did help. The mug gave me something to hold onto so that she wouldn't notice my hands were still shaking. I felt it imperative to look calm on the outside because I was about to wet my pants.

After a few tense moments, I recognized the symptoms of delayed shock sinking in. But I also felt something else mixed in with the shock: excitement. Most of the exciting things in our lives scare us to death—they wouldn't be exciting if they didn't. Still, I kept reminding myself that if I was, in fact, a stranger in a strange land, I needed to keep my wits about me. I had one chance to get this right.

The shop smelled familiar. I glanced around at the buckets and vases covering the brickwork floors stuffed with flowers in the most unusual shapes and colors. I recognized several general flower types and also noted some subtle differences. Then I told myself to stop reading between the lines. I focused again on the shoppers distorted by the wavy, leaded-glass window. At least this way I didn't feel so out of place.

The tiny bell on the flower shop door tinkled. A man and a woman walked into the shop. Not sure how Metta contacted them. They definitely knew something. I watched as the woman ran a hand over her meticulously coiled, lightly dusted gray hair, making sure everything was in place for a proper first introduction. The older balding man stepped forward cautiously. "I am Paden, which means *regal*," he said with a short bow.

The woman quietly approached me. "I am Nairne which means *tree river*."

My heart was thumping so fiercely that I could hear it in my throat. "Emily," I said, glaring at them over the rim of the mug. No idle chit-chat on my part.

The man clearly held a position of authority because I saw both Nairne and Metta defer to him with their eyes. "I want to welcome you to the planet Arden," he said.

Straight to the point; I liked that. "There aren't any planets near Earth named Arden," I said, dazed as the insane words passed my lips. "The only other planets near Earth are boiling hot or completely frozen. No one lives there. What the hell is going on here?" I concentrated on breathing properly, ignoring the feeling of dread in the pit of my stomach.

"You are not in your galaxy," Paden said, trying to convince me with his eyes that he meant every word. "You are in the Triangulum Galaxy."

I slammed the mug on the wooden counter, splashing hot tea over both of my hands. "How's this possible?"

"I know you are familiar with water travel," Paden said, his eyes widening.

"On Earth. I already went through this with Metta." I felt the blood begin to throb in my temples again.

"Then you understand that your molecules rearrange into energy, and this energy merges with the cohesive forces between the spinning water molecules." I nodded once to let him know that I understood. "And if you put yourself in the right frame of mind, you may step into a source of flowing water on your planet, fall into this cohesiveness, and travel anywhere on the planet with a source of flowing water."

"That's exactly my point. I was distracted when I jumped into the water. I know it's a big no-no, but well, I messed up." I tried not to look either guilty or sorry.

"By grasping the universal cohesive property of the water, we take this concept one step further," he continued. "Flowing water on all blue planets throughout the Universe is linked by a universal quantum cohesiveness."

I'm pretty sure I wasn't blinking. "Earth is covered in water, above and below the ground. There's no water in space."

"You are correct." Paden paused, rubbing his chin, thinking a thought. "Perception plays a big part. If you perceive the Universe as endless, and the distance between galaxies as void of flowing water, then you cannot put yourself into the right frame of mind. To us, the expanse between galaxies is insignificant because the distance is not what matters; it is your understanding of the size of the distance that counts."

"Voyaging with the water to blue planets in different galaxies is a normal condition of the Universe," Nairne added with a cautious smile. "It is just not yet what constitutes physical reality on Earth."

"No kidding," I muttered.

Paden reached down and touched a small dent in the wooden counter. A basketball size mass of whirring smoke materialized out of thin air. I jerked up so quickly that I almost fell off of the stool. "There are an infinite number of undiscovered planets in the Universe with flowing water and breathable air," Paden said before I had a chance to lose my composure.

As he spoke, the smoke inside of the whirring mass cleared, revealing hundreds of planets flying in and out of view. I couldn't believe my eyes. This village seemed so backward, but no…you touch a stupid dent, on a stupid wooden countertop, and a holographic image appears out of nowhere.

"Whenever we locate a blue planet such as Earth, the planet is placed under our guardianship," Paden said like it's a normal everyday occurrence to find a blue planet populated with humans.

As he spoke, the whirring smoky mass inside of the hologram dissolved and then re-formed, displaying a wavering image of Earth rotating on its axis. I was numb as I stared at the silent image, the skin on my forearms tingling as tiny pulses of alarm darted over it. They know about Earth and even have images. I was in deep and serious trouble here.

"Our mission," he continued, "is to assist planets unaware of intergalactic water travel to technologically and artistically prepare for mergence with The Accordance. If they so choose."

"Wait. Hold on," I said, waving a hand. "You're telling me that one day Earth will know about this…what did you call it…intergalactic water travel?"

"Yes," Paden said, folding his arms across his chest.

"When?" My tone left no doubt that I expected an answer.

"In due time," he said. "Many more factors must be in place before this step occurs."

It became clear that he wouldn't divulge any more details on this particular topic for now. Too bad he didn't know that I don't give up that easily either. "All right…all right, for arguments sake, let's say I believe you. I want to go home." I could not possibly put into words how I felt, thankful that my voice sounded steady even though my insides were doing back-flips.

"We can escort you back to Earth close to the time you entered the water," Paden said.

"Escort! I need an escort," I said. Although, if this Paden fellow is correct, and I couldn't believe that I actually believed this crap, then it's not the typical hop, skip, and a jump I'm used to on Earth.

"It is unwise to travel between galaxies without prior calculations," Paden said with a most unusual look in his eyes. "The fact that you traveled here to Arden, and not…"

"Where?" I demanded, bolting up from the stool so quickly that I almost bumped into a girl, a year or two younger than I, walking into the flower shop carrying a bundle of clothing in her arms.

"Oh," Nairne said looking startled. "Emily, I would like to introduce my daughter, DeRenne, which means *valley of red rock*."

This DeRenne girl gave me a quick smile. "Mother sent word of your arrival. She thought you might require some shoes." Out from beneath the bundle, appeared a pair of fairly new, leather skimmers.

I turned to Nairne, stunned. It's true. Compared to the whimsical patterns and bright colors in this place, I felt half-naked dressed in denim cut-offs, a white camisole, and barefoot. But how? How did Nairne contact her? And for that matter, how did Metta contact Paden and Nairne? I never saw anyone pick up a device or hear Metta say the words, "Paden you need to come to the flower shop, a strange girl just walked out from the water." Oh well, just another unsolved mystery added to the ever-growing list.

I surprised myself and took the shoes from DeRenne's hand. "Thank you," I said, dropping the skimmers on the brickwork floor. I ran the sole of my right foot against the back of my calf and slipped my foot into the shoe. And then did the same with my left foot. In a crazy way, I felt more confident. "Now what?"

"That is entirely your decision," Paden said. "We will not keep you against your will. However, I would like for you to consider staying on Arden long enough for us to answer all of your questions."

"I am happy to assist," DeRenne said. I looked deep into her soft green eyes and saw no deceit whatsoever.

My stomach dropped…Mom. She thinks I'm cleaning the storage shed behind the lake house. She'd freak out if she thought someone abducted me or that I decided to up and leave or that I went somewhere besides the usual places without telling her. "I'm not staying for long. My mother will miss me."

"Why yes, Emily," Nairne said with a pleasant smile. "Mothers throughout the Universe worry about their children." I saw DeRenne roll her eyes, a little. Good to know that moms, even in other galaxies still embarrass their children.

Paden got to his feet and said with a short bow, "I wish to extend an invitation for you to dine at my home this evening." Man, they're so formal around here. "We are earnest in our desire for you to understand who we are and to ensure your safe arrival home to Earth."

I knew I needed more information. If I was going to get this story out, and that'd be the first thing I did when I got back to Earth, would anyone believe me if I didn't have any evidence to support it? Would I even believe myself for that matter?

Leaning toward yes, I couldn't deny that I felt both petrified and elated at the idea of staying. Even thinking for the briefest moment the completely, and I do mean the completely outlandish idea that I'd landed on a planet in a different galaxy, absolutely thrilled me.

"Fine," I exhaled, knowing full well I'd done things in my life that made less sense.

δ^+

The setting sun turned the sky a smoky blue, the shadows in the lanes between the cottage-style shops transitioning from a slate gray to black. Statuesque gas lamps along the plaza periphery cast flickering light across the intricate stonework. Dodging the last of the shoppers, Paden, Nairne, DeRenne, and I walked beneath a massive stone archway carved from an enormous chunk of limestone connected a maze of leafy green passageways.

The temperature dropped dramatically once we entered the passageway, cooled by the water rushing down the culverts on either side of the path, obscured by the hedges lining the corridor. The neatly trimmed foliage, absolutely quivering with thousands of winking and flashing specks of light completed the unreal ambiance to this day.

"Emily, I hope you do not mind if I join you tonight," DeRenne said walking beside me, evening sunlight glinting off of her wheat-colored curls. "I imagine if the situation were reversed, I would want someone close in age to accompany me." She hesitated before adding, "I would consider it an honor to escort you around Arden."

"Thanks for the offer and thanks for the shoes. If I'd know I was traveling to a planet in a different galaxy, I would've done a better job packing."

"Yes," she said, barely suppressing a grin. "Intergalactic water travel requires a minimum of at least one change of clothing." Nairne glanced over her shoulder, smiling. I smiled back.

At the end of this passageway, an ancient, solitary standing stone stood sentinel inside of its circular, stacked-stone retaining wall. The thickness and complexity of the surrounding foliage implied that the plants in this area were here first and that the other passageways were added as the village grew. We veered right at the fork in front of the standing stone to a wide side corridor.

"You know, I envy you," DeRenne said, her feather earrings swaying in step.

"Seriously. You envy me, a stranger in a strange land?" I again fought stubbornly against the conclusion I was now considering even though I couldn't come up with any other conclusion that did a better job explaining the last hour to this point.

"Or, someone who is about to hear the most incredible story of their life," she said, and I saw a faraway look in her eyes. "I would gladly trade places with you right now."

I thought about that for a second. "Well, I hope you're right."

"I am," she said with a nod.

We walked through the corridor to a tree-lined street. I noted the architectural style on Arden had no sharp angles but more soft rounded lines. Well-manicured paths led to covered entryways at each of the houses painted in muted colors with sloping slate roofs and multi-paned windows fashioned in a variety of geometric shapes.

Paden stepped onto the stone stoop at the second house on the left, opened a wide plank door with sidelight windows, and moved aside so the three of us could pass. A petite woman with endearing eyes and silver hair swept to the side greeted us in the brightly lit foyer. I had the feeling she expected us even though, once again, I never heard anyone say anything to anyone about leaving the flower shop and coming here. Maybe Metta somehow got word to her after we left.

"Emily, this is my wife Ccri, which means *loved one*," Paden said, shutting the door behind him. Great, another name and another meaning—I didn't know if I could keep it all straight in my head.

"Welcome to our home, Emily," Ccri said. "I know you must be confused. So much has happened in a short time. Please come in, and have a seat." In a kind gesture, she touched my elbow and escorted me to an open-space living area at the back of the house.

Wow! The front of the house in no way hinted at the expansive interior. You couldn't tell where the indoors ended and the outdoors began, one simply flowing into the other. Their home conveyed formalness; high interior walls with exposed rafters, overstuffed furniture, and thick carpets covering the flagstone floors.

Ccri directed me to a tufted and tasseled chair next to a stacked-stone fireplace with a traditional carved marble mantle, the last of the smoldering wood chunks in the grate glowing amber. DeRenne dropped the bundle of clothing on a small settee and sat in the tub chair next to mine giving me yet another reassuring smile. She is right; I did feel better having her along.

The five of us now settled into a tidy circle around the fireplace, I decided to go for it. What did I have to lose? "Why all the secrecy?" I asked.

"I am not sure if secrecy is the correct word," Paden said. "Government officials in various countries on Earth have firsthand knowledge of our existence and future plans."

I felt nauseated. I digested that extraordinary tidbit of before saying rather harshly, "Why don't we all know?" I wanted them to understand that this was unacceptable on so many levels. DeRenne looked mortified so I guess I'd made my point.

"We dedicate our lives," Paden continued before I had a chance to completely wig out, "guiding civilizations on blue planets with human inhabitants toward mergence, and the eventual reveal of intergalactic water travel. We prefer to work behind the scene, nudging along the humans on each planet without interfering with the natural ebb and flow of their society."

I glared at Paden without saying a word. He held a hand up in a defensive position, sensing my distress, before saying, "Our one desire is to improve the quality of life and decrease illness. I am sure you studied the reveal of water travel on Earth."

"Mandatory for all middle schoolers," I said, still glaring.

The revelation of water travel changed everything. It also just about destroyed the entire human civilization. The economy tanked. The automotive and airline industries were classic examples. Personal cars and air travel were obsolete the very next day which meant so were manufacturers and suppliers, salesmen, mechanics, and on and on. About a third of the population lost their jobs in one fell swoop.

The ripple effect was widespread, more far-reaching than anyone anticipated. Real estate plummeted. The mass exodus of entire populations from one continent to another continent resulted in hoarding and infighting, crime skyrocketed.

The process was announced and explained on the internet by a group of scientists from MIT, who also explained the mishaps. No one listened. Everyone ran outdoors, jumped into the water, and either got wet or lost. A waterproof GPS device became mandatory. People needed to find their way home and keep track of their children.

I'd been taught from a young age to both fear and respect the water, to have a clear focus. Dad always asked, 'Emily, are you swimming or traveling?' "Swimming," I'd squeal, jumping full-length into the waves at the beach.

There were positive changes; a single global currency for one. Somehow, the banks were prepared, almost like they had first-hand knowledge. And now I know they did. School field trips took on a whole new meaning. Without storage costs, food prices dropped, and people had enough to eat. Fewer vehicles, because people still needed to transport their belongings from one place to another, meant burning less fossil fuel, which meant less pollution, which meant less greenhouse gasses. For the first time in several hundred years, the planet was on its way to healing itself. All of this happened when I was too young to remember. "You're responsible for the reveal?" I asked.

"If certain factors were not already in place, the fallout from the reveal would have been even more devastating," Paden said. "You cannot put things back like they were before. To add intergalactic water travel at the same time, the results…"

"And exactly how do you go about mentoring Earth?" I interrupted, the words coming out more sharply than I intended.

"Metta informed me that your stone is marked with Arden's symbol, which means the stone originally came from here," Paden said.

Okay, that comment went way past ludicrous. I sat back in the chair. "You're telling me that Pop's crazy singing stone is from Arden."

"May I see the stone?" Paden requested politely as if it's a perfectly common occurrence for someone to literally drop out of the sky and have a connection to the place where they landed.

I pulled the stone from the back pocket of my denim cut-offs and handed it to DeRenne, who handed it to Paden. I kept my face expressionless, or at least I hoped it looked that way.

"Mentors from Arden relocate to Earth in an effort to guide the inhabitants toward mergence," Paden said, placing the stone in the middle of the small wooden table to his left. "Who owned this stone?"

The smoky, whirring holographic image materialized. I wondered if every table or counter had one. An eccentric looking, elderly man dressed in vibrant colors with shoulder-length, snow white hair hovered inside of the image. He looked vaguely familiar.

"Daileass," said a disembodied voice. The arrow on the creep-o-meter swung right at the sound of that eerie voice but I kept my composure.

"His mission?" Paden asked.

"Daileass assisted the thirteen original American Colonies to establish the first Democratic Political System," the monotone voice droned. "He signed an important document, The Declaration of Independence, devoting his life guiding the members of the newly formed Assembly in its wording."

"His Earth name?" Paden asked.

"Benjamin Franklin," said the disembodied voice.

"What! I'm...I'm...related to Benjamin Franklin. He...he fathered two sons and one daughter. She's my great, great aunt or something. Pop always said this stone belonged to him...but I thought he'd made that part up." And then it hit me. "Wait! You're telling me that Benjamin Franklin is from Arden? And exactly why would anyone leave their life here on Arden to what... to live and guide the inhabitants on Earth?" I air-quoted that last part.

"We consider it an honor to guide and steer civilizations toward mergence," Nairne said with a pleasant smile.

"Yeah right," I muttered. Did they really think I'd buy this crapola? Although I can't really deny there were lots of holes and gaps in Benjamin Franklin's whereabouts, and that his work with optics and electricity seemed way ahead of its time and...

"Emily, at any time did your blood soak this stone?" Paden asked in a normal tone of voice.

The arrow on the creep-o-meter swung to the far right, landing on the extreme setting, quivering. Why would he even ask such a question? Unfortunately, I had a possible answer for him. "I think…maybe. Pop recently passed," I said, tasting the grief in the back of my throat. "I'd gathered some of his special belongings to make a shadow box, a memory box, for my mom. I was washing a few items in the kitchen sink and cut my finger along the edge of an arrowhead. Maybe some of my blood soaked it then. But it's blood, on basically a rock. What's the big deal?" I made a concerted effort not to look too horrified. From the expression on DeRenne's face, I wasn't doing a very good job.

"Since Daileass selected this stone, it is infused with his blood. Otherwise, honestly, I have no answer for you." Paden paused, drumming his fingers on the chair arm, lost in thought. "This issue requires further investigation."

Ya, think! And not just a tiny little explanation either. But a big giant explanation—big enough to satisfy an entire planet.

Paden slid the stone from the side table and stood up. He walked over and held his hand out. I took the stone from his hand, freaked out, and I do mean freaked out now that I knew Pop's stone had Benjamin Franklin's blood on it. And by the way, *EW!* Why do that?

"You don't need to keep it?" I asked, holding the stone in midair between my thumb and forefinger.

"No, the necessary information is now stored," Paden said. "I will consult with others who may have more knowledge on this topic."

"All right, all right," I said, shoving the stone deep into the back pocket of my denim cut-offs. "How close is Earth to this intergalactic mergence?"

"Closer than you might think," Paden said. "How many of your Earth years since the reveal?"

"About thirteen," I answered.

"Then perhaps, less than a couple of hundred years."

"Let's face it, when I get back, I will be speaking with someone in charge." I dropped my eyelids so they couldn't see the plan in my eyes, although I suspect everybody was already thinking the same thought.

"Again, mergence is not a simple discussion," Paden said. "I can assure you that if you choose to stay on Arden for a few days, very little time on Earth will pass."

I looked at DeRenne for support. She gave me a faint smile, nodding.

"While traveling with the water through galaxies," Paden started again before I could finish my thought, "time bends, contracts or lengthens depending on the direction and the speed of travel. What is an hour here on Arden could correlate to seconds back on Earth."

"Like time travel," I whispered, wishing it could be true.

"Not time travel, time bending," Paden said. "We can perform a series of calculations, and estimate the length of time you will appear to be gone from Earth during your stay here on Arden."

"I'm not staying long," I said for the second time.

"Understandable, dear," Ccri said giving Paden a stern look. "Perhaps you would like to rest and change clothes before supper. We can continue our discussion then."

I folded my arms across my chest, looking at each of them in turn, seeing if I could detect, oh, I don't know, perhaps a group delusion, mass hysteria, or something similar. But honestly, I saw four people who looked as bewildered as I'm sure I did. Can't really argue with that.

"I agree," I said, getting up from the chair. I could see I was getting nowhere, a headache welling in the back of my neck. I needed some alone time to gather my thoughts and formulate a plan.

DeRenne rose from her chair and gathered the bundle of clothing in her arms. "You know which room," Ccri said to DeRenne, and I saw a look pass between them.

I ran a hand through my hair a couple of times, and faked a polite southern smile. "I would say, 'Thank you and nice to meet you', but..."

"We fully comprehend," Nairne said in an assuring tone.

They had no idea how I felt. I wanted to keep it that way.

I followed DeRenne down a long, flagstone hallway softly lit by hanging sconces, to the front of the house. She entered the last door on the right, pausing for a second, brushing her fingertips on the door jamb. Tiny lights, woven into the grasscloth covering the walls inside of the room glowed brighter. I'm sure...yet again...I looked dazed and confused.

"Nanoprisms," DeRenne said, "woven into the paper, connected to solar panels on the roof."

"Cool," I mumbled, lingering on the threshold, dumbstruck by yet another piece of advanced technology in this seemingly backward place.

DeRenne walked over to a canopy bed draped with white gauzy fabric. This was clearly a girl's bedroom. She opened her arms, and the bundle of clothing tumbled across the quilted coverlet. "Now that I have met you, I see that we are similar in size." She started sorting the clothing into piles. "Let me know how these fit tonight at supper. If there is anything else you might require I can bring more items in the morning."

"I'd better be in my own bed in the morning," I said, feeling my anger rising.

"There is a warm bath," she said, nodding left, and ignoring my discomfort.

I'm not sure how I didn't notice until now. A huge floor-to-ceiling exposed rock outcrop and a bubbling pool of water covered the entire back corner of the room. Tucked into the various nooks and crannies running up and down the craggy rock wall were a variety of fluted-edge, glass bowls in bright primary colors filled to the brim with small glistening beads. Sweet-smelling, yellow flowers twisted and twined around the massive structure. The whole thing looked like something you'd find in a high-end spa at a fancy resort, not in the bedroom to the right at the end of the hall.

"The glass bowls are filled with bathing salts and shampoo," she said. "The water is siphoned from a hot spring underneath the house. You will be surprised how soft your skin feels after soaking for a few minutes."

I felt drained, empty, to the point that the thought of a warm soak in that crazy rock bathtub sounded like a good idea. "Does everyone here wear only long dresses?" I asked.

"No, we have our mission uniforms," DeRenne said, and then went stiff as if maybe she said something she shouldn't have.

"Hmm," I said, running a hand up and down the door jamb, *bright, dim, bright, dim*, pretending not to notice her mistake, filing away that tidbit for a later discussion.

"Decide on something to wear for now," she said, flicking the long curls over her shoulder. "We will most likely eat outside. The weather turns cool at night."

I walked to the bed. DeRenne had arranged the clothing into three piles; dresses, belts and shoes, and a white linen, lace-collared nightgown and robe. I ran a finger down a lavender-colored dress in the same shade as my eyes. "You don't even know me…"

"I understand," she said, touching my arm in a reassuring gesture. "I have known about intergalactic water travel my entire life, seen so many outrageous places. Yet every day, I am still amazed. I know what we are saying seems absolutely unbelievable to you. I want to assure you that it is not."

I let out a sharp breath. "I'm trying not to overthink today but my mind just keeps going around and around the same questions. I did want to get outta there, from the lake house I mean. Not to…"

"A planet in a different galaxy," DeRenne said, eyebrows raised. She scooted into the small space between the piles of clothing and the headboard, leaning against a huge pillow with tangerine piping. I crawled onto the bed near the foot rail, holding onto the corner post for strength and support. She took a moment to gather her thoughts. "As recently as yesterday, I traveled with my brother to a deserted planet, could not even tell you where, not that it matters, dumbstruck by how similar the basic design of plant life is from one end of the Universe to the other, profoundly moved by the far-reaching commonality of the water. So yesterday, I saw something new, unexpected. You need to prepare yourself for this. Around here, it is a normal everyday occurrence."

"Point taken. But putting your blood on a stone! Did you do that?" I asked, a bit guarded

"Absolutely. Never considered not pricking my finger. It is an important part of the choosing ceremony with your family. When I saw the shocked look on your face, it made me decide to research into why. Yes, it leaves your DNA on the stone. However, that is accomplished by simply by touching the stone. So what is the significance?"

"Clearly, I have no idea," I said meeting her gaze. "I'm still trying to wrap my head around the fact that there are officials in my government who know about The Accordance and intergalactic water travel."

"Again, although it seems unfair to you, I can tell you a nudge creates a ripple, and a ripple turns into a wave. Mergence is a hugely complex process, thousands of years in the making. There are numerous examples where the reveal ended in disaster. The Accordance has a strict set of guidelines to ensure the transition occurs smoothly for the unique occupants of each planet."

"Still, I'm not going to lie. The whole thing pisses me off."

"I do understand. This is why Paden's request makes sense to me, and I hope to you."

"And how come everyone around here speaks and writes in English? How did it get from Earth to here?"

"Actually, it came from here to Earth. Our English is a variant of the language spoken by the first travelers to this part of the Universe and thus, the language of The Accordance. We can verify this fact at The Assemblage. I am sure the first mentors to Earth introduced it to the planet so their families with small children could easily assimilate into the society without attracting too much attention." She rose from the bed, walked over to a set of wooden drawers built into the wall, and rummaged through the middle drawer.

"Here." She handed me a stack of pale pink, fluffy towels. "I can assure you a warm bath and some quiet time would help tremendously." DeRenne looked me directly in the eye. "There are times when you choose to believe something that would normally be considered absolutely irrational. Today is one of those times."

I took the towels from her and put them in my lap, but didn't get up from the bed. "Again, honestly, thanks."

"With pleasure," she said.

I watched as she walked toward the door, turn at the last moment, and smile before she left, quietly shutting the door behind her.

δ^+

I counted silently to ten, giving DeRenne enough time to walk all the way down the hall. I set the stack of towels to the side, hopped off of the bed, and walked to the door. I rested my head against the cool wood and listened. No one stood outside. Perfect. At least I was alone for the moment. I dashed over to a set of glass-paned doors on the opposite wall draped in gauzy fabric and pushed. The doors flew open, revealing a small hidden away courtyard with high-brick walls covered in creeping vines, two circular stone benches, a gurgling fountain, and a path leading away from the house. The sun hovered above the horizon, emitting enough light for me to see my way. I hurried down the moss-covered path until it forked. Left would take me to the front of the house and back to the passageway leading to the village. Good to know if for some reason I needed a quick escape. And right? No idea. I followed the well-worn path, wondering who'd walked this path so many times before me to an outdoor seating area defined by a curved brick edging. Paden, Ccri, and Nairne stood on the covered porch connected to the back of the house, talking. Too far away to hear their conversation, I had a pretty good idea about who and what they conversed. I smiled; the topic of my accidental arrival should keep them occupied for a time.

I took the path back to the courtyard, stopping once to make sure no one followed before walking into the room, shutting the glass-paned doors behind me. I looked in each of the wooden drawers, careful to close each one after I'd finished. Next, I opened the doors of a large wardrobe and found an extra pillow and a blanket on the top shelf. Finally, I knelt down, lifted the bed skirt, and looked underneath the bed. Not exactly sure what I expected to find but felt better for having looked. Satisfied, I went and sat on the stone ledge next to the bubbling pool of water, dipping a hand into the warm swirling water, the fragrant smell of the flowers soothing.

I needed to get a handle on today.

Thinking back to when this all started, I stood next to the creek at the lake house, reliving the emotional roller coaster ride from this past year, wishing that I could get as far away from here as possible. The words, 'Your father's having an affair', were followed by a totally unforeseen double-whammy. The other woman was Mom's best friend, Marge.

The divorce got messy–lots of lawyers, lots of paperwork, and a hurried move to Atlanta so Mom could assume some of the responsibilities caring for her ailing father. She needed a purpose and this one presented itself. Or, that's the excuse she used to convince me to move to Atlanta with her. My other option, living with Dad and Marge, wasn't working for me.

Mom threw herself into the role of a dutiful daughter, grateful to have her mind occupied. I offered to help but she kept saying, 'No, Emily. You've had more than your share of trauma this past year. Have fun. Be a kid. Enjoy life while you can.' Here's the rub: I was the adult this past year.

Pop died at the end of May, and all of a sudden, a second summer turned into a tailspin of complications. I never knew death and divorce generated so much legal work. Today, well if it's still today on Earth, Mom and I traveled to the lake house in Rabun County to start packing Pop's belongings.

We stepped out from the creek near the edge of the property late afternoon. Mom put the food in the refrigerator while I hauled in the boxes, packing paper, and tape that had been delivered to the front porch the day before. After our unannounced arrival, it took less than thirty minutes for her old ladies lake crew to appear at the door with several bottles of wine and looking for an afternoon to kill. The Divorce Squad could smell a recently wounded victim from ten miles away.

I volunteered to deal with the shed out back. I had the perfect excuse; I needed a few more items for my shadow box. Mom and I would discuss each item at length, remembering happier times in Atlanta and lazy summers spent here at the lake house. No one could argue with that. Right?

For some reason, I'd grabbed Pop's crazy singing stone from the kitchen table right before we'd left Atlanta. I can't think of a single time he didn't have it in his hand, tumbling the flat stone between his thumb and forefinger, lost in thought. He said that the stone belonged to Benjamin Franklin, didn't have any paperwork, just family stories. We always thought that the symbol chiseled across the flat surface was Native American in origin. He'd tell us that if you held the stone in your hand and stood near running water, you'd hear the music. Said that it reminded him of tiny silver bells ringing in the distance.

As his hearing went, the music faded but that never stop him from trying. He was stubborn in that way, and that's a trait I got from him.

Five boxes later, I'd found a few items to add to the shadow box. I wrapped each one carefully in packing paper and stashed them in the corner of the workbench. By the tone of their voices and the level of laughter from the screen porch on the back of the house, the moms were more than likely on their third glass of wine. There was no way I was going back inside the house. I'd just be fresh bait.

The whole process of sorting through someone's belongings from a happier time more difficult than anticipated, I decided a walk back to the creek, and then a quick trip to the dam to watch the sunset was a good idea. Mom wouldn't be at all surprised. I often did this. And, as an added benefit, I might run into some friends at their lake house for the weekend trying to get away from their parents too. I smiled; our sanctuary. At the very least it should buy me another two hours of solitude.

I headed out the door, and then promptly turned around. I pulled my cell phone from the back pocket of my denim cut-offs and stashed it next to the items I'd gathered for the shadow box. At least this way, I could honestly say that I left it in the shed and that's why I didn't answer the phone when she called. If she calls.

I followed the path to the edge of the property, admiring the sky tinged with pinkish-red light. Once I reached the creek, I kicked my flip-flops off, telling myself that it was a good plan to get as far away from here as possible. I jumped into the water feet-first.

Now that I think back, this voyage was different than any before; the crashing and colliding colors all around were so intense and vivid. But the passage of time is elusive when you are traveling through the water. You feel like you are in the water the same amount of time if you travel to a friend's house a couple of miles away or travel to Scotland for British Literature class. Maybe this time I just got lost in the colors and didn't notice. But I also have to admit that there was something strange toward the end of the voyage. First, I felt the weight of my body, never had that happen before, next there was that weird sense of emerging from the unfathomable deep water, and then that crazy push from behind.

I cringed. 'I have no idea where I landed.' The guy on the granite steps must think I'm an idiot. That entire episode was a big bucket full of awkward. Thankfully, I'll never see him again. Besides, I had too many pressing issues to deal with to concern myself with that one incident. Just forget the entire thing.

DeRenne was right; I did feel more relaxed after soaking in the warm swirling water and washing my hair with the peach-scented shampoo. I didn't realize there were two parts to her dress until I put it on. First a full-length sheath, and next a sheer overlay embroidered with iridescent metallic threads. The ethereal, light-weight dress was a perfect complement to this unreal place.

I went out to the courtyard to air dry my hair, twisting the long strands so they would curl. No more mousy brown, the red glints were back. As I stood there, I tried to dissect the last few hours, not coming up with any better explanation than the one offered to me.

On Earth, it's true that you can travel from one end of the planet to the other in the blink of an eye. So, is it really that much of a stretch to believe that there are other planets with flowing water—and I've seen one with my very own eyes—then is it possible to put yourself in the right frame of mind, and travel to said planet with the water?

Dressed and hair now dried, I went inside to check out the final effect in the mirror. I took a spin, admiring all angles of the iridescent dress, recognizing the brave face in the mirror masking the frightened face just below the surface. During my self-imposed alone time, I decided I'd listen respectfully to what Paden and the others had to say, and then kindly ask someone to escort me home. A faint smile crossed my lips; it certainly wasn't another boring weekend at the lake house. In the end, I did avoid the moms.

Mission accomplished on that front.

A soft knock on the door snapped me out of the trance. I made sure the doors to the courtyard were closed, and then walked across the room to the next part of the adventure. I paused for a second to muster a little courage before unlatching the door. Ccri stood in the hallway wearing a dove gray dress with pin tucks to the waist. "Emily dear, are you ready for supper?" she asked.

"Yes, I believe I am," I said, squeezing all ten toes in the leather skimmers.

We walked along the dimly lit hallway to the expansive open-space living area, and then out of the back of the house to the covered back porch filled with terracotta pots overflowing with herbs. I lifted the hem of the dress, feeling rather formal all things considered and stepped down the short flight of stairs, the fabric of the overlay crinkling with each step. I followed the lighted pathway lined with timbers and mature landscaping to a long, rectangular-shaped wooden table beneath the sweeping limbs of a mature tree alive with more winking and flashing specks of lights.

DeRenne walked up the short hill to meet me. She'd changed into a pumpkin orange dress with long sheer sleeves. Nairne was behind her dressed in a turquoise colored dress with an embroidered bodice. Paden stood on the outer edge of neatly trimmed grass next to the leafy forest talking to one of those fluttering lights. How crazy is that!

"DeRenne," I said, "Is Paden talking to one of those…"

"Ah, there you are, Lachlan," Nairne said.

I froze in my tracks. Did she just say, Lachlan? Not the guy on the steps. It can't be the same person. Maybe it's a really common name on Arden. Oh, please, please let it be a really common name here on Arden–and not him.

I turned slowly and then gulped.

"Emily," DeRenne said. "I would like to introduce you to my brother. This is Lachlan, which means *from the land of endless lakes*. Lachlan, this is Emily Harrison. Today she journeyed from Earth to Arden."

Absent the uniform, tonight he looked less intimidating dressed in an ivory linen shirt, loose-fitting brown pants, and soft leather boots laced to the calf. I saw the glimmer of recognition in his eyes; he knew the dress I was wearing belonged to DeRenne. "Nice to meet you," I said, trying to make my voice sound level, not too confident.

"Welcome to Arden," he said, a half-smile curving his lips. He nodded once, clearly wondering what game I was playing.

"Thanks," I mumbled, walking toward the table, making sure not to trip on the long dress.

"You three sit there," Nairne said, gesturing with her hand to the opposite side of the table.

I quickly chose the chair to DeRenne's left, which meant Lachlan had to sit in the chair across from us. At least this way, DeRenne could be my wingman. Paden sat at the opposite end of the table with Ceri to his right, which put Nairne next to her son.

I took a moment to take it all in, admiring the square-shaped glass plates on the top of the woven grass placemats, the long-stem crystal glasses filled with a dark orange liquid, and the tiny candles dotted up and down the expansive tabletop. The flickering light from the candles shimmered in the varied patterns inside of the glass plates that appeared to have more than one color at the same time. Paden started first, and then we passed the food family style. There were brightly colored ceramic bowls filled with an assortment of unusually shaped vegetables and mixed salad greens, a platter of roasted meat, and a basket of sliced bread. I tried not to load too much food on my plate. My stomach was suddenly and not unsurprisingly queasy.

Once the food made the circuit, I lifted the crystal glass and took a sip, a burst of ginger tingling the inside of my mouth. I quickly took another sip and let the liquid linger in my mouth. The taste, like Arden, was totally unexpected.

I had that strange feeling you get when someone is staring at you. I looked up to find Lachlan watching me with an odd expression. Before I had a chance to decipher his expression, he turned suddenly to ask his mother a question. I swallowed the liquid in my mouth. Okay, if that's how you want to play. Two can play at this game, and I'm in.

Our conversation stayed polite and around-the-edge of things. I could tell they avoided overloading me with the big issues, for now. For most of the meal, I decided to keep my head down, focusing on the food on my plate and on DeRenne, telling myself this can't be any more awkward than the day we found out that Dad was having an affair. Right?

This Lachlan fellow talked quietly with his mother and listened in on mine and DeRenne's conversation when he didn't think we would notice. He never once asked me a single question. By the end of the meal, I got the feeling that he considered me an insignificant bug from an inferior planet.

In my defense, I hadn't planned on traveling with the water to a planet in a different galaxy for a Saturday afternoon jaunt. Seriously, who would choose that? Okay, I would. But without this added drama. Still, I was unable to stop myself from looking at him every so often. When the coffee and dessert were served, I told myself only a few minutes more and this entire episode will be history.

I couldn't have been more wrong.

"Emily," Paden said, his gaze like a spotlight landing directly on me. "We calculated the time bending triangular relationship based on the distance from Earth to Arden, your probable route, and the estimated travel time. For you, a two-hour time span on Earth correlates to a passage of six Arden-weeks."

That concept was so farfetched that I couldn't begin to fathom if it was even possible. I looked to DeRenne for reassurance before saying, "Is this true?"

"Yes," she said, nodding her head vigorously. DeRenne set her fork on the table. She touched her hands together like a child saying their nightly prayers. "Think of Earth as sitting on the apex of an isosceles triangle and the length of my fingers as the two legs of the triangle. As you traveled with the water away from Earth, time expands equal to the width of the base of the triangle." Keeping her wrists touching, she opened her hands so that her fingers formed a wide V. "This measurement allows us to calculate the rate at which time expands or contracts."

"So the farther you travel, the more time bends?" I said, sounding like I needed to convince myself. Crap. Should've paid more attention in geometry.

"The route is extremely important," Paden said from his end of the table. "I am sure you understand that gravity is not a force that pulls on objects. Rather it is a curvature of space and time caused by the close proximity of massive objects such as planets, black holes, and stars." I forced myself to look at him and nodded once to let him know that I understood. "To the outside observer as something passes by one of these phenomena, it appears to be pulled towards that object."

"In reality, it is not being pulled at all. It is actually moving along the same straight line it was moving along before in empty space," he continued. "However, now this straight line looks curved to the observer due to gravity's warping of the underlying space-time continuum. If you bypass galaxies with fewer planets, black holes, and stars, then time does not lengthen as much. An experienced traveler wants to equalize the passage of time between their destination and arrival point, and carefully maps their route. They could also choose a route that lengthens time on the destination end if they want to spend more time mentoring a planet, and not miss too much time on their home planet."

I blinked twice, and said, "So you guys think that I…"

"Traveled a straight path between Earth and Arden," Paden said.

"Which means that I …"

"More than likely traveled through several galaxies crowded with planets, black holes, and stars. This, in turn, decreased the passage of time from your departure point, Earth."

"Sorry." I sat back in the chair. "I'm just having a hard time wrapping my head around all of this."

"Were you aware of the colors today as you voyaged with the water?" Ccri asked, sensing my distress.

"Yes. I've never experienced colors like that before," I whispered as every nuance from that unfathomable voyage showed on my face. "They were so intense, almost like the colors were alive." In my side vision, I saw Lachlan lift his head. He looked at me with what could be considered a rude stare. Or was it something else?

"As gravity slows time, the frequencies of visible light waves are affected," Paden said. "Light becomes bluer on one end of the spectrum as it approaches a massive object, and redder on the other end of the spectrum as it moves away from that object. Since you did experience the colors, this confirms what we suspected; you traveled a straight path between Earth and Arden."

"What about the music?" I asked.

"You heard music?" Lachlan asked in a hushed voice.

I couldn't believe he actually spoke to me. I turned toward him. The concentration of his gaze made me dizzy. "I…I think. More of a ringing, kind of like tiny silver sleigh bells, or maybe a tone is a better way to phrase it. Very, very faint."

"Vibrating strings of energy," he said, the lines around his mouth starting a smile. "Each string vibrates at its own frequency, producing a unique note."

"Emily," Paden said. It took a moment before I could look away. "The Universe is composed of these vibrating strings of energy, energy that has been combining and recombining since the beginning of time, implying that the connection between us and all matter in the Universe is actually quite common."

Some place in me recognized the concept. "So, have we circled back to perception?"

"Yes," Paden said, looking pleased. "Perception is the key. This is why it is important for you to consider staying on Arden for a few days so we can show you our world, and answer all of your questions."

He is persistent. And, I did have a million questions.

"Lachlan and DeRenne can serve as your guides," Nairne offered.

"That is perfect," DeRenne said, lightly touching my arm.

"As requested," Lachlan said in a flat voice, sounding more like a soldier accepting orders than a willing participant. I looked at him. His face had gone blank, except for a glint of something in his eyes.

I considered Paden's request. If what he is saying is true, and I was beginning to believe that it might be, then I needed to gather as much information about all of this as possible. "Aren't you afraid the first thing I'll do when I get back to Earth is tell anyone who will listen," I said for the second time. Come on, how could I keep my time here a secret?

"This is a real possibility," Paden said. "As we have explained, in the near future, all of Earth's inhabitants will know of our existence. Rest tonight and we can speak again in the morning."

When new evidence surfaces it demands that you change the conclusion you previously held. Besides, there are some roads you start down and can't turn back. I was already a hundred miles or so down this particular road. I stood up, placed the napkin on the tabletop, and said, "I agree."

Everyone followed suit, standing and clearing the table. DeRenne and I carried the plates, glasses, and empty bowls inside the house and put them in the sink to soak. Lachlan stayed outside with the adults. I found that a bit odd but not too surprising.

During each trip back and forth, making sure not to trip on the long dress, I didn't say much. Honestly, what else could I say? I appreciated that DeRenne respected my privacy.

The table cleared, Nairne and DeRenne each gave me a heartfelt hug and a few encouraging words. There was yet another awkward moment as Lachlan paused for a moment by the small pool of water formed by a bend in the shallow creek near the edge of the forest, seeking something to say in farewell. He finally inclined his head slightly, and said without making eye contact, "Pleasant rest."

Standing between Paden and Ccri, watching DeRenne, Nairne, and Lachlan vanish into the slowly moving current, I decided to move Lachlan to the top of my pay-no-mind list.

δ^+

Last night, after Paden and Ccri made sure that I had everything I needed and said their goodnights, I stood in the middle of the dark room wondering where in the world I'd found the courage to stay. What stopped me? The whole thing scared me enough to make me realize how stupid it'd be to step back into the water with no clear idea of which way to go. At the very least, I needed an idea of where the Triangulum Galaxy is located in reference to the Milky Way Galaxy.

This morning, I'd woken in a state of confusion, vaguely remembering that something was very wrong but couldn't, no correction, didn't *want* to remember what was wrong, convinced that the whole thing had to be a dream. Come on, traveling with the water to a planet in a different galaxy, holographic images, glowing wallpaper, ridiculous clothes. Unfortunately, I heard the water swirling in the bubbling pool and smelled fresh flowers. I also smelled fresh coffee. I pinched myself once and cracked an eye open. Everything was the same as the night before. I didn't imagine any of this.

I sat up and kicked the linen sheet to the side. From the angle of the sun streaming in through the window, I decided it was early morning. Good, I hadn't overslept and missed too much. I rubbed the sleep from my eyes and stepped into Day Two.

After inhaling three muffins, downing a mug of strong coffee, and participating in polite breakfast conversation, I now stood in the brightly lit foyer trying to look confident. "All passageways eventually lead back to the central plaza," Ccri said as she opened the wide plank door.

This entire morning was coming a little too fast for my liking. I took a step out of the door and then promptly turned around. "Left at the standing stone?"

"Yes." She paused, brushing back her silver hair before saying, "Emily, do not voyage with the water."

"Isn't that how I'll travel home?"

"Yes, of course. However, someone will escort you. It is a miracle that you arrived here safely and did not find yourself somewhere …"

"Somewhere where?" I asked.

"We will discuss the topic of your safe arrival at a later time," she said. I thought I saw a hint of something scary in her eyes. "For now, enjoy your morning, and explore our world. DeRenne will find you in the village."

The list of questions getting longer and longer with no end in sight, I headed toward the passageway. I found it odd that they were just going to let me wander around unescorted. I glanced behind my shoulder before entering the leafy green corridor to double-check that no one was following.

Earlier this morning, after trying on several different dresses, I'd decided to wear brilliant fuchsia in an effort to blend in with the village folk. I figured the gawking look on my face every other second would draw enough attention, doubly so if I wore a dull gray.

As soon as I stepped out from beneath the stone archway into the sunshine flooding the village plaza, DeRenne waved in greeting. “Good morning,” she said, walking toward me, her eyes bright with excitement. “You look well-rested, considering.”

“Intergalactic jetlag is a bear,” I mumbled. “I fell asleep before my head even hit the pillow.” That was a big fat lie. As soon as I slid underneath the quilted coverlet, I laid awake half the night reliving that awkward moment on the granite step with Lachlan, and last night’s uncomfortable meal. I kept wondering if he recognized me and decided to keep his mouth shut or simply did not give a crap.

And then I kept asking myself why I even cared.

“First, we will visit the shops in the village. Around midday, we can find a café for lunch,” DeRenne said, rattling off her itinerary for the day. “Afterwards, we can visit The Assemblage and get some answers to your questions. Where would you like to start?”

“In the middle,” I said, smiling.

The village, alive and bustling with shoppers milling in and out of the cafés and shops seemed more ordinary to me today. I heard people speaking in different languages, saw Arden’s symbol everywhere, and noticed geometric shapes incorporated in window panes, carved into fence posts, and stamped into walkways. The brilliantly painted covered entryways lined with arranged merchandise, lured customers into the shops filled with clothing and shoes, jewelry and hair ornaments, spices and kitchenware, and even a bakery.

Out in the sunlight, it hit me that the soft-curved buildings here were very old; constructed to endure. Unlike yesterday, I noticed the second-floor porches and the apartments above the shops that overlooked the central plaza. The thick layers of mature and lush foliage from the surrounding trees formed an overhang across the porches, offering the occupants privacy and shade.

Browsing the tailor's shop, running a hand down the endless bolts of brightly dyed fabric, I picked up a piece of brocade, tracing the interwoven, raised geometric design between my forefinger and thumb, the world around me spinning faster and faster. My initial impression of a medieval village splintered each time a customer made a purchase; all transactions were recorded vocally on the holographic image that seemed to pop up everywhere. I also noted that even with all the hidden advanced technology, the place had a slow and leisurely vibe.

The open-air marketplace in the plaza was twice the size from yesterday. Bin after bin housed a wide variety of fruits and vegetables, most of which I recognized as distant relatives to their counterparts back on Earth. "That tastes like a sour apple," I said, after sampling one, my lips puckering.

DeRenne pranced over to a different bin, selected yet another piece of fruit, and handed it to me. I took a bite. "And this one reminds me of a plum, but it's kind of lemony," I said, wiping away the juice running down my chin with the back of my hand. Each flavor and smell opened a small window of familiarity. I found myself relaxing more than I thought possible. Glancing over and catching DeRenne's eye, I said, "I think you're enjoying yourself way too much."

"Oh, I am," she said with a mischievous wink, handing me something that looked like a cross between a pear and an onion. "As we both now know, things are never as they seem."

My feeling of juxtaposed worlds resurfaced when we entered a large, square brick building on the edge of the village plaza near a wide, flowing river. My eyes followed the plumes of billowing smoke rising into the bright blue sky.

The inside of the cavernous structure overflowed with artisans crafting their wares; handblown glass bowls, wind chimes, clay bird baths, leather belts and shoes, textiles, and even an enormous loom with a petite woman weaving a giant section of grasscloth embedded with nanoprisms. We spent a solid hour walking the aisles, stopping to chat with several of the artists. DeRenne, of course, knew everyone.

The morning passed pleasantly, and around noon we ordered a bowl of pasta and bread from a café near the artisan's marketplace. Talking nonstop about this and that, we carried the food to a circular stone table beneath a grove of maple-like trees near the river, their crimson leaves shimmering in the sunlight. "This village is known for the marketplace," DeRenne said, unraveling the mystery of why the number of people coming and going from the large traveling pool at the opposite end of the plaza dramatically ebbed and flowed.

"So that family," I said, pointing my fork at a woman and three small children, "could be from Arden or from a planet in a different galaxy?"

"Yes," she said, focusing on my face.

I knew she expected me to respond. I had no idea how to respond, which was unusual for me. I decided a better plan was to simply shut-up and eat. “Next,” I said after we finished clearing the table.

We threaded our way through the waning lunch crowd and entered the stone archway at this end of the plaza. Once inside the leafy green passageway, I realized that the maze-like walkways were all interconnected. At the end of this corridor was another solitary standing stone exactly like the one leading to Paden and Ccri’s house. This time, we veered left. I began to make mental notes as we walked, and memorized this route, forming a map in my mind for future reference.

As soon as we emerged back into the sunshine, DeRenne caught her breath. Following her line of sight, I understood her reaction. It was the guy who called out Lachlan’s name yesterday on the granite steps. I wondered if he recognized me dressed in Arden-style clothing, and hoped that he did not. “Emily, I would like to introduce a friend of our family, Shaw, which means *slender and fair*,” DeRenne said. “Shaw, this is Emily Harrison.”

When Mr. Slender and Fair saw us, or rather when he saw DeRenne, a shimmer of muted colors distorted the fabric of his sleek, military-style uniform.

“Good day, Emily,” Shaw said, bowing crisply, a slight breeze ruffling his reddish hair. “Earlier today, Lachlan enlightened me of the unusual circumstances surrounding your arrival. I am pleased you decided to stay on Arden for a few days.”

“Has my brother returned?” DeRenne asked. I watched as she brushed the long strands of her hair over her shoulder, and then not notice when they fell back in place.

"No, and he will not today," Shaw said. A look passed between them. I wondered what that was about. "I will join him shortly."

"And me?" she said. I could tell by the tone of her voice she was a little miffed about being left out.

"You are occupied for the day," he said, eyeing me.

"And tonight?" she asked.

His eyes sharpened. "I am afraid I cannot promise to attend."

"Then we will not keep you," DeRenne said, a faint smile working its way across her lips.

"Ladies," Shaw said with a last look for DeRenne before disappearing into the passageway.

DeRenne grasped the heavy, brass handrail, and started to walk up an imposing flight of limestone steps, leading to a stately two-story building with a portico entry and a domed roof. In keeping with the symmetry of style around here, two flanking side wings offered a sheltered overhang for visitors and a place for friends to gather.

I grabbed her arm. "Wait! Am I crazy or is the fabric of Shaw's uniform, well, is it…pixelating?" That was the best word I could think of to describe the wavering and distorted shimmers in the fabric.

DeRenne looked into my eyes and detected the tiniest hint of panic. "No, you are not crazy. The fibers used to weave the cloth of our mission uniforms are harvested from genetically altered plants whose cells contain an overabundance of chromoplasts."

"Oh…" I mumbled, completely clueless.

"Bioenergetic plant organelles that contain colored pigments," she said. "Using the neurons in our skin, we can electrically excite the plastids in the cloth. This varies the amount of pigment inside each of the chromoplast and creates a chromatic aberration."

"If you get in tune with the vibrating molecules found in all living organisms, then you vibrate in tandem with the molecules. Since harmonious colors are composed of similar chromas, the pigments in the chromoplasts adjust and mimic the vibrations in your surroundings. If I set my mind to it, I can fluctuate the shades and hues in the cloth and blend into any organic background."

"You what!" I said.

"We conceal ourselves into the natural surroundings. This way we can observe humans on other worlds undetected. Since our skin always conducts electrical impulses, the cloth continuously wavers. It takes years of practice to learn how to first fade into the background and then temper your thoughts to remain hidden. Any sudden surge of emotion distorts the colors in the fabric."

I bit my lip, suppressing a smile. I'd just witnessed firsthand what happens to the cloth when a strong emotion courses through your body.

"There is one drawback," she said. "We are unable to blend into man-made materials such as concrete or brick."

"And what's with that hood?" I asked. "It's humongous!"

"The hood completely shrouds our face," she mumbled, distractedly pulling her sleeve down over her hands. "We can see through the fabric. Any exposed patch of skin would defeat the point of the illusion."

"No kidding," I mumbled. As soon as we reached the portico at the top of the steps, I glanced over my shoulder at the maze of green passageways wondering if someone was hiding in the foliage right now disguised as a tree trunk, the implication staggering and kind of creepy.

I followed DeRenne through the intricately carved wooden doors. Next, we crossed a windowed vestibule filled with huge copper urns bursting with towering flowers. The vestibule connected to a wide cross hall leading to a spacious rotunda. The curved sandstone walls were divided by twelve or so fluted columns arranged flush with the pink sandstone walls bordered by ornate relief panels depicting an exotic array of animals, insects, and flora indigenous to Arden.

This place was built to impress. Directly beneath the central dome, an intricate black and gold nautical compass star inset in the gleaming marble floors didn't denote the customary N, S, E, W directional designations. Instead, each tip of the compass arm pointed to a spiraling galaxy.

A middle age woman, her dark hair twisted into a severe bun at the nape of her neck, announced, "Now children, Berenices should come into focus any time now."

As we walked through the rotunda, I arched my head upward. A mirrored holographic nautical compass star hovered inside of the expansive dome. The galaxies at the end of each wavering compass arm continuously faded from view, only to be replaced by another shimmering galaxy. Block-style letters, engraved into the continuous frieze encircling the base of the dome read, 'The Assemblage of Knowledge Transcends the Space Between Our Galaxies'.

"You may visit The Assemblage day and night if you wish to research a topic," DeRenne said.

"Any restrictions?" I asked. Seriously, they're just handing me the keys to the place?

She turned her head, eyebrows arched. "Should there be?"

"No. Yes. Maybe," I said. "It's just that...everyone around here is so trusting, it kind of makes me suspicious." I'm sure I looked guilty, and a bit confused.

"We trust you because the water trusts you," she said matter-of-factly.

Okay, I had no idea what that meant. All I knew was that I better not do anything foolish to jeopardize that trust. And then a spontaneous applause reverberated throughout the spacious rotunda.

"Tutored children," DeRenne said with a smile. "I still get a thrill whenever the Triangulum Galaxy comes into view."

I followed her into a small anteroom behind the nearest fluted column. Five uncomfortable looking S-shaped stone recliners, each carved from a single block of quarried stone, were arranged in a tight circle. DeRenne shut the door, walked to the closest recliner and slid into the polished seat. She positioned her head against the curved headrest and crossed both of her arms over her chest. All she needed was a lily in her hands to complete the death pose. "Show us Earth's symbol," she said to no one.

The lights in the room dimmed. Inexplicably we were inside of a moving holographic image, soaring past planets, and stars. Instantly seasick, I closed my eyes.

"Emily," DeRenne said, reaching up, touching my arm.

"Sorry," I murmured. "These images are just a little intense."

"Sit," she instructed. "It takes the edge off."

Using a hand as a guide, I fumbled around in the dark until I found the adjacent stone recliner and plopped into the polished seat rather ungracefully. As it turns out, the S-shape of the curve was ergonomic, positioning your body so that you became a part of the holographic scene instead of an outside observer. An image of Earth engulfed the room to the point that I couldn't distinguish the ceiling and floors anymore. A dialogue box suspended in midair was filled with wavering words and symbols.

"It's all written in English," I said.

"As soon as you start speaking, the room configures to that language. This same information can be shown in a variety of languages." As she spoke, the wavering box vanished and then re-formed into a jumble of unrecognizable symbols. Then it vanished again and re-formed into a new set of symbols at incredible speed.

"How do you get pictures like these?" I asked, a little dizzy watching the changing images. "I haven't seen any space ships flying around or any giant telescopes."

"As I said earlier today, things are not always as they seem," DeRenne said, her voice sounding distant even though she sat less than two feet away. "On Arden, we choose to live a simpler life, more in harmony with the water. Other planets in the Triangulum Galaxy alone may have more visible signs of machinery and buildings that you would normally associate with advanced civilizations on Earth. We possess as much technology as needed to assist us in our endeavors such as the ability to project these images. Perhaps on Earth, there are noticeable gaps within different societies."

I thought about that for a moment. "I guess if you compare a tribal family living in the rainforest with a family living in a city, the contrasts would be huge. But now that I think about it, so much around here is similar to Earth."

"I would agree. Human progression, no matter where in the Universe, seems to plod along similar paths," DeRenne said. "How different civilizations progress, inventing what they need, seems to follow similar design themes. Perhaps it is the way our brains are wired. However, make no mistake, whenever we push or present or suggest from behind the scene, the process accelerates at an unexpected rate along parallel paths. Have you ever seen that symbol in the top right-hand corner? I am not sure if you noticed, it never changed."

I recognized Arden's symbol, the now-familiar oval with a squiggly loop on top. Earth's symbol was the same as Arden's except that it was surrounded by an isosceles triangle with two dots on either side of the apex. "No," I said. "But then again I never looked. It certainly isn't pounded into every sign, designed into jewelry, stamped into stone, woven into fabric designs, or etched into panes of glass and plates."

DeRenne laughed. "I guess when you put it that way we do embrace our symbol with..."

"Exuberance," I said, finishing her sentence.

She laughed again. "Yes, exuberance."

"Can the room show me how far away the Triangulum Galaxy is from Milky Way Galaxy?" As soon as the words were out of my mouth, the image all around dissolved and then re-formed.

"The Triangulum Galaxy," dinned a toneless mechanical voice, "is a pinwheel-shaped galaxy located approximately three million light-years from Earth in the Virgo cluster."

I stared at the image, speechless again. I was having trouble with the scale and pace of this place. I tried to wrap my head around how it's possible to travel so far, in such a relatively short amount of time, and survive.

"As I told you yesterday, I think you are very brave," DeRenne said.

"Either brave or psychotic," I muttered under my breath.

After a couple more rapid starts and stops, my brain adjusted to the concept. I was beginning to acquire my sea legs, so to speak. We became a couple of maritime tourists, sailing through the Universe, flying past a dying star the exact moment it went supernova, an impressive sight, as were the violent storms on an uninhabited planet near Arden.

We also looked into how English was brought to Europe during the Norman Conquest. Or so history thought. As it turns out, it was actually members of The Accordance laying the foundation so families could easily relocate and assimilate into Earth's civilization.

As the afternoon wore on, I reached critical mass from sensory overload. Stomach queasy, I slipped out of the dip in the polished stone recliner. The lights in the room brightened but my head still swirled.

"Did we really just do that?" I said, nudging DeRenne in the arm. "That! That! I can't even think of…of." What could you possibly say to someone after a day like today?

"You are most welcome," she murmured in a low voice.

δ^+

After spending my second day on Arden with DeRenne, she was called away and did not serve as my guide as promised. That also meant Lachlan wouldn't either. I'd enjoyed DeRenne's company and greatly benefited from her insight, but I also felt like I'd dodged a bullet.

Over the last few days, I'd attended way too many welcome lunches and official meetings. I also spent more hours than necessary at The Assemblage watching what I concluded were lessons outlining the rules and regulations dealing with the complexities of Planetary Mergence. And I wasn't the only one. The Assemblage was a busy place with people coming and going at all hours of the day and night. But, sitting alone in one of the anterooms and watching endless hours of boring images is not what I envisioned at supper my first night on Arden when Paden asked if I would consider staying.

"I think I'll visit a few shops and people-watch," I said as soon as we stepped out from the water onto the broad granite steps at the traveling pool in the village. Paden, Ccri, and I had just returned from visiting Ccri's mother on Keit. It was my second interplanetary voyage but not that much of a stretch. Every evening, Keit, Arden's closest planet, appeared in the night sky. Even though I looked confident, I'm not going to lie, I felt the tiniest bit concerned about getting lost or left behind. I didn't hesitate when Paden offered his arm.

Anyway, after spending the entire day only with adults, I needed a little alone time before another round of important supper guests and irrelevant chit-chat. I leisurely walked the rhombus-shaped plaza window shopping. Then I sat at the round stone table near the artisan's marketplace, watching the shop owners carry their merchandise inside and close for the evening. As Arden's sun dipped below the horizon, I made my way to the stone archway leading to Paden and Ccri's house, stopping just before entering the passageway to admire Keit peeking over the opposite horizon. I was just on that planet less than an hour ago. Earth, Arden, Keit—three planets. "Not bad for a newbie," I muttered, walking beneath the stone archway.

Tonight, the brilliant specks of lights, winking and flashing throughout the foliage tripled in number, emitting ample light to maneuver the darkening corridor. I ran a hand down the hedges as I walked, stirring the lights into a glittering frenzy. Maybe I'd relocated my mail over to crazy town. At first I thought I saw Paden, and then more times than I care to admit, I thought I saw other people carrying on a conversation with those lights. It was now time to investigate.

I found a slight indentation in a recently trimmed hedge and leaned in. A small swarm of glowing insects flew backward in equal measure. I leaned in more; they retreated in kind. And then, a few specks of light flew closer, fluttering near my eyelashes, almost as if they were as curious about me as I was about them.

I straightened my back, startled by this response. I thought about what just happened for a moment. I stood on my tippy toes, reached inside the hedge, weaving a hand through the dense foliage, making sure not to disturb several cocoons filled with luminescent eggs.

"May I assist?" a voice said from behind my shoulder.

I went stiff mid-reach. Lachlan?

Crap. What's he doing here? Why does he always catch me in these awkward predicaments? I withdrew my arm, rocked back on my heels and turned around, telling myself not to look or sound too annoyed. I didn't want to give him any indication whatsoever that I acknowledged his existence in the least. "Hello," I said, blinking back the dare before he noticed.

"Are you attempting to catch a Seren?" he asked, repressing a smile, playing along with the ruse.

I glanced over at the lights darting throughout the foliage. "Is that what you call these bugs? They remind me of fireflies…a type of insect on Earth." As usual, I felt compelled to clarify everything to everyone around here. "I thought I saw Paden talking to one of these, what did you call them?"

"The Seren are not insects," he said. I saw humor in his eyes. "They are a very intelligent life form."

"Intelligent?" I said, looking at him in surprise.

A faint smile crossed his lips as he raised a hand draped by the cuff of his long-sleeved slate colored tunic. Wait. Why did I even notice that? One of these lights swooped out from the foliage and landed on his outstretched finger.

"The Seren assist The Accordance by locating blue planets with breathable air and human inhabitants," he said. "They also gather light from the outer rim of the Universe to nourish the developing larvae inside of the cocoons that you see in the foliage. This light powers their luminescence. When they die, the light is harvested and used to either recharge an elder Seren or returned from where it was first collected. Legend says this has been going on forever, even before recorded time."

"Wow," I said. "That is truly amazing. I had no idea."

"They are not pleased you think they are insects," he said.

"Oh?" I said, swinging my head from Lachlan to the lights fluttering in the hedges, and then back to Lachlan, feeling a little guilty. "I'm so sorry…Did they tell you that? How do you talk to them?"

"With the help of this." Lachlan reached up with his free hand and touched a small circular silver disk, about the size of a dot on a pair of dice, attached to the inner fold of his earlobe. "The Seren speak at a frequency far above our ability to hear them. This device modulates their voice. This is how we communicate with them."

"I knew I wasn't seeing things. Paden was talking to one of these lights…I mean Seren."

"While we are on Arden, they deliver messages as needed." He lifted his hand. "Please inform DeRenne that Emily is on Arden tonight. We will join her shortly." I saw his back straighten as if mildly startled by the words that just came out of his mouth. The speck of light zoomed up off of his finger and darted down the tunnel back toward the plaza.

"Cool," I muttered, my eyes tracking the wavering light until it disappeared around the corner.

"We were informed that you were on Keit today," he said. "How was traveling with the water to a different planet?"

I smiled; they knew what I'd been doing. "Different. The night before, Paden gave me a pep talk and a couple of instructions. When he offered his arm before stepping into the water, I decided it was more than a gallant gesture."

"I would agree," Lachlan said. "Everyone is quite impressed that you arrived safely from Earth to Arden. One wrong turn could land you on a planet with flowing water and a toxic atmosphere or on a planet with humans unaware of water travel. You would be explaining that…"

"Yeah," I said, grinning. "They're still trying to figure that one out."

"Shall we?" he said, stepping backward.

I could tell he knew I'd dropped my guard a smidgen. "Shall we what?"

"Meet DeRenne and Shaw for supper."

"We?" I said, falling in step before I knew I was even doing it.

He glanced at me sideways. "Yes. Do you remember Paden requested…"

"Oh, I know what Paden requested and your mother volunteered. You didn't look too happy about their requests." I wasn't going to let him off of the hook too easily. Although charming right now, after mulling the entire scenario over in my head, the ugly truth was that he'd barely acknowledged my existence. I could count on two hands the total number of words he'd even said to me before tonight.

"This is true," he said with a slow nod. I could tell he was editing his words before saying them aloud. "I am sure I gave that impression. At the time I was unaware of the unique circumstances of your voyage to Arden."

I flicked a long strand of hair behind my shoulder and looked him straight in the eye. "So now you feel sorry for me?"

"Not in the least. I am intrigued." I saw his eyes flicker as he said those last three words.

"Intrigued?" I said.

"Rarely do we get an opportunity to spend time with someone who has no idea of our existence, and then a moment later, here we are." His dropped his left hand, and looped his thumb through the thick leather belt wrapped twice around his waist, holding the folds of his tunic in place. "I see that Paden's request makes sense."

"So, now I'm your personal science experiment?"

He laughed. "Since you put it that way…" He placed his right hand flat on his chest, and said with a short half-bow, "Perhaps you should consider me your science experiment. Ask whatever you like. I shall endeavor to answer."

I wasn't going to pass on an opportunity to put him in the hot seat for once. "Do you attend school?"

"We do not have formal schools. We are tutored in small groups." He brushed the loose strands of hair back behind his shoulder.

I swallowed, trying not to notice. "For how long?"

"Until the occasion of our fifteenth year at which time our training continues off-world. And trust me; this does not come soon enough."

"Ah yes, those mysterious missions," I mumbled. "Still trying to grasp that whole concept."

"As I am sure DeRenne explained, we educate societies on other planets by assisting with inventions to make their lives more comfortable."

"Don't take what I'm about to say the wrong way. At first glance, Arden appears technologically backward. I know that it isn't. But with the entire Universe literally at your fingertips, why do people around here make things? Couldn't you just, I don't know, get the Seren to go someplace and get it for you? Or go yourself?"

"Quite the opposite," he said. "We enjoy taking the time."

"If you ask me, a newbie so to speak, I'd like nothing better than to hop from planet to planet and see what's out there."

"Your comment does make sense," he said, shaking his head in agreement.

"What about money? Paden and Ccri told me to just tell that crazy holographic image to put it on their account. There are a couple of items I'd like to purchase before I go home…If that is allowed."

"We do not use money on Arden. Yes, there is compensation. However, it is more along the lines of a barter system. I cannot imagine anyone having a problem with you bringing a few items from your time spent here on Arden back to Earth."

I should have asked where we were going or showed my annoyance with him after that night at supper. Yet somehow, it didn't matter. Before I even knew it, we were walking down a side street near the artisan's marketplace. "Pleasant evening," he said to a passing couple.

"Hmm…on Earth we use roads for trucks," I said. "People still need to move their stuff from place to place. I mean you can't just carry a big sofa into the water."

"There is a device that creates a distortion field," he said.

"A what!?"

"A device that creates a small distortion around a body of water, almost like a sinkhole. You can push large items through. However, someone needs to be on the other end. Lifting and carrying are still required." He stopped, and pointed to a well-manicured path next to the bakery. "The restaurant is at the end of this pathway."

He reached the metal gate first, swung it open and stepped aside, forcing me to dip beneath his arm. I felt his eyes on me the entire time. Thankfully, knowing I would attend another series of official meetings on Keit, this morning I'd made an effort to dress a little more formal, sweeping the longer curls to the left side, clamping them in place with a jeweled barrette I'd found in a shop in the village.

We moved through a room filled with cozy sofas and a handful of customers sitting at a wooden bar to a second gate at the back of the café. This time, I opened the gate and stepped aside. "Is this where we're going?"

"Outdoor seating," he said as he walked by.

I followed him up a short flight of steps carved into a massive tree trunk, and then out onto a deck built into the tree canopy. The long-reaching limbs of the massive tree formed a ceiling over the intimate eating area. Hundreds of hanging glass lanterns filled with tiny candles illuminated the foliage with a cheery vibe. DeRenne and Shaw sat side-by-side at a small table in the corner, holding hands.

"Uh, hum," Lachlan loudly cleared his voice like an obnoxious older brother. They separated like magnets turned towards opposite poles.

"Emily," DeRenne cried out when she saw me.

"I found her in the passageway trying to catch a Seren," Lachlan said, looking at his sister side-ways.

"Were you successful?" Shaw asked, squinting both of his eyes.

"Not very," I said, grinning. Then I noticed the three place settings and the three chairs. I tasted the awkwardness in the back of my throat. "Oh. I'm sorry…I didn't mean to…"

"No, no," DeRenne said, waving her hand over the table like a sorcerer trying to conjure up a fourth place setting.

"Excuse me for a moment," Lachlan said, touching my arm in a reassuring gesture. I looked into his eyes, a little taken aback by his gesture. He looked as surprised as I did.

Shaw hopped up and grabbed a chair from an adjacent table. "Sit here," he said, placing the chair in the big empty spot across from DeRenne and next to Lachlan's chair.

"We inquired about you as soon as we arrived on Arden wishing you could join us here at the café," DeRenne said without taking a single breath, "and were informed that you were occupied for the evening."

"No big deal," I said. That lie exploded into full-blown embarrassment as I slid down into the chair, desperate to remove the attention from me. "This place is amazing. Are there lots of cafés in the trees on Arden?"

"Do they not have such places on Earth?" Shaw asked.

"Not that I know of," I said. "Perhaps I can start a whole new concept. Although, it might be difficult to find such massive trees."

Lachlan returned with his arms full, arranging the plate, silverware, and napkin on the tabletop in front of me. "I amended the order to include Emily."

"Oh! I'm sorry. I should've said something earlier." During the walk here, lost in Lachlan-land, I lost track of the time. "I'm supposed to dine with Paden and Ccri and..." I'd talked to so many people over the last few days that I was having trouble keeping things straight.

"No worries," Lachlan said, lifting his hand. A Seren zipped out from a nearby branch. "Please inform Paden that Emily is dining with me, DeRenne, and Shaw in the village tonight."

I unfolded the large white napkin and placed it in my lap, watching the Seren zip away into the night to deliver the unexpected change of plans. Not that I was sad. This was so much better than another dull supper with adults. "So where have you three been for the last few days?" They shared a look but didn't say a word. "Hmm. Is that classified? If you tell me then you'll have to kill me?"

"What! Kill you?" Shaw said, looking a little shocked. "We would never."

"Nah," I said, grinning. "It's a silly Earth saying. I was told you three were involved or let me rephrase that, unavailable. I decided that was code for doing something secretive. On Earth, they say if something is top-secret, and someone tells you the pertinent details, then they have to kill you so you don't tell anyone else."

"How very odd," Shaw muttered.

"No, what is odd," I said, leaning forward, "is spending the last few days meeting with the more senior members of Arden, not to mention the endless hours watching all of those images at The Assemblage."

"Not those?" DeRenne said, looking horrified. "The images with all the dates?"

"Coalescence Amendment," I said.

"No," they moaned in unison.

"Policy Debates for Planetary Mergence…The Ten Essential Steps for…Family Relocation Strategies…"

Shaw threw his hands up. "Enough," he groaned. "I will have nightmares tonight remembering all those examinations. I hope they did not subject you to DeRenne's old tutor, Vanor."

Completely deadpan and without hesitation, I mumbled, "You mean the guy whose lips don't move when he talks?" That got a laugh. "The worst though has to be Groth."

The three of them went stiff. "He is still alive?" Shaw asked in utter amazement.

"Barely," I said. "They left us alone in the courtyard to chat. He promptly fell asleep. I sat next to him for two hours while he sat slumped in the chair, snoring loud enough to wake the dead."

"Emily, I am truly sorry," DeRenne said her voice compassionate. "It must have been ghastly."

I sighed. "Well, I'm keeping an open mind about everything that has happened since I stepped out from the water. But things move so rapidly on Arden that I hardly have a moment to myself except when I'm sleeping."

"Good for you," Lachlan said, sounding impressed.

During the meal, I went through each event one by one, and they laughed in all the right places. Lachlan, especially attentive tonight, seemed genuinely interested in the little details over the last few days. I had to pull the reins in on my galloping hormones, trying not to read too much into this unexpected shift in the Universe.

"Lachlan, what did you mean when you said the Seren help The Accordance locate blue planets?" I asked after the coffee and dessert were served. I realized that was the first time I'd ever said his name aloud and felt a little giddy for it.

"Cannot wait to hear his explanation," Shaw garbled between bites of cobbler. "This might take a while."

"Do not listen to him, Emily," Lachlan said, sliding his chair closer to mine. "He is just plotting to eat your portion of dessert when you are not looking."

DeRenne turned her head. "Is this true Shaw?"

"That was not my intent. Now that you are mentioning it, it is not a bad idea," he said, not looking sorry in the least.

"Back to the main topic," I insisted, waving a hand in my direction.

Lachlan pushed the coffee mug off to the side, resting an elbow on the tabletop, cupping his chin in his hand, building the drama for the big reveal. "The Seren possess the uncanny ability to locate flowing water. They swarm through uncharted galaxies in the Universe checking out the conditions on any and all planets with flowing water; atmosphere, no atmosphere, inhabited, uninhabited, aware of water travel, not aware of water travel, and then report its location. At that time, the planet is placed under the protection of The Accordance."

I'd never even considered that option, everything around here seems so serene. "Planets need protection?" I asked.

"Emily, you must realize that we are not the only group out there looking," Lachlan said, keeping his voice steady.

I guess I should've drawn that conclusion after watching all of those images at The Assemblage. I took a moment, not wanting them to know how alarmed I'd become before saying, "If a planet needs protecting, then there is something or someone the planet needs protection from."

I looked over at DeRenne and Shaw who once again looked horrified. "You are scaring her," DeRenne said, ever the protector

"She should be scared," Shaw said, holding the spoon in midair.

I swung my head back to Lachlan. "In a way, they are both correct. There are certain planets that need protection. Earth, however, is under our protection. I should say under the protection of The Accordance." He glanced down at my white knuckles. Instinctively, I'd gripped the table edge.

"So why does a planet need protection?" I asked, talking over the alarm bells wailing inside of my head.

"Memorials, for one," Lachlan said. "We visit them during our tutoring. There are numerous examples where at first it appeared mergence would fail. In the end, the policies and procedures put in place by The Accordance resulted in a smooth transition and happy occupants. It is always a good plan to keep a few around for study; to learn from our success and failures. If someone or some group wanted to make a point, these planets would be the first to go. There are also planets where the reveal did end badly. It is important to never forget but risky to keep them around. The naysayers could easily point out the mistakes, and use these planets as examples as to why The Accordance should change."

"The rest of the Universe is not as idyllic as it is here on Arden," Shaw said, he and Lachlan sharing a look so that DeRenne couldn't see.

I decided right then and there, the concept of successful and unsuccessful Planetary Mergence is something I'd definitely research at The Assemblage. "I guess since Earth hasn't advanced to intergalactic water travel then..." I said, ending the sentence on a higher note.

"Earth is under the protection of The Accordance," Lachlan said, firmly.

"Good. And how do these other groups out there know that Earth is under the...protective umbrella of The Accordance?" I air-quoted that last part.

"The Seren return periodically and leave markers," Lachlan said. I could tell he was choosing his words carefully to get his point across, but not enough to scare me even more. Shaw was doing a good job in that department.

"What kind?" I asked, a barrage of images scrolling through my brain.

"The occasional human hears their energy, not really words but more of a feeling," Shaw said, wiping his mouth with the corner of his linen napkin. "The Seren turn this energy into symbols intricately woven through the dense foliage in which they thrive."

"Crop circles," I whispered. "So the Seren are the ones responsible for creating the crop circles." I sat back in the chair. This explains why crop circles seem to mysteriously and magically appear overnight. "I've seen pictures of the markers the Seren leave on Earth. They're complex geometric and celestial designs, and often considered a hoax. To know that they are real is a bit overwhelming. What do they say?"

"No magic there," Shaw said, sliding his plate off to the side, and replacing it with the half-empty bowl of cobbler. "No Trespassing; Already Taken; Go Away."

I exhaled the question unaware that I was holding my breath in the first place. "But there are instances when these warnings signs are ignored?"

"Unimaginable conflict, loss of life in the billions, entire civilizations destroyed," Lachlan said in a low voice. "There has not been a major dispute in several millennia but unrest is rumbling."

"But Earth," I said, tapping a finger on the table to emphasize my point, "in your opinion has no value."

"Yes," they said in unison.

I sat silently, this new bit of information frightening. "These designs announce to others that Earth is a member of The Accordance?" I asked again.

"That is certainly one way to phrase it," Lachlan said, doing something with his eyes to double emphasize his point.

I relaxed, a little. "You know everything around here has something to do with geometric shapes and colors. Why is that?"

Lachlan's demeanor changed at my question, becoming almost devout. "It is the basic belief that geometry and mathematical ratios, proportions, and fundamental harmonics are found in music, light, and cosmology," he said. "By studying the nature of these patterns and their interconnections, one gains insight into the mysteries and laws of the Universe. Repetition of color and geometric design is evident in our surroundings and in our clothing, reminding us of this complex and profound relationship."

"How so?" I asked, my brain becoming muddled by his words.

"It is the geometric shapes themselves," he said leaning forward, his eyes gleaming. "The square symbolizes matter and gravity, corresponding to a vivid terrestrial red. The triangle is the symbol of thought; its massless energy vibrating coherently with a sky blue. The ceaseless circle is the spirit in eternal motion, sympathetic to a sunny yellow. To us, these harmonious shapes and colors imply balance and symmetry of forces."

As he spoke, my eyes went fuzzy, vivid colors and shapes breezing through my mind as they did during the voyage here to Arden. "Too overwhelming?" DeRenne asked, sensing my distress.

I looked her straight in the eye. "Every day around here is too much. I lie awake at night trying to process what I've seen, heard, and experienced. During the day I walk around in a dream world, thinking that someone should just pinch me."

"Ouch!" I grabbed my forearm and glared at Lachlan.

"You said someone needed to pinch you."

"It's a figure of speech. I didn't mean for someone to actually pinch me."

He met my gaze looking unapologetic. "That is not what you said."

"Kill me, pinch me," Shaw said. "You sure have a strange way of talking on Earth."

"Oh, really. Using words like recanted and endeavor in everyday conversation. Saying your name, and then stating its meaning. Never using any contractions when you talk, ever, isn't?" I dropped my hands in my lap. "Everything around here is strange to me, although I'm beginning to understand why Paden asked me to stay."

"If this is true," Shaw said with a mischievous glint in his eye. "It sounds like we should schedule a little fun into one of your days here on Arden before you return to Earth."

"Works for me," I said, winking at him. "What did you have in mind?"

Unwittingly, the four of us inclined our heads together. For a brief moment, I thought the mystery of fun on Arden was about to be revealed. Instead, a tall brunette interrupted our little party.

"Lachlan!" At the sound of her voice, the three of them snapped to attention. I looked up. Wow! Her corseted, silver buttoned, flame-orange dress was over-the-top even by Arden standards. From the look in her eye, someone undoubtedly needed to cue the dramatic music.

"Raffye," Lachlan said, angling his chair away from mine. I looked at Lachlan, and then across the table at DeRenne and Shaw. Their faces were unreadable.

"When did you return?" she asked, looking none too pleased that I was the fourth person at the table instead of her.

"Earlier this evening," Lachlan answered rather curtly, shifting his chair a little closer to mine as if to make a point.

"Hi," I said, extending a hand. "Emily Harrison."

"That girl from Earth," Raffye said, folding her arms across her chest, hoisting her ample cleavage higher, and firmly turning her back.

"I am so sorry. Where are my manners," DeRenne said. "Emily, I would like to introduce Raffye which means *born of fire*."

Yep, got that name right. "One and the same," I said, withdrawing the hand hovering in midair. "In fact, this Earth girl needs to be on her way. There is something I want to research at The Assemblage."

Feeling like a square fifth wheel, I pushed the chair back and stood up. I wasn't going to hang around and be ignored. This Raffye girl and Lachlan obviously are together. I'm just a passing amusement; someone new and inexperienced to entertain with his outlandish stories. I can't believe I allowed myself to fall into this nonsense.

"Do you know the way to The Assemblage from this part of the village?" Lachlan asked, sounding concerned and looking to DeRenne and Shaw for help.

"I do," I said. "I enter the passageway next to the artisan's marketplace, take the next two rights, and veer left at the standing stone."

I could see him mapping the directions in his head. "Yes. That is correct."

"Thank you for a lovely evening," I said, forcing a polite smile. "Very informative. Nice to meet you Raffye." Allowing those last words to linger in the air, I reminded myself over and over to hold my head high until I was out of sight.

"See you soon," DeRenne called out.

δ^+

"Why did you not let me know you were on Arden tonight?" Raffye asked. Lachlan did not say a word. "Please tell me that you are not going for her."

"I have no idea what you are talking about," Lachlan said.

"From where I am standing, it sure looks as if you were trying to impress her."

"How could anything I say surpass landing on a planet in a different galaxy."

Raffye folded her arms back across her chest, and said, "You had that tone in your voice."

Lachlan glanced at DeRenne for moral support. Her face was blank. She had become adept at hiding her feelings. On the other hand, Shaw was enjoying himself way too much.

"Perhaps this is what you desire," Raffye said. "She is green, a novice."

DeRenne squirmed in her seat, raising an eyebrow.

"There is nothing between us," Lachlan said. "I met the girl twice. From what I understand, she will be gone in a few days."

"Again, you did not let me know you had returned. And, this is what I find," Raffye said, waving a hand over the empty dessert plate and mug.

"I did not let her know either," Lachlan said. That was a half-truth. DeRenne inquired about Emily's whereabouts the minute they returned to Arden. After she explained to him the details of her arrival, he found himself well, intrigued. He could not imagine what it must be like to literally land into the middle of this. She had managed well—held her ground. He observed that night at Paden and Ccri's house that she was flustered. In the end, she decided to stay. Not everyone would have made that choice.

At this moment, Raffye irked him just by the fact that she was standing here asking these ridiculous questions. Had he not clearly made his feelings known? Would he have to go over the details with her again?

"Lachlan," Raffye said, tapping her foot against the wooden decking.

"Raffye," Lachlan said.

"Care to explain?" she asked.

"I do not."

"Fine then," Raffye said, turning, and then walking away in a swell of flame-orange.

"You need to make this right with Emily," DeRenne said after Raffye disappeared down the steps carved into the tree trunk.

"I understand," Lachlan said, placing his napkin on the tabletop and rising from the chair.

"Enjoy the rest of your evening," Shaw said. Lachlan watched as he stretched his arms up into the air and then drape his right arm across DeRenne's shoulders. "I know I will."

δ^+

Running through the passageway, I couldn't see very far along the path, the hedges lining the corridor barely visible through the tears. The little voice inside of my head shouted, *Grow up Emily! How could you allow yourself to get sucked into the Lachlan mystique*? It was a fair question, and I had to ask myself, Why? Is it really his fault that he can charm me so easily? Replaying the awkward scene, I kept to my flimsy excuse of going to The Assemblage in case someone decided to check on me. Besides, I wasn't quite ready to go back to Paden and Ccri's house.

"Ahhh. What's wrong with you?" I moaned, gripping the brass handrail for support, taking the limestone steps at The Assemblage two at a time.

I blew through the carved wooden doors, ran through the windowed vestibule, crossed the rotunda without even a cursory glance at the holographic compass arm, and found an empty room in the back corner behind the nearest fluted column. I quickly entered the room, shutting the door behind me. Hands shaking from a mixture of embarrassment and regret, I slid into the polished stone recliner, the room instantly darkening. Hidden in the shadows, enshrouded by a mist of memories, the sinking feeling finally engulfed me.

Come on, he's not interested in you, the little voice jeered. I sighed. Tonight in the passageway and at supper he seemed different, almost gracious and overly friendly. That is until Raffye made her grand entrance. I should've known better, disappointed that I let those silly school girl hormones get the best of me.

After a few tense moments, my breathing calmed. I wiped the tears away with the back of my hand, whispering into the darkness, "Tell me about the Seren on Earth. Do they befriend humans?" The familiar image of Earth materialized all around, obscuring the ceiling and floor, stirring a longing for home. I should've asked about Earth's protection. But right now, I was the one needing protection from myself.

"Eamone, which means *true defender,* his home planet, Qamari, formed an alliance with The Accordance," the mechanical voice droned. "On a joint mission to Earth, The Accordance requested he investigate a young woman who had befriended the Seren. Posing as a fur trader, Eamone journeyed to Earth to meet Evening Star."

The image dissolved and re-formed into a bird's-eye view of a vast wilderness. I crooked an arm behind my head and settled into the curve of the recliner, grateful for a chance to focus on someone else's memories instead of making more unwelcome ones of my own.

Flying through a whirl of colors, the image zoomed down onto a river meandering through a grove of widely spaced trees, the scene so vivid that I felt the wind blowing through my hair and smelled the faint scent of pine. A handsome man dressed in layers of thick fur, stepped out from the water, his dark complexion and sturdy build thoroughly looked the part of a rugged mountain man. "And in time he fell in love with her, and she with him," the mechanical voice dinned.

"Why do you stare, my beloved?" Evening Star murmured, her lilting voice sliding along the night wind.

"I keep waiting to tire of your beauty," Eamone sighed. "Still, my eyes refuse to waste a single nanosecond gazing upon you to relish the setting Sun."

"Your words are foreign to me," she said, rocking back on her heels, "though I cherish the sound pouring forth from your mouth." Gathering a sweep of dark black hair in her hand, she brushed the long strands over her shoulder.

There was a silence to this place at dusk when the natural world bedded down for the night. From his vantage point on the top of the boulder, Eamone watched as the delicate swarm of Seren guided Evening Star's hands, helping her select *digitalis* to cure her uncle's failing heart. She smiled at the winking and flashing lights before adding the herb to her grinding bowl.

How the Seren loved her. He would research their unique relationship upon his return to Qamari but felt confident the literature would not reveal another relationship equal to this special bond. Eamone knew the Seren assisted The Accordance in this part of the Universe, customarily keeping to their own company. But here, near her, their radiant lights glowed even brighter. This he understood.

Evening Star was a remarkable human; her perception of the restorative power of the water was unsurpassed. She trained under her mother's tutelage, matured into a truly gifted healer. He smiled. No one from Qamari would believe it to be true unless they met her themselves. Just the mere thought of bringing her to his home planet sent a desperate desire to be near her spreading across his chest.

"Will you walk with me, my love," he said, gliding off of the boulder and making his way to her side.

Evening Star glanced up at him and nodded. She poured the crushed herbs into a leather pouch and then stacked the grinding stones. Eamone extended his hand. Evening Star accepted his invitation, rising to her feet with an unhurried fluid motion. Standing face-to-face, he marveled at the night on her hair as he lifted the long strands and inhaled deeply; fresh clean water, momentarily satisfying his ever constant thirst for her.

Eamone captured the nape of her neck in his hand and felt the steady beat of her heart in his fingertips. With the gentlest motion, he tilted her head back, and her striking beauty consumed him like a flash fire. Arching his head downward, catching the glint of moonlight shimmering in her dark eyes, he kissed this remarkable creature, rushing headlong into her colors, and giving himself over to the wildness of the night.

Later that same evening, Eamone stood alone in the slowly moving river, water waves lapping at his knees. The *River of Whispering Rocks*, Evening Star called the gently moving tributary winding its way through the lush valley, paramount to the survival of the humans living along the sandy shore. He considered the unusual circumstances impeding their relationship. The Accordance would never officially sanction their union, neither would they prohibit it.

'I am the spiritual leader of my tribe. I cannot abandon my own,' her non-negotiable words came flooding into his mind. Nor would he ask her to until a time of her choosing. He knew that Evening Star would never leave her old life behind and begin a new life with him until these issues were resolved.

And then there was her father.

When Evening Star declared her love for Eamone, her father did not relinquish her from her duty to join with the elder chosen for her from the neighboring tribe, going so far as to publically beat Evening Star for her insolence. She begged Eamone with her eyes not to interfere. That single act tore his soul to shreds as he stood by her side, willing himself with each lash to honor her wishes, knowing full well the sound of her cries and the sight of her cowering body would haunt him for the rest of his life.

A week later, swimming in the still pool of water between the branches of a large oak tree, Evening Star surfaced from the water like a welcomed change of season. She draped her cool arms around Eamone's sturdy shoulders. "I cannot bind myself to this elder when my heart beats only for you."

A lump caught in Eamone's throat and stayed. Now is the right time. He wrapped his arms around Evening Star's waist and pulled her close. Basking in her exquisiteness in this moon-kissed night, he whispered, "There is something I must share with you—I am not from your world. I come from the world of the Seren. Together, we pledged to protect your planet, respecting the natural ebb and flow of its inhabitants."

Evening Star gazed at him, her eyes filled with ancient wisdom. "They have shared your story," she said, beaming at the lights fluttering all around her face. "As soon as there is peace between the tribes, I will join you. Together we will journey to your world. There we will begin a family of our own."

In the end, her father banished Eamome to no avail. Evening Star would sneak away nightly to meet with her one true love. On the eve of the day before she was to be taken to the neighboring tribe to join with the elder, Evening Star made her decision.

Standing in the slowly moving current beneath a canopy of shining stars, Evening Star wore a newly fashioned buckskin garment embellished with mica and colored stones, the plush feel of the leather rough in comparison to her silky emotions. Tonight she'd tamed the long, black strands into a tight braid that lay down the center of her back. Facing one another, Eamone reached over and took her hand carefully into his, soothing *whooshes* from the flowing water echoing their buoyant mood.

"I freely give my heart to you and to no other," she proclaimed into the night, thousands of Seren quivering excitedly as she spoke aloud the words that would change his life forever.

Keeping her hand in his, Eamone knelt and dipped his free hand into the silvery ripples. Breathing deeply, he turned Evening Star's hand upward. He placed a small wet stone in her cupped palm. "This symbol represents my home world and now yours," he said, running his thumb across the unusual symbol chiseled across the flat, honed surface of the stone.

Eamone reached into the side-pocket of his jacket and removed a small, chipped freshwater mussel shell. His eyes never leaving hers, he pricked Evening Star's thumb with the shell, allowing a single drop of her blood to soak the surface of the wet stone. "Keep this with you at all times," he said, looking deep into her eyes. "The Seren will guide you through the water."

Over the next few weeks, they visited each of the neighboring tribes, emphasizing their love for one another, expressing their desire for peace in the valley, always keeping just a hair's breadth ahead of her father's warriors. Each elder willingly met with them, listened, and then expressed their concern about possible retaliation. Never in the history of the tribes had a daughter of the chief refused her duty to join with the man chosen for her. But they also recognized the need for change. Strange settlers from the north brought tools and medicines to ease their lives and to heal their children's illnesses.

One evening after a long day of heated discussions with the elders from two neighboring tribes, Eamone and Evening Star made camp in a thicket of feathery ferns. Before the moon crested the night sky, the Seren woke the lovers from their deep sleep in a panicked flutter. Her father's warriors were near.

Evening Star pushed herself into a sitting position, the set of her back indicating there would be no argument tonight— she would go alone. "I must be the one to speak with them," she said, teetering on bended knee, running a hand through Eamone's unbound hair, her thumbs tracing the determined crease in his steady face. "No one can deny the depth of love I have for you once they look into my eyes."

Eamone knew that he did not have to like what she was about to do but neither did he have the right to stop her. "Call for the Seren if you need help," he pleaded. "Get to the water to keep yourself safe."

As soon as Evening Star disappeared into the seamless night, he quietly followed, keeping a safe distance, making sure the light from the campfires in the clearing didn't reveal his position. Hidden in the shadows, every nerve straining, Eamone waited.

"I will be safe," Evening Star said to the agitated lights darting near her face. "Stay here." Head held high, she walked into the clearing.

"Your father sent us," a warrior scowled. But all Eamone heard was…

"Stop," I shouted, bolting up from the stone recliner, the image dissolving into nothingness. I already knew how the story ended. Eamone lived up to his name, defending Evening Star in the one true way he could…with his life. "Where is the stone?" I asked, breathing heavily. "The one Eamone gave her."

The image re-formed to a small, grass-covered mound nestled in the middle of a lush green valley surrounded by gently rolling hills. "The Seren cherished Evening Star and Eamone, a love unparalleled in the Universe," the disembodied voice purred, now oddly compassionate. "To this day they regard their resting place as a sanctuary to those who made the ultimate sacrifice, for love. The stone given to Evening Star is buried with them, signifying a solid link between their two worlds. Nightly, the Seren guide their souls back to the mound to greet the rising sun…Earth's life-giving star."

I swallowed slowly, allowing the words to form in the back of my throat before asking the question aloud even though I already knew the answer. "What's the policy on relationships between members of The Accordance and the humans on the planets they mentor?"

An image of a petite elderly woman materialized. She was smartly dressed in vivid magenta and standing on a short plinth in front of a sleek and angular, two-story marble building. I sat back in the recliner and braced for the reveal.

The woman raised her hand and a hush settled over the small crowd before her. "We would never presume to forbid relationships between sentient beings," she said in a rather loud voice considering her stature. "However, we cautiously urge mentors to proceed with a clear view of the probable outcome."

Well, there you have it; doomed from the start. I'd been braced to hear the answer but it was a blow nonetheless. My limp posture admitting defeat, I slid from the recliner and walked out of the room, lost in a hundred colliding thoughts. I breezed through the rotunda and windowed vestibule without really seeing anything or anyone. I hurried down the limestone steps, surprising a family of deer-like animals grazing near the passageway.

Outside in the cool night air, my resolve vanished. I found myself shaking. Standing on the bottom step, watching the small herd scurrying into the surrounding woods, the decision I'd been avoiding solidified inside of my head.

After a few tense moments, I entered the passageway, entranced by the hedges quivering with thousands of glittering Seren now that I understood their role, aware that even at night, the twists and turns inside of the maze were already second nature to me. But isn't this how life is? Doesn't it turn you around and you find yourself further along the path without really noticing how it is that you got there in the first place?

I took my time walking through the corridor, memorizing each and every detail of this magical place so that I'd never forget, running a hand along the closely cropped hedges, stirring the swarms of Seren into a glittering frenzy. I stopped for a moment to admire the standing stone at the end of the passageway, softly lit by the gas lamp, and my signpost to veer right. I jumped onto the circular, stacked-stone retaining wall, and patted the rough-hewn rock face. That's when I saw some symbols carved into the thick bottom portion of the stone that I never noticed before because honestly, I never stopped to look. I expected them to be geometric like everything around here, but these symbols were blockish, slanted, and partially connected.

I felt a slight pang in my heart remembering how trance-like I felt listening to Lachlan describe the importance of the geometric symbols and colors.

And then I remembered Raffye.

I pushed all thoughts to the back of my mind, hurried through the side corridor, shoving my embarrassment down deep. I stepped onto the stone stoop at Paden and Ccri's house, and unlatched the wide plank door, pausing for a moment in the doorway to consider the enormity of the decision I'd just made, and was about to tell them. It was hard to wrap my head around the fact that I'd been on Arden for just six days. Six whirlwind days filled with a lifetime of memories; memories that I'd never share with anyone for the rest of my life. The sound of Ccri's light footsteps racing into the foyer jolted me out of the trance.

"Emily," she cried out when she saw me hunched against the door jamb. "Have you been hurt?"

"Not physically," I murmured. "But…I think perhaps it's time for me to go home."

"Paden," she called out, gripping my hand tightly into both of hers.

Paden dashed into the foyer, a concerned fatherly look in his eyes.

"I don't want to sound ungrateful," I said, a faint smile working its way across my face. "There's been so much to absorb. I've been trying. Tomorrow, though, I would like to discuss my return to Earth."

"Whatever you need. First, come into the house," Paden urged, helping me around the corner to the open-space living area.

And there I saw the only thing in the Universe more far-fetched and outrageous than traveling with the water to a planet in a different galaxy. Lachlan stood by the fireplace with his hands folded behind his back, a pained expression on his face.

"I am so sorry, Emily," Ccri said, gently stroking my hair. "I did not have a chance to tell you. Lachlan stopped by. He has been waiting to speak with you."

Her words should have been a song in my heart but felt like a knife to the gut.

δ^+

Our eyes locked, Lachlan's meticulously picking away at the padlock I'd so painstakingly fastened around my bruised heart during the walk through the passageway.

"Lachlan, our Emily has returned," Paden said, guiding me to the tufted and tasseled chair next to the stacked-stone fireplace, the blazing fire crackling in warning. Just his presence made me weak-kneed. I sank into the seat wishing that I could disappear deep into the protective crease. Instead, I swished my hair over my face so that he couldn't misread the true reason for my swollen and blotchy eyes.

Why is he here? Did he need to speak with Paden? Ccri said he came to see…me. Didn't she? Isn't this my silly secret wish? One I dare not allow myself. Granted he'd been animated and overly charming tonight. That is until the lady in orange made her grand entrance. I cringed, recalling his reflex reaction; angling his chair away from mine. But then again, he moved it back, a smidgen. Not a grand gesture still…

"Emily…Emily," Ccri said. My head jerked up at the sound of her voice. I watched as her eyes landed first on me, and then on Lachlan. "I will get you some hot tea. Paden, please give me a hand."

Paden stood in the middle of the room looking confused until an inkling of comprehension dawned. “Right away, dear,” he said, hurrying into the kitchen.

After their hasty departure, the inevitable silence engulfed the room. Maybe I was making it up, I couldn’t really be sure. In my side vision, I thought I saw Lachlan open his mouth to say something. I took a deep breath and counted silently to ten before risking a covert peek through the long strands. I surprised myself, I wasn’t normally this patient. By now, I would’ve already said something stupid that I couldn’t take back. But desperate times call for desperate measures. So I took the risk and glanced at him. Lachlan assumed a wide stance near the fireplace still taking notes with his eyes, flickering firelight shadowing his all too refined cheekbones. He appeared the picture of ease, not his most endearing quality I might add.

I felt inclined to take this whole evening as a bunch of hooey; such things just don’t happen in real life. I’d had many shocked moments since stepping out from the water. The worst though was tonight. I thought of feigning illness and remaining in my refuge, but dismissed the idea. The ugly truth is there’s little point in delaying tactics, unless I had something to delay for, and I didn’t. I decided to go first. Why not! I certainly had nothing to lose. Tomorrow I’ll be back on Earth and this entire episode will be nothing more than a dim memory. Won’t it?

A huge wave of disappointment crashed all over me at the thought of never seeing him again…ever. I was surprised by the depth of feeling. I’d met him, what, three times and the first two times didn't even count. How did it get to this level so quickly? Just glance at him; no harm no foul. I sighed and sat straighter in the chair. "You came to see me."

He took his time before answering. "I wanted to ensure you arrived here safely. You left the café rather abruptly."

I noted the subtle distinction in his word choice, he *wanted*, not *needed* to ensure I arrived safely. Eyes fixed on a spot on the wall behind him, I said, "As you can see I'm fine. How long have you been waiting?" I felt it imperative to gather more information before drawing the wrong conclusion, my usual pattern. Another awkward silence filled the room until a log in the fire shifted, distracting us both. I folded my hands in my lap, waiting to see what came next.

"A little over an hour of Arden time," he said the set of his lips unreadable.

I did the math and looked at him. That meant he left the café soon after I did. This meant that he didn't hang around the café talking with Raffye. I bit my lip, thinking.

And then miraculously, he took two steps forward looking pleased that I'd decided to acknowledge his existence. I brushed the hair back from my face, and scooted to the edge of the chair, wondering why I'd done that. "As I said before I left the café, I had something I wanted to research at The Assemblage." I was offering this absurd excuse as a reasonable explanation for my seemingly irrational behavior. Hopefully, the misdirection worked.

"What is it that you so desperately needed to research?" he asked, a faint smile crossing his lips, an interest in his eye. He wanted to know what I'd been doing.

And snap! Just like that, we'd managed to skirt the real issue. My body revolved in the chair toward the sheer magnetism of his presence. All the while his calculating eyes assessed my every move. I was undeniably riveted by those *come hither* eyes. Actually, come to think of it, every single part of him was strategically placed.

A weapon of mass destruction, the little voice growled.

"Emily, I came to ask…"

He paused.

We're at a critical tipping point here, Lachlan. Come on already.

"Will you consider delaying your meeting tomorrow—to discuss your return to Earth?" His lips puckered at those last few words, almost as if he'd tasted something sour.

"Can you give me one reason why I should?"

"Yes," he said.

I waited; impatient as usual. What is this elegant power he has over me?

He closed his eyes as if editing his words before saying them aloud. "Two actually…Shaw and DeRenne decided to take tomorrow afternoon off. They…I mean, we," he said with a nod, almost like he was giving himself permission. "We want to show you the underside of Arden."

I threw back my head in surprise. "The underside of Arden?"

For the second time tonight, Lachlan had my full attention, and he knew it. "It would be best if you did not mention those exact words to Paden and Ccri." Like Shaw earlier tonight, there was a mischievous glint in his eyes.

Well, how about that! How could I possibly pass on such a stealth adventure? "Exactly who's going on this mysterious outing?" I asked.

He hedged this time. "You, me, Shaw, DeRenne and..." I swear if he says her name, I'll punch him right in "...the Seren."

My mouth fell open. I didn't see that one coming. "Really?"

At that exact moment, Paden and Ccri walked into the room. Lachlan's jaw tightened imperceptibly. Ccri set the tray on the small side table to the left of my chair. Lachlan sat in the empty tub chair to my right, bringing the smell of the fire with him. From some detached place, I watched as Ccri poured four mugs of tea. "Thank you," I said taking the mug from her hand, relishing the warmth against my palms.

"Lachlan," she said, holding a second mug for him. He accepted the mug from her without directly looking at her, his eyes were currently holding mine hostage, trying to get a read on the state of my emotions.

"Emily," Paden said. "What do you wish to discuss?"

I slid around in the chair to face him. "For starters, I...I'm worried that when I return to Earth will Arden then seem like a dream to me? Maybe I'll think I've gone schizophrenic wondering if any of this even happened. I want to know if it's possible to stay in touch with someone here on Arden." In my side view, I saw Lachlan's back stiffen. "Are there other situations like mine? Is some form of communication possible through...the Seren?" I was grasping at straws, hyper aware that once I left Arden, the chance of seeing any of these people ever again was a big fat, zero.

"Emily," Paden said with a reassuring smile. "We have no intention of escorting you to Earth and having no further contact. As you know, there are individuals on Earth aware of our existence and future plans. Perhaps, you might help steer Earth toward intergalactic water travel."

"Oh." That certainly put a whole new spin on the issues at hand. "Is Earth that close?"

"In the morning I will speak with those in charge and determine a timeline before your departure," Paden said, throwing Ccri a guarded glance.

Lachlan sipped his tea. "I have asked Emily to clear her schedule tomorrow afternoon. I have not yet had a chance to spend time with her as requested."

Once again, I looked at him in surprise. Clever boy! He was playing 'the request card' to save face.

"Is that agreeable to you, Emily?" Ccri asked.

"Yes," I answered straightaway, surprising myself at the speed at which I agreed. Thankfully, she and Paden weren't that shocked by my change of heart nor did they ask where we were going on our little outing. Good, best to keep the details vague.

"Excellent," Paden said. "The additional time will give me an opportunity to gather more information on Earth's timeline."

"And additional time for you to watch more images at The Assemblage," Lachlan added.

"Yes, not a bad idea," Paden mumbled.

I shot him an exasperated look.

"If you are going to assist after your return to Earth, and considering our discussions from earlier tonight, then I cannot stress the importance of knowing what you are going up against," Lachlan said, relaxing his shoulders.

"I will wait to see what Paden finds out first before making any rash decisions."

"Hmm," Lachlan said, sipping his tea again. I could tell he was ordering his thoughts.

"I want you all to know that I'm open to any and all suggestions. I also want you to know that it's important for me to go at my own speed. I get the feeling the progression of Earth's mergence with The Accordance is just the tip of the iceberg."

"Which is why a day away from meetings before delving into the details is perhaps overdue," Lachlan said as soon as the words were out of my mouth.

"I agree," I said so that there'd be no doubt.

Lachlan stood from the chair and set his empty mug on the tray. "Either DeRenne or I will come here after lunch, depending on who is free," Lachlan said, sharing at look with Paden, who nodded.

"I need to cancel with…with. "What do I have tomorrow?" I wish I had my cell phone so I could keep everything straight.

"Nothing that cannot be rescheduled," Paden said, drumming his fingertips on the chair arm, lost in thought.

"I bid you goodnight then," Lachlan said with a short bow to Ccri and a last lingering glance for me.

"Until tomorrow," I said in a faint whisper.

Off like a dirty shirt, he maneuvered his way to the back of the house and vanished into the night. Watching him in action, it became abundantly clear that Lachlan was a smooth operator. I made a mental note about that particular character trait for future reference.

δ^+

"Oh! There you are," DeRenne said, kicking her feet in a sort of happy dance, bouncing down the short flight of stairs from the covered porch at the back of the house, her feather earrings swaying in step. "I knocked on the front door and no one answered. So, I let myself in. I am sorry I did not get here any earlier. The morning got away from me. Are you ready?"

I had been waiting outside Paden and Ccri's house, pacing and counting the seconds until someone came to fetch me. Seeing DeRenne so carefree, I decided not to be annoyed. I didn't want to spoil her good mood. "Sure," I said. "Do I need to bring anything?"

"Not that I can think of." DeRenne had an air of someone up to no good wavering all around her.

"Have you been on Arden all day?" I asked, figuring I at least had the right to know what kept her occupied all morning.

"I have not traveled off-world today if that is what you are implying. None of us have. Spending the afternoon with you worked out perfectly."

"So, now I'm an excuse," I said, regretting the words as soon as they came out of my mouth.

DeRenne's smile faded. "I am sorry that did not come out as intended. You are certainly not an excuse. The Accordance would never approve of the three of us staying on Arden for the day, with one exception."

"That girl from Earth." Damn. There it was again. Get with the program Emily.

DeRenne's eyes widened; she knew to whom I referred. "Exactly. That girl from Earth is as equally important as any mission." She pivoted on her heel and headed toward the small traveling pool behind the house. I guess she'd decided to ignore me.

"At least give me a hint as to where we're going," I said, walking behind her.

"And spoil the surprise. I think not." Her back stiffened, and by now I knew that was her tell. I wouldn't get any more information out of her so I shouldn't even try. "The sooner we get going the sooner you will know the answers to your questions." She touched my elbow, and I followed her into the water.

"The two of you should go inside and change," Shaw said as soon as we stepped out from the stream into a small clearing surrounded by tall, willow-like trees. "Lachlan sent word that he will meet us here in a few minutes."

Yikes! The thought of seeing him again after the roller coaster night both excited and frightened me. And now, I find out that we're changing. Into what? Since I already deflated DeRenne's mood once, I didn't want to do it a second time so I kept my mouth shut.

"The house is up the hill," DeRenne said, turning on her heel for a second time.

I followed her through the tidy vegetable and herb garden where the path took a steep curve. At the top of the short hill, the ground flattened into a grassy lawn and wide stone walkway connected to a covered entryway. DeRenne easily folded, and then pushed three accordion-style doors that disappeared into the side wall. Unlike the homes in the village, their sprawling single-story house went on forever. Less formal, the high glass walls and low furniture with clean lines and muted colors drew your eyes in every direction to the outdoors. This must be country living on Arden.

We walked through the open-space living area, past a double-sided river rock fireplace with a granite slab mantle that was open on the opposite side to a central kitchen. "My room is on this side of the house," she said, veering right and walking down a sunny hallway.

DeRenne's bedroom was extraordinary; layer upon layer of every imaginable shade of eggplant, mint, and pumpkin imbued her colors throughout the spacious room and delicately draped curtains. A pair of floor-to-ceiling, outward-swinging hinged doors with triangular-shaped windowed glass panes, opened onto a private patio surrounded by intricate wrought-iron fencing. Lying across the footboard of the white cottage-style bed covered in squishy pillows were two sets of…?

"Do I even want to know?" I asked, lifting one of the limp, silvery garments, the insubstantial fabric cool and slippery to the touch.

DeRenne's eyes narrowed. "Perhaps a survival suit is a good way to phrase it. The fabric keeps your core body temperature constant in extreme conditions."

"Extreme conditions!" I shot her an exasperated look. "Exactly where are we going that I need something to keep my core body temperature constant?" I air-quoted that last part, causing the limp garment to flail through the air.

She threw her right hand up like she was about to take a pledge. "Sworn to secrecy. You change. I will return in a moment." DeRenne disappeared back into the sunny hallway before I could question her further. I noted that she and Lachlan shared that skill of conveniently vanishing into thin air whenever they wanted to avoid answering any of my questions.

I stood alone in the room, staring at the iridescent garment. This is so not what I expected. Not that I had any idea of what to expect. Just like my room at Paden and Ccri's house, a rock wall and bubbling pool of water filled the entire back corner. But unlike my room, she had a large walk-in closet filled with a variety of mission uniforms hanging on one side of the closet and long dresses arranged by color on the opposite side. I found it a bit unnerving that the fabric of her mission uniforms didn't pixelate. The hanging garments looked more like over washed gray prison uniforms. Anyway, I told myself not to look because I had more pressing issues to deal with: Where are we going? Why am I wearing a survival suit? When will I see Lachlan? There it was again, that twinge of doubt sneaking in through the back door.

What if this morning, he woke up and realized that he'd made a huge mistake asking me to go today. Maybe he regretted his decision to come to Paden and Ccri's house in the first place. That part still confused me. How do I really know he left the café right after I did and went straight to their house and waited? He could've come to The Assemblage, and seen me contorted in a fetal position in the stone recliner, watching the ill-fated love story of Evening Star and Eamone. I did say that I was going there, and I did shut the door? Right?

"Get a grip Emily," I mumbled, stepping inside of the closet. "Too late. You're committed."

I slipped the dress over my head that I'd decided to wear after trying on every single piece of clothing I'd accumulated over the last few days, now a complete waste of time. But the mini fashion show at least occupied an hour of not sitting outside, alone. I stepped into the silvery survival suit; the intangible outfit light as a feather and quite pliable, almost a vaporous silk. I fastened the sleeve tabs, walked out from the closet, and looked in the mirror. I ran my hands down my sides and hips, turning around to check the rearview, grateful the fabric didn't reveal any unsightly bulges. Gilded in a metallic sheen, each and every time I moved, rainbow colors refracted through the fabric in a subtle shimmer.

At that exact moment, DeRenne walked into the room carrying two pairs of reef-runner type shoes with suction-cup bottoms. "Here you are," she said, assessing the outfit. "I thought that would fit."

"Does this survival suit allow me to fade into the background?" I asked, the tone in my voice making it clear that I really didn't like being the odd-man-out.

"No," she said, lifting her silvery survival suit from the footboard of the bed. "The cloth is woven from an organic polymer coated in diamond dust. Diamond is an excellent insulator; its crystalline structure gives the fabric its sheen."

"Interesting," I said, eyeing her on the way out to the patio so she could change in private.

I sat on the stone bench, slipping my foot into the suction-cup shoes, racking my brain as to why I needed to wear these crazy shoes in the first place. I pressed my foot into the brick pavers. Thankfully, the suction cups didn't stick. Good, at least I wouldn't trip accidently on the cumbersome shoes.

DeRenne's voice from the doorway made me look up. "There is a short-cut," she said. "The guys are waiting for us near the path."

I gulped. No more delaying tactics. I was about to find out the answers to the endless barrage of questions. I walked through the bedroom, down the sunny hallway, past the open-space living area, and into the central kitchen. She opened a glass door in the far corner. Seeing nothing but blue and green, I realized that we were in the tree canopy. Their house sat perched on the top of a mountain. You wouldn't have a clue entering the house way we did except for the steep climb at the end.

I'd say it was a suspension bridge walkway built from the rib bones of a whale skeleton but the floorboards and side rails were definitely made of wood. Anyway, down we went through the twisting and descending walkway, admiring the view of the treetops and the blue sky. I kept steadying my gurgling stomach the entire way, telling myself that everything would work out just fine.

The walkway ended in a rather impressive straight wooden staircase with double handrails leading to an intimate, circular-shaped, outdoor eating area bordered by the leafy forest. The guys waited for us at the bottom of the steps.

I realized with the exception of that horrible one-minute encounter on the granite step my first day on Arden, I'd never seen Lachlan in the daylight. The normally pale, pale eyes morphed into a searing green against the great outdoors; the loosely gathered strands of blond hair glistening in the sunlight.

I suddenly felt very insignificant, again.

"Ladies," Shaw said, his eyes melting like warm butter on a hot pancake when he saw DeRenne. Without breaking stride, she took hold of his outstretched hand.

"This way," Lachlan said, gesturing to a path disappearing deep into the forest. I fell in line behind DeRenne with no idea of where we were going or what we were doing. And since no one bothered to offer an explanation, I decided it best to follow along.

And then it hit me. I stopped dead in my tracks and glanced over my shoulder. "We're going to …walk!"

"Our destination is not that far into the woods," Lachlan said, suppressing a smirk.

"I'm not at all worried about the distance. It's just well… peculiar."

"We have the day off, remember?" he said, reaching around my shoulder, holding back a branch, his piercing eyes tracking my every move.

"Thank you," I said in a faint whisper, having once again lost the ability to speak in his presence.

We went on like this for a couple more twists and turns, going deeper in the woods before switching directions. The day was cool and quiet, except for my heart pounding away in my chest. We hiked a gentle slope past a shallow waterfall feeding a slowly moving stream. The leafy forest encroached all around until we entered a small clearing of ancient ruins. My heart sank. The tangle of vines curling up the stacked-stone walls and attached columns reached for the few rays of sunlight that managed to filter all the way down through the thick foliage.

"I hope we're not going in here," I mumbled, peering into a dark and dank sinkhole in the middle of what at one time must've been the central plaza. It was a sheer drop into obscurity.

"No, over there," Shaw said, pointing to a jagged opening in the side of an earthen bank. "We are going down a lava tube."

"A who?" I asked.

"A…lava…tube," Shaw sang the words, unable to conceal his excitement. "The lava river continues to flow after the volcanic eruption stops, leaving an underground tunnel. This particular lava tube connects to the vast system of Arden's underground caves."

Lachlan's face, alight with the knowledge that something big was about to happen, and I do mean BIG, didn't conceal his amusement.

"Is this what you meant by the underside of Arden?" I asked, never having done any real spelunking. Unfortunately, his face broke into a wide grin. "Do we at least have lights?" I noticed that none of them carried a pack or had any supplies. If I was forced to spend a beautiful day down in the dark, I at least wanted to see exactly what I'd gotten myself into.

"Come on," Lachlan said, gesturing with his hand. "You will see."

Last in line, I turned sideways, squeezed through the narrow opening, and made a slight turn to the right. The air inside of the small space felt damp and warm from the water vapor condensing on the earthen walls. Our lights waited just beyond the entrance; thousands and thousands of Seren, their glowing bodies throwing glints and glimmers in every direction. "This first part is a little tricky," Shaw said. "We slide down the lava tube to a subterranean cistern. True, we could have traveled with the water, as you so kindly suggested, but what is the fun in that?"

"Well, there's nothing like a baptism by fire," I said, gawking at the pitch-black opening just wide enough for us to slide down one at a time. "I guess if I can travel to a planet…in a different galaxy…then I can certainly throw myself down a rabbit hole on that planet."

"I will go down the lava tube first, and wait for you in the water," Shaw announced. And before I could utter a single word, he threw himself feet-first into the tunnel, a swarm of Seren zipping alongside.

"They light the way," DeRenne said, her eyes wide with excitement.

I looked from Lachlan to DeRenne and then back to Lachlan, Shaw's yelps of joy growing weaker followed by a faint splash, and then another muffled yelp. A dozen or so Seren promptly zoomed out from the mouth of the lava tube.

"He is ready for you," Lachlan said, pointing to the opening.

I walked the short distance and dutifully plopped down on the rock ledge with as much grace as possible under the circumstances. A briskly moving stream of water spilled out from underneath the rock ledge, disappearing down into the dark tunnel. Lachlan knelt behind me, reached his arms around my shoulders, and firmly grasped each of my wrists. He positioned my hands flat against the sides of the slippery lava tube. "Straighten yourself so that you are more in the middle," he ordered all bossy-like.

I managed not to roll my eyes, scooted left, and centered my body on the ledge, extending both legs out in front of me. "How's this?" I asked, my voice echoing inside of the lava tube.

"Perfect," he whispered, and I could feel his breath, warm and moist against my ear. "The Seren will guide you."

I inhaled a deep breath, counted to three, and fired off. Almost immediately, I entered a dramatic right-hand curve. Centripetal acceleration threw me against the side of the slippery tunnel. Zipping down through the darkness surrounded by the dazzling lights, blood pounding furiously in both of my ears, I screamed from the sheer rush of fierce joy.

The tunnel changed directions and I banked left, airborne for an instant before plummeting even deeper into the tunnel, and then airborne again. All too soon, I shot out of the lava tube, suspended in the air for a shining second inside of the swarm of glittering Seren before plunging feet-first into the cool water. I surfaced a moment later like a slippery seal.

"I have you," Shaw said, reaching out and grasping an arm. "And?" His eyes were bright with anticipation.

"Incredible!" I said. "Absolutely incredible!"

"As promised," he grinned, turning toward the swarm of Seren. "Tell the others to come on." A blur of lights disappeared into the tunnel.

It was a cave of crystals, shimmering faceted giant columns, stalactites, and stalagmites of every possible description, almost as if someone went around and sprinkled the surface with finely crushed mica. Hundreds of thousands of Seren darted and dive-bombed the deep pool, sending tiny wavelets rippling in every direction. The Caribbean-blue water, internally glowing from the presence of this luminescent life form, created a strange and haunting illusion of floating inside of an immense jewel. I swam around in a large circle trying to take it all in.

DeRenne's high-pitched squeals reverberating from the inside of the tunnel made me look up. She catapulted out of the lava tube, hovering in the air inside of the glittering swarm of Seren before diving into the water, smoothly, with no splashing. She shot out from the water a second later into Shaw's waiting arms.

"Come here you," he said playfully, pulling her off to the side.

Next up were Lachlan's triumphant howls. He careened out from the tunnel head-first, gathering speed for a spectacular dive, the pursuing Seren streaming a brilliant tail to the human comet.

"Pretentious," Shaw coughed.

Lachlan shot through the water like a torpedo, stirring the shoals of swimming Seren, leaving a glowing wake behind him. He exploded out from the water next to the group, looking as if he didn't have a care in the world.

Crowded together, treading water, my hands and face registered the water as cold. The survival suit adhered to my body like a glove, keeping me toasty warm. "How did you find this place?" I asked, my voice resonating around the high cavern.

DeRenne made an impertinent noise in the back of her throat. "Shaw and Lachlan's old tutor used to bring them down here to look for buried treasure," she said. "I had to stay home and memorize the names of the planets in the Triangulum Galaxy." She stuck her tongue out at the pair of them.

I laughed. Poor DeRenne, it must've been trying growing up around these two.

"This is true, DeRenne," Shaw muttered a little darkly. "You must also remember that we never found any treasure he considered worth keeping."

"Follow me, Emily," DeRenne huffed before submerging beneath the surface, still clearly annoyed.

We swam to the side and hopped out of the water onto a flat rock shelf. I now understood the point of the suction-cup shoes. True, they make a wet swishy noise negotiating the slimy rocks but at least you didn't slip.

One by one, we squeezed sideways through a narrow lopsided fracture in the stone wall, meandering through several twisting side tunnels and passageways, poking our heads into various empty alcoves and chambers. Off in one side chamber, twenty-foot long, limestone chandeliers, eerily glowing from the presence of the thousands of alighted Seren, created a supernatural feel to this otherworldly place. I stopped for a moment, hypnotized by the endless patter of milky, rose-colored water droplets falling from the tips of the hanging chandeliers. "Glad you stayed on Arden for the day?" Lachlan asked from behind my shoulder.

I whirled around on the squishy shoes, and said a little too eagerly, "Yes. The ride through the lava tube and these caverns are definitely worth the trip." His pleased smile sent my heart into a pounding frenzy. I discreetly placed a hand over my chest, convinced that he could hear it beating in this silent world with that silver disk stuck to the inside of his ear.

"Ladies," Shaw said, jumping over a couple of steps crudely cut into the stone, a wobbly boulder as a make-shift handhold. A huge swarm of Seren zipped past us in a blur of light trails, illuminating the tunnel ahead.

DeRenne went down the rickety incline first. I went next, and lost my footing, toppling forward. A now familiar pair of hands gripped both of my shoulders. "Careful," Lachlan said, enjoying his role as savior way too much.

"Yeah, yeah," I mumbled.

Safely deposited on the landing, Lachlan touched my elbow. I walked with him around a clear pool of water outlined by a serpentine deposit of white, iridescent minerals. Shimmering like glass over the black volcanic sand, the absolutely still surface caught our reflection; the mirrored image of our silvery suits made us appear angelic.

Stepping over a jumble of stones, and then squeezing through another narrow fissure, we marched single file across a natural stone bridge connected to a subterranean lake housed inside of an enormous underground grotto. “There is an opening beyond those stalagmites,” Shaw said, pointing to a grouping of spiked columns with thick trunks on the opposite bank.

The lake was big but not impossible. The moving water meant that it was fed by an underground stream. I estimated a three to four-minute swim at most. Not a problem. We approached the edge of the lake. I dove into the water, surfaced, and then launched into a breaststroke. Moving along at a pretty good clip, I seemed to be taking the lead. Feeling smug for once, I glanced backward on the next breath to see how far ahead I’d gotten.

No one swam behind me. How did that happen? No one had passed me. I stopped swimming. That’s when I saw the three of them on the opposite bank doubled over with laughter. Oh, crap! They didn’t swim the length of the lake; they traveled through the water. And here I was, the lone Earthling all impressed with herself. “Stay there,” Lachlan yelled through his cupped hands. “I will come and get you.”

Before I could answer back, he popped out from the water right beside me. “Whoa!” I cried out, rocking backward in the small waves.

The strands of wet hair flattened against his high forehead, accentuated his mischievous eyes. Without asking first, he reached out and seized me around the waist. Of their own accord, both of my arms floated upward and securely grasped his shoulders. I stared in horror at those traitor arms.

I swear a satisfied smirk crossed his lips but I couldn't really be sure. A fraction of a second later we were standing on the opposite bank next to the others. Lachlan easily held me at eye-level which meant that my feet dangled about four inches above the wet ground. "Oh! Sorry," he said, setting me down.

I landed on the slimy rocks with a drippy *squish,* immediately taking several steps backward. Out of the corner of my eye, I saw that DeRenne and Shaw were having a hard time holding in their laughter. "Oh, go ahead," I grumbled. "I imagine from your point of view it was comical."

We all looked at each other and kind of lost it. All four of us started to laugh, and once started, it was impossible to stop. "I thought you had the day off," I said, still stung by having appeared stupid.

"I am…so…so sorry, Emily," DeRenne howled, placing a hand over her stomach, unable to stop laughing. "I forget, and then…and then…I turned around and you were…swimming."

I folded my arms across my waist, shaking my head back and forth in disgust.

"You are all right for an extraterrestrial," Shaw said, yanking my wet hair as he walked past.

"Thanks!" I grumbled, again. "I think."

Behind me, a portion of the cavern wall belled out forming a small ledge. I hobbled over, sat down, and slipped my left shoe off. I tipped the shoe over; a tiny pebble pelted to the ground.

"Wow, this cave is breathing," I said, rubbing the sore spot on my heel, shivering from the cold air blowing on the back of my neck. "There must be another series of caves or an opening to the outside on the other side of this." I twisted my waist and patted the massive stone wall with my hand.

"Are you certain," Shaw asked in a surprised tone. "We explored the entire cave system."

"Then come on over and see for yourself," I challenged, slipping the shoe on. Never one to be dissuaded, Shaw made his way toward me, squishing the suction-cup shoes the entire way. He butt-bumped me off to the side, leaned forward, and put a hand over the narrow crack.

"She is correct," he said. "Air is pouring out."

Several hundred Seren zipped through the tiny crack, zooming out a minute later, hovering around Shaw's, Lachlan's, and DeRenne's heads. Almost like they were tuned into the same frequency, they each reached up, and touched the silver disk in their earlobes.

"Are you sure?" Lachlan cried out.

No one had said a word.

"Breathable air," DeRenne inquired.

"Should we alert anyone?" Shaw asked. Oddly he and DeRenne turned to look at Lachlan. They waited for his answer and I found myself doing the same.

"No," he said. "We will take a look first before getting them involved."

“Yes, you are probably correct,” Shaw said.

“Would somebody please tell me what’s going on!” I insisted. It was like listening to a one-sided conversation.

“Sorry… sorry… sorry,” their voices echoed around the high ceiling.

“It seems that you have located a previously undiscovered cavern,” Lachlan said with a new-found authority. “And one we should investigate.”

Shaw pretended to sit on me and lost his footing, dropping straight to the ground. “Why?” I asked, getting out of the way just in time. “What’s the big deal?”

“Apparently, the Seren saw some inscriptions on the cavern walls,” DeRenne said.

“In that case then,” I said, spinning around on the spot, and avoiding Shaw’s prone body. I leaned forward to examine the crack. “If there is a way to get some heavy equipment down here, we might be able to...”

“Emily,” Lachlan said my name with a teasing intonation.

“What?” I said, still studying the massive stone wall.

“Are you or are you not on a different planet besides Earth?” he asked.

“Tsk, tsk,” Shaw said, getting to his feet. “And right after the swimming incident no less.” He’d never miss an opportunity to rib me if one presented itself.

“Oh! Right!” I stood, turning towards the swarm of fluttering Seren. “Hmm, any water inside there guys?” I glanced over my shoulder at Lachlan. “How do I know if they heard me? Any chance I could get one of those silver ear thingies?”

“Perhaps,” Lachlan chuckled.

I turned back to the stone wall mumbling under my breath, "Are you sure we're not going to materialize inside of solid rock or worse."

"Welcome to our world," Shaw said, crooking an elbow and standing with one foot in the lake. I debated for a moment, deciding if I should trust him. "Ready?"

I walked to his side, snaked an arm through his. "Let's bounce."

"Are you sure?" Shaw asked with a lift of the brow.

I took a deep breath. "I don't know about how sure, but yeah, let's do this."

"Better," he said, grinning.

Several Seren flew to his side to assist. As soon as my big toe touched the water, the cavern dissolved into a kaleidoscope of brilliant colors. The next instant we stood ankle-deep in water inside of a cathedral of dazzling multicolored minerals and faceted crystals. There weren't any tall and thick stalactites and stalagmites or endless dripping, only the constant hum of blowing wind.

My senses told me we'd entered a sacred place. "Guys, I think this is a wind cave. I visited one in South Dakota with my aunt a few years back. The Lakota called it a breathing hole; a doorway from which the first messengers or sacred beings arrived. Let me see, how did the park ranger phrase it? Something about how to become human, heal the sick and let me think... Oh! See visions."

"The inscriptions on the walls could very well be the work of our ancestors," Shaw said, walking around in a tight circle.

"Their stories refer to a cavern used by the first travelers as an arrival and departure platform."

"Before they had the ability to blend into the natural surroundings," DeRenne added for my benefit.

Swarms of Seren zoomed into the expansive space, throwing light in every direction, illuminating a mind-boggling number of words, pictures, and symbols chiseled and hammered across the steep stone walls. The pattern, scale, and archetypal quality of the inscriptions hinted at their age, and at the sophistication of the people who carved them. The whole thing must have taken untold numbers of man-hours to complete.

"Here," Lachlan said in a hushed tone, gesturing to us with his hand. DeRenne, Shaw, and I edged our way around a cluster of boulders riddled with angular cracks.

Five sets of inscriptions of equal length were etched across the smooth stone walls. I figured they were more than likely the same message in different languages and writing styles. One set of inscriptions reminded me of the symbols I saw on the standing stone in the passageway leading to Paden and Ccri's house.

Ever so slowly, I moved forward, hesitated, made my mind up, took two more tiny steps forward, and inched around in front of Lachlan for a closer look. As if it was the most natural act in the world, he stepped back a smidgen to make room for me. "Can you translate these symbols?" I asked, my voice *swooshing* along the wind.

We all watched as Lachlan traced the set of inscriptions to his right with his finger, the wavering silence was broken only by the wind gusting through the immense cavern almost as if the wind itself was a physical presence in this place. "They are instructions on how to control the elements," Lachlan said.

"The Generating Elements

Wood feeds fire
Fire creates the Earth
Earth bears metal
Metal collects water
Water nourishes wood"

"Overcoming the Elements

Wood parts Earth
Earth absorbs water
Water quenches fire
Fire melts metal
Metal chops wood"

Lachlan looked down at me and said, "Remember last night at dinner you asked about the colors?" I nodded, sensing his nearness with every fiber of my being. "They also apply here: wood is represented by a verdant green, fire is a flame red, earth a sunny yellow, pure metals are pristine white, and water is a starless black."

"Black for water?" I said in a subdued voice, the air definitely tinged by magic.

"Black is the absence of color," Lachlan said and there was something in his tone. "Water sparkles with clarity and life due to its ability to bend light waves, not because of its ability to reflect wavelengths of colored light. And, we must always remember water is the compound that vanquished the blackness of empty space, forever linking all galaxies in the Universe."

He had a point. Given a choice, I'm not exactly sure what color I'd assign to water. I'd choose silver or some other sparkly color, although those choices seem trite to me now. Lost in the thread of my own unspooling thoughts, I didn't follow when they moved on to peruse another set of inscriptions on an adjacent wall.

After visiting the wind cave in South Dakota, I understood that ancient places have whispers and secrets. I had a feeling that whatever happened down in this cavern significantly influenced Arden's development. Standing still, watching the Seren darting in and out of the vertical cracks and crevices running up and down the craggy stone wall to my left, something gleamed in the light. I hopped over and then squeezed through the cluster of boulders riddled with the angular cracks.

I hesitated for a heartbeat.

"Guys," I said a little hoarsely. "You might want to see what I found." Draped over my pointer finger was a silvery survival suit exactly like the ones we were wearing.

Three things happened at once.

First, Lachlan hissed the name, Jokull, with such a menacing timbre that I instinctively took a step backward. Second, he turned to Shaw, whose demeanor instantly transformed, assuming an almost reverent posture. "Organize the Seren to keep watch," Lachlan ordered like a general announcing the battle plan to his staff. "Instruct them to remain hidden but to alert The Accordance the moment anyone enters this cavern."

"At once," Shaw said, eyeing the large swarm of Seren that suddenly gathered near his face.

Third, he locked DeRenne in his sights. "Take Emily back *Now!* Wait for us at the house. I will report the Bradwr."

At his words, DeRenne literally walked up into the air, and over the cluster of boulders I now cowered behind. The look in her eyes clearly indicated that she was coming…for me. I didn't have time to react. She snatched me into her arms as she streamed past. The next instant we stood in the middle of her bedroom surrounded by a puff of smoke. DeRenne released her grip, and I toppled to the floor like a ragdoll. "Oh!" Her hand flew up to her lips. "I forget."

"What happened to the part where you step into the water?" I mumbled. As soon as DeRenne grabbed hold of me down in the cavern, I had the strangest sensation of being stretched like a piece of taffy, and then shoved feet-first into a meat grinder; a harsh electric groan of metal grinding against metal still clattering away in both of my ears.

"We evanesced through the gaseous water vapor in the air," DeRenne said, wearing a horrified expression.

"Evan who?"

"Evanesced," she said, enunciating each syllable. "True, it is not as fluid as flowing with the liquid water. It allows you to travel short bursts in a tight situation. When Lachlan said, *'Now!'* he meant right then. I did not have time to get us back to the water."

I rocked over onto my side, sat in a sitting position, and pushed the hair plastered to my face off to the side. "We need to have a little chat but first I would like to change."

DeRenne looked distressed. Indisputably, I'd just watched her walk through the air, and overheard a conversation I probably shouldn't have heard. There is no way she was going to get out of answering my any questions this time. And she knew it.

δ^+

Lachlan stood in front of the massive cavern wall covered in inscriptions from top to bottom and from side to side. The coloration in the deep grooves left little doubt that the inscriptions were very ancient. This type of stone is not easily worked implying that whoever did this meant for it to last. The entire wall was lighted by a well-like opening in the ceiling that also allowed the moaning wind to pour in.

"What do you make of this," Lachlan asked, running his hands across the linear grooves. "Is there some hidden meaning, something we need to decipher?"

"No idea," Shaw said, studying the wall. "We need to find out as much as we can before alerting those in charge. Looks older than anything I have seen before or studied at The Assemblage. You will most likely be allowed to return but not me."

"What about Emily?" Lachlan asked.

"I would love to hear DeRenne's explanation," Shaw said. "Honestly, we looked for this cavern for years, and she what, drops out from the sky and…"

Lachlan looked at Shaw. "This is what concerns me. She has no idea what she has gotten herself into the middle of. I would like to keep it that way."

“That one, my friend, is on you. You should have seen her face when DeRenne started to evanesce.”

“I am going to need to talk to DeRenne about showing her hand.”

“I think it was just instinct,” Shaw said. “After all, we have been practicing.”

“True, yet this adds another layer,” Lachlan said, shaking his head.

δ^+

Whack...whack...whack. DeRenne stationed me at the kitchen counter near the double-sided river rock fireplace so that my hair would dry. I was dicing several odd-looking root vegetables into bite-size pieces to add to the stew. I'd changed back into the plum-colored dress, grateful now that I'd spent the time deciding what to wear since I was staying for supper.

"And if you do not mind, this too," DeRenne said, setting something that reminded me of a tomato on the cutting board.

"I'm ready," I announced.

She appraised the knife in my hand. "While evanescing through the gaseous water vapor, you can decrease your velocity, giving the false impression that you are walking through the air instead of traveling through it." She quickly threw her hand up into the air when my brow furrowed. "I did not want to overshoot and miss bringing you here."

"Why the puff of smoke?" I asked, scooting the square chunks off to the side. I started chopping the celery-looking vegetable.

"A cloud of water vapor, actually," she said, not doing a very good job keeping her voice level. "The energy released when you come to a stop blows apart the moisture droplets in the air forming a gaseous cloud."

"How?" I asked, my adamant tone leaving no wiggle room.

"Years of practice and intense concentration. In truth very rare; not something we want others to become aware of. To say that it is sanctioned by The Accordance would not be a complete truth." She hesitated before adding, "Let me just say there is another use besides the added convenience of traveling short bursts through the gaseous water vapor if you find yourself in a difficult situation."

"Care to elaborate?"

She looked up from her stirring. "If I did, then I would have to kill you."

Me and my big mouth. "What's a Bradwr?"

"A traitor," she whispered.

"And what does this traitor have to do with you three?"

"The traitor's name is Jokull, which means *ice glacier*," DeRenne said. "He was Shaw and Lachlan's tutor."

I looked at her, the knife hanging in midair. "The guy who had them looking for buried treasure in the caverns?"

"One and the same," she muttered, adding spices to the big copper pot.

"What?! He had them searching for that particular cavern when they thought they were treasure hunting?" I pulled back on the chopping; pulverizing the vegetables into tiny pieces was not the intent.

"It seems so," she said. "That cavern was always considered a legend until today. With your discovery, I bet everyone must be beside themselves right about now."

"So much for keeping a low profile," I said.

"They will most likely question you." Her lips formed a thin line. "I am sure Lachlan is trying to stall them."

"I don't mind talking to them, although I had the impression from Lachlan that he would've preferred keeping today's destination under wraps." Now I was mortified. "Guess that's not going to happen. I'm sorry if I got anyone in trouble."

"The caverns are one of the few places on the planet where we can get away," she sighed. "No one else ever goes down there."

"Your sanctuary?" I mumbled, nodding in solidarity at the loss of their safe haven.

At that exact moment, Lachlan ambled into the kitchen still wearing his silvery survival suit, looking like he didn't have a care in the world. At the sight of him, a jittery sense of anticipation fluttered in the pit of my stomach.

Somehow, he managed to squeeze his lean body into the small space between the river rock fireplace and the section of kitchen counter where I was still dicing. He selected a square piece of vegetable from the pile off to the side and popped it into his mouth. "Have you been busy?" he asked.

"I have, although I wager you've been busier."

"A very interesting conversation," he said, and there was something in his tone that I couldn't get a read on, "Paden may have a few more questions for you later tonight."

"Anything I should try to conceal?" I asked.

"The swimming incident for sure," Lachlan said, raising a single eyebrow.

DeRenne made a snorting noise in the back of her throat.

"Very funny." I scooted over a root vegetable from the pile and *whacked* it in half in one fell swoop.

"Noted," Lachlan said, eyeing the knife in my hand. "How much longer, sis?"

"The preparation will go faster if you help instead of distract," she said without looking up from her stirring. Lachlan made an impatient noise in the back of his throat this time.

"Thank you, by the way," I said in a low voice. Lachlan tilted his head to the side, his eyes intrigued. "Today was my best day on Arden so far; the Seren, the colors, the unexpectedness of the entire experience."

"My pleasure," he said, reaching around my waist to grab another square chunk from the pile.

"Emily, do not let him eat everything before I have a chance to add it to the stew," DeRenne teased. "You have to watch him every second."

"You heard your sister," I said, brandishing the knife.

Lachlan contorted his body so that DeRenne couldn't see, reached across the cutting board, and scooped up a handful of vegetables.

"Hey, stop that," DeRenne said.

"Eyes in the back of her head," Lachlan mumbled under his breath, disappearing down the sunny hallway to his side of the house.

"Interesting turn of events," Shaw remarked as he passed. He was now dressed in regular clothes. "What, six days on Arden, and you find *the cavern.*"

"Beginner's luck," I said, watching him gently place a hand on DeRenne's back, and then lean forward to get a whiff of the stew.

"That smells delicious," he said. "I am starving."

Whack...whack...whack. I went back to chopping to give them some privacy.

In the end, we pooled our various culinary skills to finish preparing the food. At his request, Lachlan and I carried the napkins, silverware, and candles down the twisting walkway in the tree canopy, now softly lit by the lanterns hanging inside the arch formed by the curved side rails. I lifted the hem of the dress before walking down the wooden staircase leading to the outdoor eating area bordered by the feathery forest.

It was not as dark as I expected it to be inside of the woods at this time of day. Life seemed to broadcast a different frequency tonight; a composition with a mellow timbre. Somewhere beneath the raised flower beds, you could hear flowing water and chirping insects. "That throws me every night," I sighed, nodding up at the sky. "During the day Arden and Earth seem so similar, and then every night at dusk, there's this." Keit filled the night sky with a soft coral glow.

"During this season of our year, Keit is in perigee causing it to appear closer to Arden than normal," Lachlan said, wobbling the plate in his hand back and forth, a muted radiance glinting in the colors embedded in the glass. "We call this Keitlight."

"Keitlight," I whispered, a blank look settling across my face. "Light reflecting off of a planet instead of a moon. Who would've thought I'd ever see such a thing?"

There was a long silence in which the breeze picked up, rustling the leaves in the willowy trees. "Is it happening?" Lachlan asked, edging around the circular wooden table to where I was standing. He'd changed from the silvery survival suit into a white linen, long-sleeved shirt, brown pants, and the same laced leather boots he wore to supper my first night on Arden. He kept his hair loose tonight, the slightly wavy strands just touching his shoulders. Out here, in the Keitlight, I had to admit that he was easy on the eyes.

"Happening?" I muttered. If his plan was to befuddle me, it had worked. I watched as he set the last glass plate on the tabletop, edging a shade closer to me. I finished doling out the silverware in my hand, gravitating to him like a compass needle pointing north.

"The part where everything about Arden overwhelms you?" he asked, concern coloring his voice.

"Well," I sighed. "To be perfectly honest, I'm just dandy, and then someone throws me a curveball."

"A curveball?"

"Something that seems to comes out of nowhere. Does that ever happen to you? I mean you've probably traveled to countless planets and seen a ton of… of unbelievable sights."

"Today someone did throw me a curveball, taking me by surprise," he said, his voice suddenly low and pleasant.

"Finding the cavern?" I said, waving a hand. "Naa. That's just old-fashion luck."

"True, that was certainly a surprise," he said, smiling about something. "However, your discovery is not the surprise I was referring to."

I looked at him, puzzled.

"What is going on you two?" DeRenne demanded, walking down the wooden staircase carrying a tray of food, Shaw behind her with the drinks.

"No idea," I said, still looking into Lachlan's eyes. "Your brother is talking in riddles."

"That is nothing new," DeRenne said, giving him a quick wink. "Give it some time. You will grow accustomed."

"Okay. Whatever," I mumbled. Lachlan still smiled, and against my better judgment I found it contagious, and smiled back.

We all got to work. Lachlan lit the candles while DeRenne arranged the purple ceramic bowls filled with stew at each place setting. Shaw followed DeRenne, placing two pieces of thickly sliced bread on each glass plate. I noticed that the basket and the remaining slices of bread ended up next to his plate. The four of us settled nicely into the cushioned rattan chairs in the perfect boy-girl-boy-girl configuration tonight.

The evening became a delightful event; good conversation, good refreshments, and a wonderful distraction from what was really on our minds. Everything was going along swimmingly until Lachlan said, "Emily, we will be off-world for the next couple of days."

The curls in my hair wilted along with my good mood. "I thought that might be the case," I said, trying not to sound too discouraged. I dabbed the corner of my mouth with the napkin, hesitated, and then blurted out before I could stop myself, "I thought perhaps, maybe…there's something I could do to…"

Lachlan's back flexed. "That is impossible. The Accordance would never…"

"Relax," I said, giving him a friendly jab to the shoulder. "I know they'd never approve of me going off-world with you three. I was thinking more along the lines of…er…research."

"What kind of research?" Shaw asked his interest piqued.

I set the soup spoon on the glass plate. "I could profile Jokull for you."

Lachlan threw DeRenne a disapproving look.

"She asked," DeRenne said, shrugging her shoulders. "After all, Emily is the person who discovered the cavern."

"It's no longer a secret," I said, moving my pointer finger in a circle to get the spotlight back on me, holding Lachlan's comment at bay for DeRenne's sake. "Anyway, I'll be here on Arden, all alone…by myself, and I really don't want to spend any more time sitting next to a snoring Groth."

That got a smile, Lachlan careful not to meet my eye as he dipped his bread in the stew.

"What is a profile?" DeRenne asked, handing Shaw her uneaten bread, the basket now empty.

"My father is a profiler for a law firm. He researches a person's life and puts together a psychological profile." I sat back in the seat without turning around to meet the hot eyes I felt focused on my back. "He talks about his work at home; says the best defense or offense is to learn as much as you can about someone. I've never met the man…the only thing I do know is…is that he's considered a traitor."

Shaw looked disapprovingly at DeRenne. She had the good sense to ignore him too.

"I don't have any preconceived notions," I continued. "I'd search the archives at The Assemblage for any information pertaining to his life, and then present you an unbiased view."

"Not a bad idea," DeRenne said.

"I'll go crazy here, missing out on all of the fun," I said, the desire to make this place a part of my life growing by leaps and bounds. I didn't want them, especially Lachlan, to know how involved I'd become.

"Or you could return to Earth," Lachlan said, setting his glass down on the table with a decisive *clink.*

I turned to glare at Lachlan. He had a tight set to his lips. My galloping emotions whisked me down a dark path that I really didn't want to travel. "Excuse me??"

"So you are safe," he said, meeting my gaze.

"Am I in danger?"

"No," Shaw answered straightaway. DeRenne sat stunned into silence.

What happened? Why the about face? I was caught in a tailspin with no idea of how to regain control. I looked to Shaw and DeRenne for a little moral support. None was forthcoming. I turned back to Lachlan, blinking back the embarrassment.

"I see now that my suggestion was a bad idea," Lachlan said, keeping his thoughts well in check, his charm carefully in place. "Please continue explaining your profiling idea."

There was one little problem; none of us were buying any of it. And if he thought Earth girls folded like a card table at the first sign of danger then he was in for the shock of his off-world life! I angled my head, flipping a lock of hair past his nose. "My father says that you compile information about ordinary topics such as hobbies, family history, education, where they lived, and then look for a pattern. See if something jumps out at you," I said, talking over the alarm bells wailing inside of my head. "Information that might shed new light on an old subject and reveal any hidden strengths or weaknesses. You all know him, but do you really know what makes him tick? Sometimes it's difficult to see the forest for the trees when you're so personally involved."

I looked hopeful. The thought of several days with nothing to do was swallowing me whole, especially after Lachlan's comment.

"She does make an astute observation. What do we really know about Jokull?" DeRenne asked her eyes enormous and lost in the past. "At the time he was an authority figure in our lives. We simply accepted him at face value…never questioned his motives."

Shaw's head bobbed up and down, as he absentmindedly wrung his hands. I'd certainly hit a nerve.

"I will speak with Paden first," I said, giving Lachlan a sideways glance.

I could feel him thinking, the air between us heavy with his deliberating. "I shall escort Emily back to the village tonight," Lachlan announced with an increased intensity in the line of his mouth.

My head was reeling from yet another abrupt change of course. I begged DeRenne with my eyes to rescue me. She rose to her feet and dropped her napkin on the tabletop. "In a few minutes, big brother," she said. "There are a couple of items Emily needs to take with her...in my room."

I followed DeRenne up the wooden staircase, hoping to drag this out long enough to get some answers, but not long enough to let her know that her brother was breaking my heart.

"What was that all about?" I asked, once we reached her room and shut all of the doors.

"No idea," DeRenne said, twirling a lock of hair around a forefinger. "Maybe something happened when he went to report the cavern."

"Maybe something with the girl in orange?" I pressed.

DeRenne looked at me. "Raffye? Not anymore," she said, disappearing into the closet. "What do you need?"

"Pants," I answered, wishing that I could've gotten more information out of her. Something brown came whizzing past.

"Better take these too," she said in a muffled voice from deep inside the closet, tossing out a pair of chartreuse slippers. The slippers were so outrageous that I didn't know if I could actually take them with me let alone wear them. I kicked each slipper under the bed one at a time making sure that she wouldn't notice until it was too late.

"Anything I can do to help?" I asked, feeling a little awkward standing alone in the middle of the ever-growing mound of clothing.

She came out from the closet saying really fast, "Lachlan is very guarded with his emotions. Sometimes it is difficult to get a fix on exactly what is swirling around in that big head of his. One thing I do know."

She hesitated.

"You're keeping me hanging, DeRenne. And…?" Her brow furrowed.

"DeRenne!" I cried out, no longer caring if my true feelings were about to be exposed. "You surprise him," she said, her eyes boring a hole through my heart. "After his comment tonight, I thought you should know what is in front of you because there is something going on with you as well."

"That noticeable?"

"Seriously," she said with a sly smile. "The two of you are equally stubborn so the next few weeks should be interesting. Let us not tarry in here too long; he has a suspicious mind. You should know that about him. His brain never stops, even when he is sleeping."

"I'll take that under advisement," I said.

Strictly for the effect, I picked a few random items from the pile. Ten minutes later when DeRenne and I made our appearance at the outdoor eating area, Shaw tended the fire. Lachlan waited for me next to the stream. "Wish me luck," I whispered, giving DeRenne a quick hug goodbye. "See you in a few days," I hollered at Shaw.

"Have a nice evening, you two," he said, tossing another log on the fire. I saw DeRenne give him an admonishing look, raising a finger to her lips, signaling to him to hush. "What? What did I say? Is it not obvious?"

"Did you get everything you needed?" Lachlan asked, eyeing the unnecessary bundle of clothing in my arms.

"Yes," I answered without hesitation. In truth, I'd gotten the information I needed.

"I see," he said, holding his hands out.

"I've got it," I bridled.

"I thought we could take our time, and walk part of the way."

Furrowing my brow, and adding a smile, I handed the bundle over. "Lead on, then."

δ^+

We emerged from a small pool of water near the artisan's marketplace. The village was subdued, the stonework now softly lit by the light from the gas lamps, several couples from the late supper crowd were window shopping. Lachlan headed toward the passageway at the opposite end of the plaza leading to Paden and Ccri's house, and also to the end of this most unexpected day.

"I wanted an opportunity, in private, to explain my comment from earlier tonight," he said. "This issue with Jokull is complicated; the effects of today's discovery far reaching. DeRenne, Shaw, and I pledged to assist The Accordance. We have trained our entire lives." He paused for the longest second. "Emily…for a brief moment I pictured you close to Jokull, in the middle of…"

"So you assumed that I'm better off on Earth, out of harm's way, oblivious to the turmoil," I said, not doing a very good job hiding the sarcasm. "Listen, I respect and appreciate your concern. You should know that I do understand my place in this crazy situation. What I don't get is what you seem to know that no one else does."

"The unknown is what has me worried," he said, looking down at me with the most peculiar look. "Do you truly understand your place?"

"Am I confused? Yes, you bet I am. When I found that silvery suit in the cavern, everything changed. The speed and suddenness with which you three flipped into different roles…I have no idea what that was all about. I now understand this Jokull fellow should be taken very seriously."

"So seriously, DeRenne dragged me through the gaseous water vapor. You may think that I'm naïve according to Arden standards. And it's true that almost everyone on Earth is unaware of The Accordance and intergalactic water travel. But I feel confident that human nature is the same throughout the Universe. Evil is still evil, even in the Triangulum Galaxy."

"Just this morning, I discussed some of the memorials you mentioned with Ccri; even looked at a few of them on the holographic images. They are sobering. Now that I know what I know, I'm prepared to go back to Earth and help. But I still I need more time. I've got to squeeze years of study into just a few short weeks."

"For once, Shaw is correct. You are exceptional for an extraterrestrial," Lachlan said, and I heard the surprise in his voice.

I laughed. "Never in a million years could I have imagined that someone from Earth would be considered the extraterrestrial. Here I am talking like a pro. But trust me, deep inside, I'm very scared."

"A good dose of scared is often not a bad thing," he said as we passed beneath the stone archway leading to the maze of darkening tunnels. Walking closer once we entered the leafy passageway, Lachlan was just a sultry wish away for the second time today. I kept both of my arms pinned to my sides. Otherwise, I might be tempted to coax a nonexistent desire from him.

"How dangerous?" He knew what I meant.

"Enough to pay attention and reasonable enough to take the risk."

"And for DeRenne?"

"DeRenne is very well trained, and trust me, she is quite talented. Actually, she is a little frightening at times." He glanced at me sideway. "Do you think Shaw would ever allow anything to happen to her?"

I thought about that as we passed the standing stone at the end of the corridor, veering right. "Yeah, you are probably right. What about Earth?"

"Earth is of no importance to Jokull," Lachlan said, stopping mid-step, seizing my left arm, and swinging me around until we faced each other. The Seren fluttering in the foliage switched direction like a shoal of startled fish. "And I would like to keep it that way. I do not want to give him the tiniest reason to draw his attention in that direction."

"Got it!" I said, unnerved by his intensity.

"Earth has no reason to become involved. However, the fact that you discovered the cavern completely changed the equation," he said in an authoritative voice. "I have seen enough to know that events can turn in the blink of an eye. Something that seems of no consequence today becomes paramount at a later time."

Well, his explanation certainly justified his abrupt change of behavior earlier tonight. But honestly, I didn't have the slightest idea how it could spiral so out of control. We walked in silence to Paden and Ccri's house. Now somewhat anxious, I quickly stepped onto the stone stoop so he wouldn't see the shocked look on my face. I went to unlatch the door.

"Emily," he said softly.

I swallowed the lump in the back of my throat, pivoting on my heel until I faced him. His entire posture relaxed as he stepped onto the stone stoop. I could tell something out of left field was coming simply by watching his face and because he'd been talking a little less formal during the walk. I stood perfectly still so that I wouldn't miss anything.

"You are correct about one point," he said, dropping his head until we were eye-level. "You are already inadvertently involved. We suspected and anticipated that Jokull would attempt to sneak back onto Arden. That particular question now answered, the cavern is now under constant surveillance."

Lachlan glanced around like he was looking for someone hidden in the shadows, listening in on our conversation. "I asked the Seren to watch you…merely as a precaution," he added when he saw the alarmed look in my eyes. "As DeRenne and Shaw so eloquently stated; you are safe here on Arden. However, these new events allowed me to convince those in charge to give you this."

He opened his right hand. A tiny, silver disk attached to a square piece of white parchment, rested in his palm. "You asked for one, remember? It is modified for you to hear only the Seren and no other communication. Ccri and Paden will also approve once I inform them whom you will be researching over the next few days."

"How does it work?" I asked, totally freaked out by yet another change of events.

"May I?" His enticing eyes were hesitant, unsure.

Without delay, mine answered, *Yes!*

Lachlan smiled. He handed me the bundle of clothing. I wrapped my arms around the mound, grateful to have something to hold onto, and if I was being totally honest, to hide behind.

"This device is extremely sensitive," he said, peeling the tiny silver disk off of the piece of paper.

"Exactly how many Seren do you have keeping tabs on me?" I asked, a bit of a mutinous look in my eye.

"Only one," he said, reaching over, and sticking the silver disk to my earlobe. "At my request, the Seren began keeping tabs on you, whatever that means, the moment you and DeRenne left the cavern." Lachlan's eyes shifted left. A bright light swooped out from a nearby tree hovering in the air near my face. "The Seren are very discreet."

I bunched the clothing into my left arm, reached up with my right hand, and touched the disk with my finger like I'd seen them do. It was as if someone adjusted the frequency, and turned the volume up on life; the sounds all around enhanced in a richer and more fluid tone.

"I am Nazca," the Seren said in a lilting voice

I was blown away. "It's nice to meet you, Nazca. I…I look forward to working with you." I know that sounded stupid but I had no idea what else to say.

"It is an honor to serve The Accordance. If you require my assistance, simply speak my name aloud."

"Thank you, Lachlan," I said, watching the brilliant light disappear into the foliage. "Is Nazca male or female?"

"A female gender is more appropriate, although the males are the ones who tend the larvae. May I ask a favor?"

He knew I couldn't refuse him after that. "Absolutely."

"Try not to draw attention to yourself," he said, scanning my face for any hint of hysteria.

"Sure. Whatever, that means," I huffed, figuring that must be Arden-speak for lacking a proper perspective.

Lachlan smiled about something, stepped around me, and opened the wide plank door, keeping his hand on the top corner, forcing me to dip beneath his arm as I crossed the threshold. Dizziness threatened from a combination of gratitude, shock, and wonder.

He closed the door, took a deep breath, switched into the *official mode*, and walked around the corner to speak with Paden and Ccri. I hurried down the hall to my room, arranging the new batch of clothing in the wardrobe to give him ample time to fill them in on all the gory details related to the Jokull dilemma.

When I made my appearance in the open-space living area, Lachlan stood by the fireplace, once again the picture of ease. My reaction was a complete 180 from the previous night. I went and stood next to him.

"I have informed Paden and Ccri of this evening's…revisions?" he said, and his eyes were steady.

I glanced at Paden and Ccri who were sitting side-by-side on the sofa near the fireplace wearing stern expressions. Nervous, I bit my lip.

"They may have a few more questions in the morning," Lachlan said, sounding relieved that he wouldn't be around to answer any of those questions.

"I will walk you to the stream," I said, desperate to get away from Paden's glare.

"Good evening then," Lachlan said with a low bow. He touched my elbow and turned me toward the back of the house.

"Today certainly wasn't boring," I said as soon as we were outside. "This morning, I waited out here for someone to fetch me with no idea of what to expect. Never in my wildest imagination could I have predicted any of this. DeRenne said that I should get used to it though. Let me think, oh yeah, she said, 'it is a normal everyday occurrence around here.'"

"You have no idea. And for once, Paden was at a loss for words—never seen that before," Lachlan said. "He is giving you leeway so watch your step. Do not let his calm manner fool you because the man is a quick study."

"Point taken," I said. "They've really gone out of their way for me. The last thing I want to do is upset them."

"Stay focused; he will never argue with a determined attitude. I have no idea what the profiling will yield. It is true that we never questioned Jokull's motives. Perhaps the process will garner new insight for us all." He stepped backward into the slowly moving current. "I will send word with Nazca when we return to Arden."

I reached up, tapped my ear, and smiled. "Again, thank you."

He smiled back and nodded once before disappearing into the water.

I took my sweet time walking back inside of the house, desperately wishing that Paden and Ccri had gone to bed. No such luck. They were still sitting on the sofa. Paden's disapproval was palatable. Ccri was taking her time before drawing a conclusion.

"Guess I better get to bed," I said, mouthing a fake yawn. "Busy day and all." I'd rehearsed this pitiful scene a few times back in my room. Hopefully, my performance was convincing. To be on the safe-side, I made a quick escape.

I found myself ready for bed a few minutes later even though I didn't remember brushing my teeth or washing my face. Punching the feathery pillow into a comfortable shape, I snuggled down under the quilted comforter, and drifted off to sleep, the strangest sensation enveloping me.

This Lachlan character floated through my waking dreams all night long.

δ^-

"Jokull's a ruthless renegade, the likes of which you have never encountered," Paden scowled the next morning at the breakfast table. "If you go around digging up someone's past, then you run the risk of unearthing things that should never again see the light of day."

Suffice it to say, he wasn't thrilled with my profiling idea. Our usual pleasant morning routine became a tumultuous affair. Each time I felt the urge to argue with him, I popped a piece of food into my mouth. By mid-morning, we'd reached a compromise, of sorts.

Paden would block access to several key pieces of information that he felt should remain buried. Intuitively, I knew those juicy tidbits were more than likely the most pertinent details into Jokull's personality. This meant that I'd have to dig a little deeper. But I also knew that I had little choice in the matter, politely muttering a couple of 'Yes-sirs', 'of-course-I-will', and 'that-is-not-a-problem', at the appropriate times.

Game and set to you Paden, but not yet match.

The next issue to resolve was how to store the information. "Does anyone on Arden ever write?" I asked, swirling a hand through the air.

"All information at The Assemblage is recorded," Ccri said with a harsh look at her husband. I got the feeling that she wasn't exactly on my side but a bit more supportive than Paden. This morning while she was pouring the coffee, I thought I heard her mumble something about 'needing to face the truth no matter how painful'.

"Ah…I know this might sound strange, I like to write on paper." I shrugged my shoulders. "Writing helps me organize my thoughts."

"Would this work?" Ccri asked, holding a roll of parchment.

"I was thinking more along the lines of a journal or a book."

Ccri rummaged through a kitchen drawer. She placed something that looked like a twig on the top of a book bound in blue leather. "It is a writing utensil. The interior is soaked with a concentrated ink. Never has to be sharpened or refilled."

"This is perfect," I said, flipping through the blank pages made of handmade paper.

In the end, I promised to either personally check in with them several times a day or send a message with Nazca. I was surprised that they weren't surprised by the fact that Lachlan arranged Nazca to watch me. This meant they also thought it was a good idea. That worried me a bit. I pushed that worry to the back of my mind. I had more pressing matters to deal with.

I finally blustered my way out of the house after a light lunch, navigating the leafy green passageway to the far side of the village, stopping in the corridor twice to jot down a few notes as they jumped into my head. Tucking the book under my arm, I exited the passageway back into the sunlight, grabbed the brass handrail, and took the limestone steps at The Assemblage two at a time. I entered the windowed vestibule, stopping for a moment to admire the urns of towering flowers; the petals of a brilliant red flower unwinding right before my very eyes.

As I crossed the rotunda, I made a mental note to ask someone when the Milky Way Galaxy would appear on the holographic compass arm. I avoided the room I'd used two nights ago after that awkward encounter with Raffye, deciding to keep those desolate emotions sealed away.

I slid into the polished stone recliner and propped the book on my lap. I was worried the angle wouldn't work but once again, the ergonomic S-shape positioned my legs and head so that I could both watch the images and write notes. For a brief moment, I pictured a much younger Lachlan, Shaw, and DeRenne doing the same thing for their tutoring, and grinned. Now that's not a bad idea. I should search for some images of them when they were younger, feeling a little giddy for it. "Family history of Jokull, Lachlan and Shaw's tutor," I said in an official tone in case someone could read my mind. They could have a silver disk for that too.

The room darkened, enveloping me inside an image of a small boy standing between two adults dressed in bold colors. "Jokull, originally from the planet Sagmine," the monotone voice droned, "is the only son of Ilar and Tagna, who are known for spearheading a bill to amend the general premise of The Accordance. Their proposal rejected the tenet of noninterference, supporting an immediate reveal for each newly discovered planet with a source of flowing water and established human inhabitants."

The image blurred to a meeting convened in a pristine white outdoor amphitheater, the day sunny without a cloud in the sky. Ilar stood poised on the dais facing the audience, the tailored hem of his scarlet tunic flapping in the breeze. "I feel the policy of noninterference is antiquated. It is not necessary for planets currently experiencing any level of industrialization," he bellowed as if he needed to emphasize every word. "These clandestine missions give the false impression of membership into a secret society."

"Ilar," a member of the audience called out.

I gasped. In the middle of the image sat a much younger Paden…with a full head of black hair. "A detailed study of the history annals reveals that an early disclosure invariably results in one or two individuals rising up to answer the siren's call to power. And once someone assumes such a powerful position, they rarely choose to relinquish control of that power."

The younger Paden rose to his feet. He purposefully made his way to the dais. The crowd hushed as he took center stage, reached out, and touched a stone pedestal next to the fuming Ilar. A holographic image materialized, displaying three rotating planets. "All of these worlds are solid proof that an early reveal simply does not work. In each case, a few individuals establish themselves as rulers, controlling trade, the economy, and even worse, water travel."

A displeased murmur rumbled through the crowd.

"The fault lies with us," Ilar retorted with a flippant wave of his hand. "We need to better prepare those in charge of each newly discovered world. If we keep our presence a secret, the cream does not rise to the top so to speak. We might miss involving individuals who could sway others to accelerate the reveal."

Almost as if staged, a group sitting near the front broke into a spontaneous applause.

"If we arrive flashing our abilities," Paden said, raising a hand to *shush* the obvious plants, "they are often misinterpreted as magical or worse, sorcery. And Ilar, you know because you participated in several of the more recent reveals, we seek out and place influential people in these prominent positions to assist with the transition."

Ilar didn't say a word but shared an interesting look with his wife, Tagna.

Paden paused for a moment, before saying, "We attempt to guide the inhabitants of each newly discovered world to the point where power and money are no longer the objectives. The goal becomes the desire to share in the liberating and healing power of the water; to comprehend that our existence is not a random event. Primitive societies cannot fully grasp what we have to offer. Often in more advance civilizations we must allow the technology to surpass the desire to let it go."

"Paden spins a colorful tale of intrigue and mayhem," Ilar said, whirling around to the audience in a dramatic sweep of scarlet. A lady in the back row shrieked at his sudden movement. "If we relied on technological achievement as our sole guideline, then his home planet of Delmar would currently be unaware of The Accordance."

"Exactly my point," Paden countered. Several spectators exchanged anxious glances. "Delmar's early reveal and ensuing power struggles demonstrate why too much, too soon, often fails. It is imperative that each world's unique customs last through the ages. We should pass through a planet's history, not erase it. They should be given the right to choose for themselves."

The argument intensified on both sides with no clear winner in sight. I got the impression that this particular topic had been continuously and passionately argued over and over in more than one arena. What else hit me was that with an entire Universe to explore, there's no telling how many more populated worlds were out there. Not to mention that there are new planets forming every single day. "How many planets are currently in some stage of, I don't know the right words, guidance toward intergalactic mergence?" I asked.

"Currently, 1,217,195,506,201,556 planets are aware of intergalactic water travel with another 244,051,992 within a thousand years or less of their reveal," the auto voice droned. "In addition, billions of planets have been identified as livable, although no humans currently reside there. Today alone, the Seren discovered and cataloged 818 more planets."

I thought about those numbers because that meant countless families would soon volunteer, pack their belongings, and relocate to one of these newly discovered planets to help prepare the humans who lived there. It also meant that the Seren were still out there looking; the scope and logistics of the entire process staggering. "Bring the lights up," I said, reminding my curious self to stay focused.

I flipped through the book, checking the few notes I'd scribbled on the first page during the walk here, adding in the margin a note to look into the relationship between Arden and Earth. I wanted a firm timeline of not only when the Seren discovered Earth and cataloged it with The Accordance, but exactly who on Earth knows about The Accordance. I underlined that last part several times. The whole thing still pissed me off. These topics could wait because I had no idea when Lachlan, DeRenne, and Shaw would return. They'd gone out on a limb for me. I wanted something of value prepared when they returned.

"Did Jokull attend a University, or perhaps institution of higher learning associated with The Accordance?" I looked around the room again, feeling a little silly talking to myself.

"Jokull was identified as a gifted orator. He was selected to participate in Coalescence," the monotonous voice started again as the lights dimmed.

"The what?" I slid back down into the recliner.

"Coalescence is a gathering of diverse minds into one body or forum designed to bring together the young and passionate from various worlds in an attempt to focus less on what separates us, and more on what we can learn from our differences."

"Interesting concept," I said, making a few notes. "While attending Coalescence what clubs or organizations did Jokull join?"

Over the next few days, I spent the morning at The Assemblage, lunch in the village, and then back to The Assemblage for more research. This dramatically cut down the number of important meetings I had to attend. I also managed to sneak in a couple of childhood images of Lachlan and DeRenne. I felt a little guilty peeking into their lives without permission. I couldn't resist either. Even back then, DeRenne, her hair as white as snow, followed her big brother around, hanging on his every word, trying to outrun him every chance she could. I also saw that on several occasions, Shaw lived with Lachlan's family to finish his tutoring while his parents and sisters were away mentoring a planet.

One image showed Lachlan, DeRenne, and Nairne standing arm-in-arm with a man in front of a beautiful waterfall. Even in the wavering image, I detected a perceptible air of authority all around him. It had to be their father. Lachlan shared his height and facial features. DeRenne had his thick hair and a wide smile. I wanted to find out his name but quickly changed the image, worried that I'd already seen more than I should.

Every night, I honored Paden's one request and discussed the day's findings with him. As it turns out, his knowledge of the procedural wording in The Accordance, and a lifetime spent traveling the Universe helped me grasp the complexities of mergence. Lachlan was right, even though Paden wasn't pleased that I was researching Jokull, he realized that the research forced me to ask the hard questions, to consider issues I would've never considered without delving into these topics. And for me, it sped up the learning curve.

Several days later, sitting on the grassy knoll next to the traveling pool in the village, eating a slice of cheese and bread from the bakery, scribbling some thoughts in the book while ignoring the curious stares at my writing, Nazca swooped down and landed on a sturdy blade of grass. My hand soared up to touch the disk in my ear. "Lachlan and the others will return to Arden later today," she said in her lilting voice. "They desire to meet with you this evening."

"Thank you, Nazca. Please tell him, DeRenne, and Shaw to join me at Paden and Ccri's house around dusk for supper," I said in a forced calm voice even though my insides were jumping up and down for joy. "And by the way, how many planets did the Seren discover today?" I loved asking this question, her answer so joyous.

"Only three," she said. "They searched a newly formed galaxy and did not expect to find many. None of the cataloged planets were populated with humans."

"Do the Seren have a plan or just go wherever?"

"Daily, my kind swarms the far corners of the Universe to gain insight into the transformative power of the water. We have seen what no others have seen, relished in the brilliance that sparkles just beyond the vanishing point at the outer rim of the Universe. Many travelers attempt to reach the end of this light. What they do not comprehend is that there is no end to the light. There was never a time its luminescence grew dim or less perfect—the light simply folds and fans into shimmering hues of radiance. We harvest this energy to nourish our larvae."

"Yes," I said, getting all excited. "Lachlan told me about this."

"Did he also share with you that the Seren taught the humans how to travel with the water?" she asked, her luminescence glowing brighter.

"No." I closed the book, giving her my full attention. "I would love to hear the story if you have the time."

"Before The Accordance, the Seren joined with a small group of humans who heard the music within the flowing water," she said. "Not musical notes as you are accustomed, more of a pleasing tone or vibration. We are intuitively drawn to these tones by the energy emanating from our subatomic particles. They identified sources of flowing water where these tones intensified and stacked piles of small river stones to mark the location."

"We taught them to listen for, and fall into these vibrating water molecules. At first, they traveled between sources of flowing water on their home planet. As they became more adept, we shared with them the exhilaration of traversing the entire Universe in less than a moment."

"Nazca, do you think this is where the concept of a water stone started?" I asked, opening the book to make a note so I wouldn't forget to tell Paden.

"It is frightening the first time someone falls out of the world they know into the energy between the spinning water molecules, leaving the memory of their solid body behind. The familiar feel of the stone gave the first travelers courage."

"So true," I said, pulling Pop's stone out from a side pocket in my skirt. "This stone gives me the courage to stay and to try and figure this all out. Thank you for sharing the story."

"It is my pleasure to serve The Accordance," she said, fluttering up into the air.

"Before you go, I want to ask a favor. Please notify me before Lachlan, DeRenne, and Shaw arrive to Paden and Ccri's house."

"I will," she said before disappearing in the noonday sun.

δ^+

"I do not understand why we have to wear these ridiculous outfits," Shaw said, kicking out the folds in the heavy, knit overtunic.

"In a word, tradition," Lachlan said.

"When you are the person in charge, this is the first thing that needs to change," Shaw huffed under his breath.

Lachlan watched as DeRenne scooted sideways across the crowded row of chairs, and then slid into the empty chair next to Shaw. "Everything is ready for the next practice run," she said.

"I still have not recovered from yesterday's course," Shaw said, grabbing his right shoulder. "When do you have time to arrange them?"

"Organization," DeRenne said. "As of today, three others are in place. I have been thinking about a perfect planet for a fourth."

Lachlan lifted his hand to his mouth, and coughed, "Told you."

"I am sitting right here," DeRenne said.

"Fine by me if you want to give the whole thing a rest," Shaw muttered.

"With Emily's discovery," Lachlan said, "I think we should practice more."

"No surprise there," Shaw said, looking sideways at Lachlan. "Did you get her to calm down that night after you escorted her back to the village?"

DeRenne craned her neck and tried to look innocent. Lachlan knew better, and took his time before saying, "You should have seen the look in her eye when I told her about the Seren."

"I wish I could have been there," Shaw grumbled.

"You need to be careful what you say to her," DeRenne said. "She gives the impression that she is not paying attention. If you look close, you will see her mind turning."

"Yes, I noticed that too," Lachlan said. "I sent Nazca to inform Emily that we will be on Arden for the night. I am curious to hear what she has to say."

"Curious about her profiling or curious about *her*?" DeRenne asked, her eyebrows rising in an obvious dare.

"*Shush* sis," Lachlan said. "They are about to begin."

"As if you are interested in another boring presentation," DeRenne said, settling back into the chair.

δ^+

Don't ask me where this crazy thought came from. I'd decided that when Lachlan, DeRenne, and Shaw returned to Arden, I would prepare supper for the four of us. Now that I knew tonight was the night it would happen, I put my plan into action.

I packed my belongings and waded through the late lunch crowd to the open-air marketplace in the center of the plaza. I picked through the bins of fruit and selected several ripe apples for the pie. Next, I decided on a purplish oblong-shaped vegetable that reminded me of squash, a variety of mushrooms, and some small potatoes that would skewer nicely.

"Pleasant afternoon, Emily," Metta said when I entered the flower shop. "What may I help you with today?" Sunlight streamed into the shop through the wavy leaded-glass windows. I stared at the wooden counter and smiled, remembering my first day on Arden, sitting on that very stool. "I am hosting a small gathering tonight," I said. "We're eating outside. I wanted to see if you have something special for the table."

"I do," Metta said, setting the twine in her hand on the countertop. I followed her around several buckets filled with the usual assortment of flowers crowding the aisles, to the back of the store. She leaned over, opened a small wooden box, folded the cheesecloth back, and lifted out a handful of the most delicate flowers I'd ever seen. "I picked these early this morning; one of a kind. They grow for a few short weeks on the west side of the mountains."

The arched stem and bell-shaped flower reminded me of the Lily of the Valley blooms that grew near Pop's lake house. "Are they glowing?" I asked.

"Yes," Metta said, looking pleased. "They will change from this translucent opal to a deep sapphire as Keit rises in the night sky."

"Thanks again," I said before leaving the flower shop, careful not to crush the delicate flowers wrapped in brightly colored, thick wax paper. Last stop before entering the leafy green passageway was the bakery. I decided on a dozen rolls to ensure that I had enough filler to satisfy Shaw's appetite.

Ccri and I had discussed the possibility of hosting a small gathering at the house a few days ago. She helped get the food started before she and Paden left to meet friends at a café in the adjacent village. Standing alone in the middle of the kitchen, I couldn't deny the pace was getting to me. I wiped my hands on the dishtowel, considering what was about to happen, the aroma of possibilities filling the air.

After sorting through a new batch of clothing Ccri acquired from a friend, I'd chosen a taupe colored dress that wouldn't show any accidental stains. I'd already set the table outside and lit the fire. It smelled pretty good in here but I also knew that doesn't necessarily always translate into tasting good. A twinge of doubt rattled at the back door as I watched Nazca fluttered in through the open kitchen window. "They are preparing to leave," she announced in her lilting voice.

"Okay," I gulped, noting that my stomach was suddenly queasy. I seasoned the meat smoldering on the rotisserie one last time and then stirred the vegetables and mushrooms, breathing in full gulps of air to calm my beating heart.

A minute later, Lachlan walked into the kitchen dressed in an amethyst shirt, gray pants, and my now favorite leather boots laced to the calf. The all too familiar lump in the back of my throat doubled in size. I watched as he draped an armful of heavy, velvet cloaks across the back of the kitchen chair. "Are we going somewhere after we eat?" I asked, sort of stunned. "I hope there aren't any more mysteries to solve."

"Not tonight," he said, the tone of his voice and a look in his eye hinting at a surprise. "Tonight's outing is strictly for your enjoyment." I opened my mouth to say something; no words came out. In the meantime, Lachlan's stomach growled. "I apologize. Unquestionably, I am ready for supper."

"As am I," Shaw said, towing DeRenne into the kitchen.

"Me too," she giggled.

My head was reeling. "If you could all give me a hand, the food is ready."

Everyone got to work. Lachlan arranged the meat on a glass platter I'd found on the top shelf of the pantry that matched the glass plates. DeRenne ladled the vegetables and mushrooms into a wide, ceramic bowl while Shaw…"Oops," he said, catching the small round roasted potato before it hit the floor. He blew on the potato before tossing tossed it into his mouth.

"You know that I hate to waste food." Under DeRenne's watchful eye, he carefully removed the remaining skewers and the apple pie from the wood fired oven.

Lachlan picked up the drink tray, Shaw the double-handled ceramic bowl, DeRenne the platter of meat, and I grabbed the skewers of roasted potatoes with the mitts. We made our way to the covered porch at the back of the house and then down the pathway to the rectangular wooden table beneath the sweep of gnarled trees. A quick assessment confirmed that the glass plates reflected the light from the flickering candles dotted up and down the long tabletop; the delicate bell-shaped flowers now glowing a royal blue as Keit peeked above the horizon. I looked around. The sounds of the night cranking up, it seems that the climate, the breeze, and more importantly, the disappearing rain clouds conspired to give us an enchanted respite in this little corner of today.

I blew out a breath, relieved. At least I didn't burn anything.

Our conversation idled in generic topics, purposely skirting the real issues of where they'd been for the last five days and my research. Not a problem. I enjoyed the time with my new friends. After everyone finished eating, Shaw graciously volunteered to devour any remnants. After he finished, DeRenne and I loaded the trays. We carried them inside while Lachlan arranged the chairs around the fire pit.

I put the dishes, glasses, and silverware in the sink to soak while DeRenne sliced the pie. Shaw, who appeared out of nowhere, poured four mugs of steaming coffee. "What's this?" I asked, lifting the collar on one of the heavy velvet cloaks, tracing the raised woven symbol with my thumb; three interlocking triangles embroidered in gold, silver, and copper metallic threads.

"The emblem of my lineage," DeRenne said. "Do you remember down in the caverns that Lachlan mentioned the five generating elements?"

"Wood, water, metal, fire, and Earth," I said, recalling that moment for a totally different reason—Lachlan's silky voice.

"On Arden, there are five family lineages. My family's lineage is Water. Our emblem is three interlocking triangles forged from pure elemental metals.

"Five lineages on Arden," I mumbled, heading back outside carrying the dessert plates and forks, wondering which lineage Benjamin Franklin, I mean, Daileass, is descended from.

"Emily," DeRenne said, handing me a plate overflowing with apple pie, "were you able to get Paden to calm down that night after your big discovery? Lachlan said he had that look in his eye."

"Ooo," Shaw said. "I've been on the receiving end of that look. Not fun. Notice, I used a contraction."

"And correctly," I said, settling comfortably into the chair next to Lachlan. "If you're referring to the night the rat abandoned the sinking ship, they were in shock and didn't say much. Well, really, I didn't give them much of a chance to say anything. Trust me, the next morning Paden was not happy." Lachlan's face contorted into a sympathetic but horrified expression. I handed him a fork, grinning at his fake concern. "He restricted a few pieces of information from my research. I think I can still shed some light on Jokull's personality." I opened the book, running a hand down the middle crease, the leather spine crackling in response.

"You wrote the information on...paper?" Shaw asked.

I decided not be annoyed by his comment. For once they were getting a glimpse into my world, a sliver of who I was instead of me always being the one two steps behind in the dark. "I did. I find it helpful to take notes. Writing helps me sort my thoughts and then make changes. I like the tactile sensation of writing...must be the Earthling in me."

Lachlan's gleaming green eyes, steady over the rim of his mug, didn't hide his enjoyment as he sipped his coffee and quietly listened.

"Anyway, I am sure you are aware that his parents formed a group to amend the general premise of The Accordance." They each nodded. Good, this would save time. "Jokull was identified as a gifted orator and chosen to attend Coalescence. While in residence, he connected with several questionable fringe groups who also petitioned The Accordance to ease up on the noninterference restrictions. Which, by the way, I spent many hours researching," I said, pointing the twig pen at Lachlan. DeRenne and Shaw exchanged a confused look but didn't utter a word. "Interestingly, no matter which group he joined, even if the group already had an established leader, eventually everything revolved around him."

"After watching several hours of images from various meetings while he was at Coalescence, I concluded that Jokull must be an exceptionally charming man, quite beguiling actually. Someone who could bluff his way into any situation, gain everyone's trust, bend them to his point of view, and then easily persuade them to follow him. Games were his favorite pastime. One, in particular, reminds me of a game we play on Earth, chess."

"That's true," Shaw said, clapping his hands gleefully. "Our daily lessons included these games of strategy. And daily, he would lose spectacularly to our Lachlan here. A sore loser, I might add—not that I minded watching him lose."

I looked over at Lachlan. His eyes narrowed as he said, "Trust me, he never let me win."

"Anyway, at Coalescence he met a young lady, Orlaith, chosen to represent Arden," I said, flipping through the pages. "Yes, here it is: chosen for her ardent desire to faithfully serve The Accordance. I liked that, her ardent desire and she's from Arden. Get it?" They shared a look but didn't say a word. "Okay, moving on. Tough audience." On the same page, I'd scribbled a note in the margin, underlined it three times. "While in residence at Coalescence Jokull struggled with horrendous headaches."

"That continued to be a problem for him here on Arden as well," Shaw said. "We could never understand why he wanted to go down in the caverns in the first place. The dampness always aggravated his headaches." Shaw glanced at Lachlan with a disgusted look on his face. "Remember how it would start, first the sniffling and then the gagging. That is when his voice changed, urgent and frantic, telling us to go deeper; squeeze into smaller places, always forging ahead. He never told us what we were looking for, never took any direction from the Seren, treated them like they were beneath him. We were just doing his dirty work. I hate that part now, especially the way it all turned out."

Lachlan nodded. "He would pop out of nowhere, scolding us, always tottering on the verge of hysteria."

"Apparently, he's skilled at persuading others to do his bidding," I said. Shaw flinched in his chair. "A trait I believe he inherited from his parents. And of course, he ended up on Arden because of..."

"Orlaith," DeRenne whispered her eyes suddenly somewhere in the past. "He fell in love with her at Coalescence. She always said there was another side to him. A kind side he felt the need to hide. We all loved her and trusted her judgment."

"I believe that he never completely changed his views on the noninterference argument," I said, tapping the twig on the book, lost in thought, "but perhaps he set them aside for her sake."

"I would agree," Shaw said. For a brief second, he and Lachlan exchanged a serious look. A disturbing kind of look that can only be shared by two boys whose tutor later became a known enemy of their planet.

"From my perspective of a young girl of thirteen, I can tell you he worshiped her," DeRenne said, brushing her bangs away from her eyes, oblivious when they fell back into place. "Orlaith said he fought with his parents over his decision to move to Arden. For his sake, I want to believe that Arden is the first place he was ever happy."

"On the surface," I said. "This particular bit of information was of special interest to Paden." Unwittingly, they each leaned in a little closer. "The headaches continued and as a result, he rarely slept. They had a house in the village so Jokull spent most nights at The Assemblage until the wee hours of the morning. I was able to recover his usage. I discovered that during those endless nights, he'd search for information about the first travelers to Arden and more importantly, the hearsay of their abilities to control the elements."

That comment hit a nerve.

"Of course, he did," Shaw snarled, leaping to his feet. "I told you he was up to no good. Telling us those ridiculous stories, insisting we research the first travelers to learn about our ancestors. What a bunch of rubbish."

DeRenne tugged on Shaw's hand. "He fooled us all," she said in a little girl voice, forcing him to sit back down.

"You may be more right than you think." I paused, building the dramatic effect for the big reveal. "Apparently, jewelry-making was a hobby of his. I found evidence that in reality, it was a misdirect for his obsession with metallurgy. He tested the malleability of different elemental metals and metal alloys, experimenting with them in novel ways. At least, that's what I think Paden said."

"Paden tried to explain to me that pure metals amplify the waters cohesive properties…let me see." I flipped through the pages in the book until I found the page in the middle with the corner turned down. "This went way over my head, but here goes. The crystalline lattice structure of elemental metals forged at very specific temperatures, and then folded in precise steps, and something about a superconductor magnet that I didn't understand, creates an electromagnetic field that amplifies the spinning water molecules in the surrounding air.

This narrows the waters focal point, opening a small window for water travel in an area where water travel has been restricted."

"Never in a million years would I think someone would restrict water travel. Paden went through this elaborate discussion. Technically, it's possible to create a distortion field around a source of flowing water that would realign the electrons in the atoms. This stops some of the water molecules from spinning, cancels their cohesive property, and restricts water travel in that area." I looked toward Lachlan, and blinked. "Maybe it's a reverse to the sinkhole you said people transport their belongings through. Paden said the process is very difficult to accomplish and maintain, although the whole thing reminds me of a force field."

Now they were all angry.

"How dare he?" Lachlan hissed in the same menacing tone he'd used down in the cavern. This time, I held the cringe in check in the presence of his fierce words. "He worked on his plan while living on Arden!"

"Up to no good the entire time," Shaw said, slapping both of his knees.

"Poor Orlaith," DeRenne murmured, curling into a ball in the middle of the chair. "She loved him so."

"I guess the old saying holds true here on Arden as well as it does back on Earth. If you want to hide something so that no one else can find it, just hide it in plain sight." I let things simmer for a second before saying, "There's more."

"Continue then, Emily," Lachlan said, apparently calmed down now.

"Paden seemed vague on this one point. The final straw broke when Jokull begged Orlaith not to go on a specific mission. Well, 'ordered' her not to go might be a better way to phrase it. She went without his permission and was killed in the chaos that erupted after the reveal went terribly wrong. But not many people knew that she was pregnant."

"No!" DeRenne cried out. "She never had a chance to share this with me." The book dropped to the ground as I bolted out of the chair to hug her, Lachlan right beside me, Shaw already there. We all held her in our arms as she quietly sobbed until Lachlan gestured to me in my side vision. He reached for my hand. We both returned to our seats. Shaw kept DeRenne safely enfolded in his arms. Lachlan didn't say a word but he didn't let go of my hand either. I saw the concern for his sister in his eyes, and maybe something else. I didn't dare move a hair.

"Is there more?" Lachlan whispered after DeRenne returned to her seat.

"Yes, if you want me to continue."

Shaw glanced over at DeRenne, who nodded once. Lachlan released my hand but not before DeRenne noticed. I sat back in the chair and opened the book. "Jokull is obviously a charming man, charming enough to convince others to satellite around him. He thinks of them as pieces to move about to satisfy a game of strategy, and do his dirty work."

"He sees himself as particularly clever, superior, and smug." Lachlan went rigid in his chair as if my words hit a nerve. "I believe if you were to ask him his weapon of choice, he'd tell you that it's his mind." I leaned forward a bit. "But this could prove to be his one major weakness. I feel confident that he now believes he has the advantage since discovering the cavern, using its power and…"

Lachlan looked at me with the strangest expression on his face, almost like he was mad. "What did you say?"

"The cavern and the inscriptions covering the walls obviously have something to do with the waters energy." I sat straighter in the chair to checkmate his unrelenting gaze, absolutely positive that he was filing away this new piece of information to use against me at a later date. "Anyway, Jokull did try to make a home here on Arden with Orlaith, indicating that perhaps down deep, he may harbor some regret."

"From what I understand, whenever they profile someone back on Earth, they look for a theme, a signature riff running through the personal story of someone's life to give them leverage to distract that person in a tight situation. Perhaps, his is the regret. As soon as you see the hesitation in his eyes, feelings rising to the surface of their own accord, that's the time to strike. You'll only get one chance."

Lachlan turned to Shaw, and said, "That does make sense." Shaw's head nodded in agreement but he didn't utter a single word.

"There's one more little odd observation," I said after a few moments. "I was reviewing the images, and something struck me as peculiar. He always wears one color, a dark blue, and not a single geometric symbol in sight."

I glanced at the three of them and bit my lip. Each of the mother-of-pearl buttons on Lachlan's shirt was a different geometric shape. Shaw wore a paprika-colored, gabardine waistcoat with copper piping on the cuffs. And DeRenne, well DeRenne put them both to shame in her iridescent pink dress.

To embrace the extraordinary culture herè on Arden is to embrace the exuberance of color and geometric design. I loved the pulse, the pace, the excitement, the way each new day stretches out before you. It makes me feel…happy. But, to be perfectly honest, back on Earth, these three could easily be mistaken for circus gypsies.

On a whim, I decided to research the psychological influence of colors and geometric shapes on the human psyche. I flipped the book over, turned it upside down, and opened the back cover to reference my notes. I often did this whenever I had a totally different train of thought.

"Okay, here it is. Colors are forces, radiant energies that affect us whether we are aware of them or not. The color blue is passive, considered cold like that of deep winter when all life is hidden in darkness and silence. Midnight blue, in particular, is always shadowy, the color chosen by someone who keeps to the side streets and alleyways, not by someone choosing to walk down the middle of the street in broad daylight…someone with a damaged pride." I ran my finger down the page. "Here is it. Blue beckons our spirit with the vibrations of the coming dawn…it also creeps close to superstition, fear, and desolate grief, so close to black."

"This may not be important but somehow it just seemed to fit his personality." I shut the book with a loud *thwack*. "The rest of the information is stored as images."

Lachlan leaned back into the chair, resting his elbows on the chair arm, tapping his fingers together, lost in thought.

"Listening to you tonight reminds me of something Paden instilled in us during our tutoring. There are lines that should never be crossed, rules put in place to prevent the misuse of power. We have sworn to uphold all of the tenets in The Accordance; not pick and choose which ones to obey. Jokull deluded himself into believing that the rules no longer apply to him, and lost sight of the common goal."

"So true, my friend," Shaw said, standing from the chair to stretch his legs, a wordless conversation passing between him and Lachlan in a way that DeRenne wouldn't see. He dragged over a small side table and then reached for the vase of flowers now glowing sapphire. "I have only heard of these," Shaw said, fingering the delicate flowers.

"When Nazca informed me you three would be on Arden tonight, I went to ask Metta if she has something special for the table. These are certainly something special."

We bunched the chairs together in a tight circle to search through the images and rehash the details. I offered clarification wherever possible. Shaw and Lachlan were particularly interested in the meeting held in the pristine white amphitheater, listening with keen interest to both sides of the noninterference argument. DeRenne, still clearly troubled, offered her views from the perspective of a young girl watching the relationship between Jokull and Orlaith, her mentor and dear friend, develop. For her sake, I hoped that his time spent on Arden was more than compromise and convenience.

An hour or so later, unexpected but not unanticipated, the lights inside of the house suddenly came on, announcing Paden and Ccri's arrival home. "I will return in a moment," Lachlan said, getting up from the chair, his gait indicating that he was a man on a mission.

"DeRenne," I said, inclining forward a bit. "What does Orlaith mean?"

"Gold princess," she whispered, tears welling in the corners of her eyes.

"I'm so sorry. Jokull does seem to have a laundry list of character defects but he did try." I watched as DeRenne's lips formed a faint smile. "Not very successfully mind you. At least he made the effort for her sake." I stood to give her some time, stacking the dessert plates and forks.

"Where do you think you are taking that?" Shaw asked, reaching for the half-empty pie plate.

"Nowhere now." I handed him the plate along with the serving spoon. DeRenne shook her head but I also saw a smile. At that same moment, Lachlan appeared out of nowhere carrying the heavy, velvet cloaks from the kitchen chair. "We're not going back to the cavern tonight?"

"Quite the opposite," he said. I saw a look in his eyes that I'd never seen before. Shaw and DeRenne weren't as subtle; their bodies shook with quiet laughter. Everyone except me was in on the game.

A shaft of awkwardness pierced my heart at the abrupt change of step in our carefully choreographed dance. "Help me clean the dishes first," I said, not doing a very good job hiding my displeasure at once again being the odd-man-out.

We emerged from a vigorously moving stream on the top of the mountain beneath a ceiling of densely packed stars. I pushed aside and stepped out from beneath the hanging hemlock branches, my hair flying in curls around my face from a gust of wind. I drifted across the thick undergrowth to the edge of the precipice, the texture and feel of this unreal place so intense that I felt off-balance, almost like walking inside of a dream.

I gasped in wonder as the world at my feet sloped away in a breathtaking view, convinced that I could reach out and touch the face of Keit, looming large and regal in pastel shades of coral in the night sky. Literally standing on the top of the world, blinded by the intense star-shine, I could feel the Universe in motion all around. I took a moment to take it all in, knowing there were no words that could possibly describe the wonder and awe before me.

"You will need this," Lachlan said from behind my back. With the gentlest motion, he draped the heavy cloak across my left shoulder. Next, he gathered my hair into his free hand, brushed the long strands to the side, and draped the cloak across my right shoulder. His hand lingered for a moment on my forearm

"Thanks," I murmured, unable to suppress the giddy thrill in the pit of my stomach.

Lachlan walked around in front of me, a second cloak draped over his arm. "Let me help with that," he said, scanning my face with intent eyes. He fiddled with the metal clasp on the collar of the cloak until it *clicked* together in the center of my throat. "The weather turns cold rather quickly."

Tonight his voice sounded alluringly wicked. I'm not entirely sure if that was his intention or just how it sounded to my overactive, light-infused brain standing here in the heavens. "Another unexpected turn of events," I said, grateful my voice didn't sound all woozy like my insides. "Is this a particular talent of yours?"

I saw a slight glimmer in his eyes. "There is a meteor shower tonight," he said, running his hand down the full-length of my right arm, taking hold of my hand as if it was the most natural act in the world.

Lachlan turned and pulled me with him across the thick undergrowth to a protective granite overhang notched into the side of the cliff. Talk about your front-row seat! Several thick fur pelts spread across the craggy stone floor surrounded a neatly laid fire.

"Now I know what you two were doing when you suddenly disappeared as soon we stepped out from the water on Arden," DeRenne said, sounding both impressed and appreciative, her eyes huge in the firelight. She nudged Shaw in the side and then smiled when he slipped an arm around her waist, and kissed her cheek.

"To keep you ladies warm in the cool night air," Shaw said, looking pleased, sliding down into the curve of the granite overhang.

Giggling for the second time since our early discussions, DeRenne settled sideways into his arms. "Emily," she said, patting the fur pelt next to her. "Sit here next to me."

That shaft of awkwardness winkled itself a little deeper into my heart. Timidly, I collapsed into the lushness, molding my body into the stone's natural contour with absolutely no idea of what to expect next.

Lachlan threw the thick velvet cloak over his shoulder, knelt down, and kindled the fire, flooding the interior of the overhang with a warm, milky light. I guess I must've gaped open-mouthed because DeRenne caught his eye, and grinned at Lachlan. Thankfully, he had the good sense to ignore his sister, sliding into the overhang to my left.

"Comfortable?" he asked, fussing with the folds of my cloak, making sure that I was completely covered by the supple fabric.

"Yes, very," I whispered, every neuron in my skin sizzling at his nearness, almost certain my closeness caused the same stirring feelings in him tonight. I even tasted the infatuation on the tip of my tongue.

"What do we have here?" He reached over and picked a small stem of hemlock from my hair, gliding the back of his hand across my cheek, leaving a lingering feeling where he'd touched me. I gave him a swift smile, and his answering smile caused a fluttering sense of happiness to spread across my chest. Up here, in the stars, I was trapped in his world and he knew it too. I saw the tiniest smirk of satisfaction twitch the corners of his lips.

"How long till the show?" I asked, not that it really mattered. I could've easily stayed here for the rest of my natural-born life.

"Soon," he said, his eyes focused on mine.

Slowly, magnificently, and in complete silence, as if the sky had been touched by a magic wand, the show began. At first, a few brilliant but short-lived bursts of light skipping low along the horizon leaving light trails evanescing into the darkness. Building to a crescendo, it rained fire in the night sky complete with blazing meteor tails hundreds of miles long. This was a sensory overload of a good kind.

Lachlan seemed pleased when I quietly "oohed" and "awed" at the dazzling colors. "The cosmic winds bring the solar dust," he said, smiling.

That dust added a whole new dimension to the show, refracting the streaming tapers into a cosmic display of galactic proportion. Consumed by the heightened reality, I unbridled those prancing hormones for once, burrowing my head into the curve at the base of Lachlan's neck.

Tonight his reflex reaction was to reposition me, folding an arm around my waist, pulling me closer. You couldn't have slipped a single sheet of paper between us.

From start to finish, the entire evening was truly out of this world.

δ⁺

I stared at the folded sheet of paper, propped against the plate of neatly arranged muffins, *emilY harrisoN*, written across the flat front. I unfolded the stiff sheet, pressing the crease out with my thumb, hardly daring to breath.

good morninG /

i thought the earthlinG would enjoy the tactile sensation of papeR / if you are free later today, would you care to join me for an afternoon picnic luncH?/ if your answer is 'yes', then meet me an hour after the midday sun near the standing stones in the village plazA /

send your reply with nazcA /

lachlaN/

I was so glad that I'd decided to stay on Arden for a few more weeks. I lifted the paper, held it near my nose, and inhaled. It was there, the smell of the fresh mountain air. I closed my eyes and relived every incredible moment from last night; the feel of Lachlan holding my hand, the dazzling brightness from the shooting stars, the weight of the thick velvet cloak.

I opened my eyes and reread the message. Well, truthfully, to read between the lines. How thoughtful of him to write a note instead of simply sending Nazca to deliver the invitation. This meant he'd listened to me, that what I said mattered. I reached up, touched the silver disk in my ear, and said in a faint whisper, "Nazca." She would hear me.

Uncertain of the time, I poured a cup of coffee, grabbed a muffin off the plate, and rushed back down the hall, the cold flagstone floors against my bare feet a stark contrast to the warmth melting down to my toes. Practically skipping over the doorway, movement near the window made me stop and look. A brilliant blur streaked into the room, zooming back and forth, twice. I grinned at Nazca's exuberance. "Please inform Lachlan that I graciously accept his lunch invitation."

I arrived early at the standing stones in the village plaza so that Lachlan wouldn't have to wait for me. A calm day on Arden, the sun was warm to the skin with a fresh breeze caressing my face. I had no idea where we were going for our picnic but assumed somewhere outside and not down in the caverns. I'd chosen a more casual dress, periwinkle, and sturdy shoes.

I realized that I'd never walked inside the enclosure formed by the three standing stones and massive capstones. I stepped into the shady space, surprised by the style of the fountain, half-circle low stone benches, and by the unique pattern in the stonework. Not the usual geometric symbols you see everywhere on Arden; the patina of the whole place somehow older than anything I'd seen so far.

The steady streams of water shooting up into the air from the fountain, looked more like glass rods than water spray and didn't splash when they hit the basin. And even though the standing stones were near the traveling pool and open-air marketplace, it was eerily quiet inside of the enclosure with just a soft babbling of running water from somewhere beneath the layers of plantings. The varying shades of green were designed in a coordinated color pattern with such great detail that the foliage looked almost like embroidery work.

Transfixed, my eyes followed one of the glass rods as it leaped into the air. It should've been surprising to see that bold swipe of blue framed by the three capstones in so quiet a place, but somehow, it seemed to fit.

I walked around the flat rock face of each of the three standing stone, admiring their girth and the flecks of mica catching the midday light. Immutable giants, whoever put them here meant for them to last. I kicked aside the leaf litter covering the circular, stacked-stone retaining wall of the pinnacle standing stone. The blockish, slanted letters and symbols looked similar to the letters and symbols I'd seen on the solitary standing stone in the passageway leading to Paden and Ccri's house, implying that these standing stones and the solitary standing stones in each of the three passageways were erected at the same time. I wish I'd had my book to jot down a reminder note to ask Paden.

I considered sitting on the half-circle bench to watch the dancing glass rods of water but quickly dismissed the idea. I didn't want to miss seeing Lachlan. I walked out from the shady enclosure back onto the plaza, my eyes dazed by the sunlight. I leaned against the rough, flat surface of the pinnacle standing stone, infusing my queasy stomach with its solid strength. I had the perfect view of all three archways in the plaza.

Wait for it…Wait for it…Now!

A tall drink of water, Lachlan spilled out through the central archway onto the plaza looking like he didn't have a care in the world. Today he wore a burgundy tunic and had his hair unbound with a simple tight braid on the right side holding the longer strands in check.

At the sight of him, I bet I looked just like my dog did when he was chasing seagulls at the beach; eyes rapidly blinking and a big goofy dog-grin. I waved to him, an indescribable feeling of excitement pulsing through my veins. Before I could even count to three, he stood right in front of me. Leaning in, he placed his right hand flat against the rock face above my left shoulder, sunlight glinting off of the metallic threads woven into the fabric of his tunic.

He let his gaze wander lazily until our eyes met. My mind became muddled. True, he'd been this close last night but under the cover of darkness, his relentless green eyes didn't interfere with my ability to think. "Did you bring your appetite?" he asked his voice bewitching even in the daylight.

"Yes," I said, glad that I could sound so steady.

The corners of his lips curled into a smile. "Do you know that it is possible to decrease your velocity while journeying through the water to enjoy the colors?"

"No," I gulped. One word answers. That's the best I could do.

"Today, I want to voyage to the other side of the planet. There is something I wish to show you." For a brief moment, a secret floated to the surface of his eyes.

"Well, let's see," I said, concentrating on not batting my eyelashes. "I've gone to the underside of Arden, and to the tippy top. What next?"

"No guessing," he said.

"Are DeRenne and Shaw coming?"

"Not today." He didn't sound disappointed.

"Should we at least take some food and water?" I asked, my feelings sizzling at the realization that it just might be the two of us. "Will we be gone for the afternoon?"

"As planned, and not to worry," he said, patting a sturdy pack made of some type of bark, slung across his back. "Shall we?"

Lachlan stood upright, smiled about something, and lightly touched my elbow. Together we threaded through the late lunch crowd milling around the plaza. In no time at all, we stood on the top landing at the traveling pool. He reached over, and took my hand into his, causing an electric jolt to skip down my spine at his tender touch. It was everything I remembered from last night on the mountaintop, and oh, so much more. Hand-in-hand, we approached the bottom granite step and stopped. A chatty group of girls, their arms overloaded with purchases from a day spent shopping in the village blew past us and disappeared into the sparkling water.

"Close your eyes," he said, tightening his grip. Immediately and without hesitation, I did as requested, feeling the excitement of this moment stretch out before me. I gave my full attention to the task at hand, concentrating on the sound of the water waves lapping against the bottom granite step. "I will not let go," Lachlan said, squeezing my hand.

Together we poured into the swiftly moving current, an odd tingling effervescence disintegrating our bodies into their constituent molecular components. This sensation felt different, almost like I stalled right before slipping between the cohesive spinning water molecules, and got stuck in a swirling whorl off to the side. Surprised by this new experience, I opened my eyes for a little moral support.

With each heartbeat, vibrating colors radiated outward from Lachlan's incorporeal form in a continuous wave front. They were the most vivid colors I'd ever seen; whizzing around one another at fantastic speeds. Worried that my own colors must look hideously dull in comparison to his, I dropped my head, secretly wishing that I hadn't so readily agreed to today's outing.

Tangerine sparks flashed near my face.

I ignored him.

He did it again.

Pesky person.

Annoyed, I glanced at him through upturned eyes. Lachlan smiled, the energy from his smile forming a silvery rivulet in the moving current of vibrating molecules. I knew I shouldn't but couldn't seem to stop myself either. I reached out with my free hand, and lightly touched the moving shimmer with my pointer finger. I watched in fascination as the steady stream of energy undulated up the full-length of my vaporous arm, relentlessly tapping at the edge of my consciousness.

I let him in.

The concentrated colors combined, and then exploded, sequentially firing millions of neurons in rapid succession like the finale of a parade, waking up areas of my brain that I never knew existed. Maybe it was because my brain was too small or maybe it was because I was so unprepared. It didn't matter. I couldn't seem to stop from free-falling through the spinning whirlpool of brilliance. An absolute color assault in every sense of the word, I passed out from sensory overload.

"Emily," Lachlan said. Dazzling after-images erupted behind both eyes at the sound of his voice.

"Yes," I whispered the one word. I could that feel my feet were on the dry ground even though I didn't remember stepping out from the water.

"Open your eyes." I heard something in his voice this time.

"I'm afraid." It was true. Not only was I afraid of what just happened but quite honestly, of what might be coming next.

A hand that was cradling my neck, and another hand around my waist, tightened. "I have you," he said.

"Are you sure?"

"Yes, I am sure," he said, and I could tell he was getting a little impatient.

"All right then." My eyelids fluttered open.

In a skillful move, Lachlan swung me upright, forcing both of my hands to rest flat against his chest. I could feel his heart beating slow and strong beneath my fingertips. "Thank you," I murmured, the intensity of his nearness once again making me lightheaded. “I’m not really sure what happened.”

“The process takes practice,” he said, widening his stance, pulling me a shade closer. Pressing his hands into the small of my back, ten fingertips finding the space between my ribs, caused my heart to skip a beat. I really should’ve know better especially after what just happened. Before good sense kicked in, I chanced a quick glance upward. A pair of intent green eyes regarded me without flinching; a look of anticipation attempting to coax a smile out of me.

I thought I heard the sound of someone’s guard dropping, and then realized it was mine—I felt the plunge in the pit of my stomach. In a protective reflex, I pushed against his chest, backing away quickly, horrified by my childish behavior.

“Steady,” he said, looking disappointed.

I didn’t blush, but the embarrassment was a hot mess on my cheeks nonetheless. I inhaled deeply. We’d emerged from the water in the midst of a vast hardwood forest, a rich fragrance of fertile earth and woodsy smell hinting at its age. Only a few diffuse rays of sunlight managed to penetrate the thick foliage, all buttery and warm. Lakes of vibrantly colored wildflowers grew within those pools of light, the adjoining shaded areas overflowing with patches of coppery red undergrowth. “The forest is magnificent, how…”

“I often come here with my family,” he said, that secret of his peering out from beneath his lashes. “The spot I had in mind for our picnic is a short walk from here.” He turned, and headed into the forest. I guess I’d made my point, and he’d decided to play along.

I lifted the folds of the skirt, still having trouble negotiating these outfits, especially in the great outdoors. I followed him along a barely-there path running alongside a slow moving stream, the water glinting clear tumbling over and around the small stones covering the streambed. As he did the day we walked to the caverns, he kept an ever attentive eye on me, holding back branches so I could easily pass, or offering a hand so I didn't slip.

After a few minutes, we emerged from the widely spaced trees onto a rock ledge cantilevered over a deep, grayish-blue pool of water lined by a jumble of boulders. A waterfall tumbling down the sheer rock cliff continuously fed a fine cool mist boiling up from the swirling water. Lachlan stepped beside me and dropped the sturdy pack on the rock ledge.

I found myself a lichen-covered spot, and sat down with as much grace as possible under the circumstances. Lachlan crouched over the pack. He flipped the lid open and removed two brown paper packages; crusty whole grain bread and a block of cheese. Next, a container of raspberry-like fruit, a cloth bag filled with nuts, and then something wrapped in brightly colored, thick wax paper. I looked at him in surprised. He'd visited Metta's flower shop.

I watched as he carefully unfolded the paper, and picked up a single purple flower. "Edible," he said twirling the stem between his forefinger and thumb, obviously pleased with himself. "A sour melon flavor."

I relaxed a little, deciding that I might as well enjoy the day. After all, he did invite me and planned a rather well-thought-out picnic. I unfolded my stiff legs, basking in the warming shaft of sunlight filtering down through the thick canopy. I smiled. Out from the seemingly bottomless pack came plates and napkins made of handmade paper, and two ceramic flasks. Wiggling the cork loose from one of the bulbous flasks, Lachlan handed the flask to me along with a wooden-handled knife.

Humming quietly, stretched at length across the rock ledge, he riffled through the pile of raspberries until finding one to his liking. Tossing the raspberry high into the air, it landed perfectly in his open mouth. Show off! Suddenly aware that he was looking at me looking at him, I picked the flask up, and took a sip; pomegranate juice, rich and robust.

Head down, I tucked the flask into the folds of the skirt, sliced a piece of cheese, and tore a chunk of bread from the loaf, arranging them on the plate. I leaned forward a bit, chose a single raspberry from the top of the pile, and popped it into my mouth, the astonishing potent taste unexpected.

Good grief, even the food tastes better around him.

"I am curious," he said reaching for the knife. "Will you tell me about your life on Earth?"

I finished chewing, and swallowed. "What would you like to know?"

"How does Earth differ from Arden?"

I thought about his question for a moment. "The plant and animal life here and on Earth are almost the same. DeRenne says these designs work best when water is readily available in a liquid form." I chose another raspberry from the pile, anxious to experience its exquisite taste again. "Like I know this is a raspberry but the color is a deeper red."

"I agree. Life seems to vibrate at the same frequency across the Universe," Lachlan said, tearing a chunk of bread from the loaf, and putting it on his plate. "No matter where I travel, I see the commonality of structure in the flora and fauna."

"And, it's very quiet around here. No machinery, no background noise."

He took a sip from his flask. "As we already discussed, this is what we prefer on Arden."

"Slow and organic," I said, reaching inside the cloth bag. "The only other planet I've visited besides Earth, and of course Arden, is Keit. Although I still got the medieval vibe on Keit, the buildings there are taller, and the planet seems a bit more, well, industrial." He sliced a piece of cheese from the block, lifted the knife to his lips, and ate the piece of cheese. "And, the stars here are amazing," I said with a sly smile. "Last night, on the mountaintop, truly might be the first time I've experienced a night sky filled with stars as it meant to be seen." I looked him straight in the eye. "Thank you for that."

A half-smile curved his lips, "My pleasure." He selected a single flower from the top of the pile. "So how old were you at the reveal?"

"Two. So, I really don't remember much."

"I witnessed several reveals during my tutoring," he said. "In a single minute, the world you know changes. No more haves and have-nots. The entitled felt they had earned the right to have more and keep it. They felt it unfair to lose everything they had worked for." He glanced at me with upturned eyes. "My first real glimpse into power and ownership. The entire process was shocking. The have-nots went berserk. They could finally visit the places they thought were unattainable and off-limits. Thousands stormed the shores like a swarm of insects. They trampled the plant life and destroyed the dunes. However, there were guards in place." I looked at him in surprise. "Can you image what would have happened if there were no guards?"

"Good point," I said. "I read that the first year after the reveal everyone pretty much stayed inside, and feared for their lives. After a while, the confusion calmed down, a pattern formed. Whichever part of the planet had summer was always packed so they started to better prepare for the crowds."

Chatting and eating, he asked about my family, where I lived, school, music, the usual array of generic topics. We talked the entire time. I couldn't deny that he appeared totally absorbed by the little details of my life back on Earth. It all felt so…so natural.

As we talked, liquid images of Lachlan on Earth poured through my mind, and my breath caught on the possibilities. I really wanted my friends to meet him; no one would believe me unless they saw him with their own eyes. But I didn't dare allow myself any false hope, not even a little. And in one of those mysterious ways, the afternoon passed in a blissful blur. "Any chance I'm going to hear about that secret you've been keeping?" I asked when I couldn't think of anything else to tell him.

Silence fell upon us for the first time since our arrival. "Let us walk closer to the water," he said, getting to his feet in one quick move. Lachlan leaned forward and stretched out his hands; the suddenness and completeness of the gesture catching me off-guard. I accepted his invitation, rising upward with an unhurried fluid motion. Standing face–to-face for that first awkward moment, our eyes met. Slowly, almost hesitantly, he let go of my left hand. With a gentle motion, he lightly twisted a stray curl back into place behind my shoulder.

Satisfied, he pivoted on his heel, gliding across the rock ledge, the force of his personality magnetically pulling me along with him. In a skillful maneuver, he jumped off of the ledge, whirled back around, and grabbed me around the waist. Never fully taking his eyes off of mine, Lachlan lowered me down the short drop.

Feet firmly planted on the ground, we walked hand-in-hand down the steep slope. He guided me around a few small bushes, and a shallow ravine with smooth, decisive steps. I didn't have to think to follow. We emerged from the mist onto the grassy landing near the base of the waterfall. The hidden world of the glade, drenched in shades of watery blues and greens, imbued magic; enchanting sounds of running water, shards of vanishing light, and of course, Lachlan.

He'd certainly bewitched me.

Standing beside me, both of us now facing the waterfall, he started. "As you know, it is not necessary to carry a water stone while traveling through the water. However, for teaching purposes, small children find it reassuring to hold onto something solid. On the occasion of your second year, you enter a source of flowing water on your home planet and choose your stone. My father helped me select my stone along this very shore."

"On the occasion of your tenth year, you pledge your mergence with the water, building on its four principles. The first principle is harmony, forming an accord with others and with nature. This establishes a bond with the dynamic properties of the water. From then on, you and the waters energy vibrate sympathetically."

"The second principle is respect, upholding and defending your esteem and regard for all life forms. This kinship forever binds you to others who also chose this path. The third principle acknowledges the waters ability to both refresh and renew the mind and the spirit. It is imperative that the life-giving properties of the water are available to everyone…no matter the cost." Lachlan looked down at me with the most peculiar expression. "Even if the price is your life or the life of others who have joined with the water."

"Which is why there are memorials," I said.

"The last principle is tranquility," he said, nodding. "This is a calm and quiet serenity that fills the mind with an ardent appreciation of nature's abundance. It is truly the peace that passes all understanding."

"The history annals reference that the first travelers to this part of the Universe brought stones with them from their home planets. They would leave these stones alongside stones gathered on each newly discovered blue planet, chiseled with the symbol assigned to that planet."

"So, they're the ones who came up with Arden's symbol, like the one on Daileass' stone?" I asked.

"Yes," he said. "The history annals describe a ceremony where the first travelers would dip these newly chiseled stones into a source of flowing water on the planet. They would prick their thumb, and allow a single drop of blood to soak each wet stone, honoring those who shed their blood defending these four principles, and as a symbolic gesture bonding them in an accord with the transformative power of the water."

"Since visiting the cavern, I now feel the ceremony is more than symbolism," he said, shaking his head imperceptibly. "And you discovered the cavern."

"New eyes on an old subject," I said, once again astounded by my luck, thus entrenching me deeper into his world—not that I minded. "Lachlan, I accidentally cut my finger and some of my blood soaked Daileass' wet stone. Paden thought, maybe, since I'm related to him and because his stone had traveled hundreds of times between Earth and Arden, that when I stepped into the water unfocused, the stone brought me here to Arden."

"And I will thank the stars nightly for all the little steps that went wrong," he said, reaching over and taking my hands into his. "Or should I say all the little steps that went right. Without that one mistake, you would have never flowed into my life."

"How…how do you know you are in accordance with the water, and these four principles?" I asked my words now as jumbled as my emotions.

"It feels natural, frictionless," he said, lifting our entwined hands.

Out of the blue, the hairs on my arms fluxed, almost like the build-up of energy before lightning strikes. Granted all of this was over-the-top; the story, Lachlan, the glade. Yet, this felt different. “Did you feel that?” I asked, the skin on my forearms prickling into goosebumps.

“I am sorry.” He released my left hand and touched the silver disk in his ear. “I set this on resonating.”

I blinked several times, trying to grasp the opposing contrasts of his world. Okay, there’s this Lachlan, almost regal in appearance and voice reciting the oral traditions of his lineage. But, there’s another Lachlan. One trained for clandestine missions on other planets, in other galaxies, to the death. How is it possible to tell the difference between the two versions? Would I ever get a chance to meet the other Lachlan?

“Here on Arden,” he stated, sounding rather official.

Silence.

“Emily is with me.” His features softened a bit as he said my name.

I felt the flush on my cheeks.

More silence. This one stretched on interminably.

“Wait for us near the traveling pool in the village,” he sighed, touching his ear again. A curious glint flashed in his eyes as he gathered my free hand back into his. “There is another reason I wanted to bring you here today.”

I looked around at the intense colors and shimmering water inside the hidden glade. “What else could you possibly add?”

“You do not know what Emily means.”

Okay, at first I found it odd how everyone around here says their name, and then states its meaning. But now, I enjoyed their quirky custom. Anyway, I had no idea what Emily *meant*. “I’m named after my grandmother. That’s all I know.”

"On Arden, there is an ancestral name, Emlyn, which means *a rare waterfall*. When I see and sense your colors in my mind, I am reminiscent of this waterfall."

I flinched, recalling my dull colors in comparison to his during the voyage here today. That flinch did not go unnoticed.

"I experienced your colors last night as we traveled to the mountaintop—you have no idea how exquisite they are. They strike a chord in my heart reminding me of this special place filled with pleasant memories," he said, swinging our entwined hands back and forth. "To me, you and this waterfall now vibrate sympathetically; it feels right having you here beside me."

Lachlan released both of my hands, and skimmed his fingers up my arms, tenderly but confidently caressing my face in the palms of his hands. "You are my rare waterfall," he said, and I knew he had to feel the way that my pulse was hammering away beneath his fingertips. I sighed deeply as my arms slipped up and around his shoulders. I didn't see my arms as traitors this time. Lachlan lowered his mouth, stopping an inch before contact. "Do you have a problem with me being from a different planet?"

"No," I whispered, closing my eyes.

He brushed his thumb lightly against my trembling lower lip. Detecting no hesitation on my part whatsoever, his mouth was on mine. I found myself locked in an unforgettable kiss. The kind of kiss every girl dreams of. My heart took a spin on the colossus roller coaster, careening down the highest hill at the speed of light. Flying out of the seat, I dug all ten fingers into his strong shoulders, holding on for dear life. I suddenly felt all prickly again.

How could I not?

"Unbelievable," he murmured, gliding his moist lips across my cheekbone, a tingling following the path he traced, leaving my skin flushed but in a good way.

Unsure if he was referring to the fact that they had the nerve to contact him again so soon or to our first kiss, I decided to go with the latter. Lachlan leaned his forehead against mine for a fraction of a second, and whispered, "I will return in a moment."

And like the evanescing mist, he vanished into thin air.

Everything in the glade went silent except for the faint rush of wind, and the sound of my heart pounding away in my ears. I took two slow breaths, in and out, allowing the cool air rushing into my lungs to calm my breathing. I attempted to put this day into perspective, anxious thoughts about our first kiss racing down the path of second guessing.

And that's when I realized I was in deep and serious trouble here. Did I kiss him back? Did I reveal too much? Does he think I'm inexperienced? Before I had a chance to argue the questions out to their logical conclusion, he stood in front of me with the pack slung across his shoulder, twirling an iridescent turquoise feather between his thumb and forefinger.

"I found this on the granite ledge where you were sitting. A keepsake from our time spent here today."

I took the feather from his hand and tucked it inside the pocket of the dress. "Lachlan, in case I don't get a chance…" I demurred, embarrassed by my inability to talk in his presence once again, allowing my hair to swish across my face so he wouldn't see. "I want to thank you for sharing today with me."

Impossibly charming as ever, he leaned his head down and swept back the long strands with his fingertips until our eyes met. There was no escape; he'd seen to that. Without warning, his lips brushed mine for the briefest moment, leaving the memory of our first kiss lingering. "I meant for us to spend the entire afternoon together," he said with complete and absolute sincerity. "I promise to rectify this missed time upon my return."

That promise energized the air between us, simultaneously stimulating every single neuron in my skin like I'd just downed three cups of strong coffee. Without saying a word, he slipped his hand down to mine, and I went with him into the water.

δ^+

"The man is nothing but annoyingly industrious," Shaw said in a discouraging tone. He and DeRenne met us on the grassy knoll next to the traveling pool in the village plaza. DeRenne's eyes were as big as saucers at the sight of her big brother stepping out from the water, pulling me along with him.

"Will you walk with us to The Assemblage?" Lachlan asked, tugging my hand, avoiding his sister's curious gaze.

"Of course," I said, smiling at him. "There're a few topics I want to research."

We all turned. DeRenne was holding Shaw's hand, walking backward. "Are you still profiling Jokull?" she asked, eyeing the pack slung across Lachlan's shoulder, a glimmer of recognition crossing her face.

"No, Benjamin Franklin," I said, "a.k.a Daileass, my distant relative." Since the profiling was finished, unnecessary research was always my emergency backup entertainment plan if I suddenly found myself without anything to do…like this afternoon.

"Hold up," Shaw said, stopping in front of the bakery near the artisan's marketplace. "DeRenne and I enjoyed a late breakfast and no lunch. How about you two? Hungry?"

"We're good," I said. "Lachlan fixed us a picnic lunch."

"That is why he has the pack!" DeRenne blurted out looking both shocked and pleased, now that she knew what they interrupted. "He actually put together a picnic lunch?"

"Yes, he did!" I said, giving Lachlan a quick wink. "And the meal was delicious."

"Never would have predicted that," Shaw muttered, dragging an open-mouthed DeRenne into the bakery.

"That was priceless," I said, glancing up at Lachlan.

The leopard, however, changed his spots and went all somber. Lachlan towed me to a nearby tree, dropped the pack on the ground, leaned back against the wide trunk, and appraised me with pale, papery eyes. Oh no! Here it comes. "I am not sure how long I will be gone," he said without really seeing me. "And your time here on Arden is limited."

I winced as a huge wave of disappointment crashed all over me. Unlike the cool and shady glade, the glaring sunlight highlighted the ugly truth. I desperately wanted to say something but honestly, there was nothing to say. I ran a hand through my hair a couple of times and dropped my head. After the wonderful picnic, I wouldn't let him see the disappointment.

As usual, it seems we were tuned into the same wavelength.

Reaching for my free hand, Lachlan twirled me closer, resting my back against his chest, our interlaced arms coming to rest across my waist. He rested his chin on the top of my head. I felt the steady thump of his heart against my shoulder and the slight stir of breath in my hair each time he exhaled.

Neither of us said a single word, lost in our own thoughts. A few long minutes later, Shaw and DeRenne waltzed out from the bakery laughing and talking, until they saw us. The only two people in the entire Universe who understood our predicament of limited time walked toward the stone archway at the far end of the plaza. Lachlan and I separated and followed, keeping our distance.

All too quickly we reached The Assemblage, and the end of our time together, for now. I turned to face Lachlan and met troubled eyes focused on my face. I gave him a faint smile. He smiled in response, lightly touching my arm before walking to join Shaw.

I felt cold and exposed without him near, folding my arms back across my waist, cherishing the memory of his embrace for a little longer. DeRenne and I now stood side-by-side, watching the two soldiers stoically accept their duty and troop away without a single backward glance, our thoughts running over different but converging paths.

"Wait! You're not leaving?" I said, looking from DeRenne to Lachlan and Shaw.

"Not this mission," she murmured.

"Don't you always go with them?" I asked, recognizing the faraway look in her eyes.

"Not necessarily." She hesitated as usual before adding, "I have more training to complete. As I accomplish each new skill level, and if Lachlan deems the mission safe, I am allowed to join them. Otherwise, I accompany a different group or work on a project of my own."

"I take it since you aren't leaving then they consider this a dangerous mission."

"Suffice it to say, I will sleep better upon their return." She gripped my forearm. "Do you mind if I accompany you to The Assemblage?"

Intuitively, we both knew the best place to seek solace on Arden today was with each other. "I'd hoped," I said, patting her hand, thankful for a friendship that transcended words.

Arm-in-arm, supporting one another in our common cause, we slowly walked up the limestone steps to the portico. "Exactly where did Lachlan take you today?" DeRenne asked as we passed through the windowed vestibule, her tone uncharacteristically nonchalant, for her.

"The waterfall where he chose his water stone," I said, ending the sentence on a high note.

She stopped in the doorway of the rotunda. A mother and her two small children almost ran into us. "He did?"

"Yeah? Why?"

"Emily, he only goes there alone. I...I."

"Not even Raffye?" I wasn't sure where that sarcasm came from.

"She is a childhood friend. At one time…perhaps…but not now."

My heart skipped a beat at this revelation. One other piece of information Lachlan mentioned today was that his father helped him select his stone at the waterfall. I'm pretty sure that was their father in the image I viewed a few days ago. I was curious to learn more about him but I also knew that today was not the day to discuss the past when the phantom future loomed so large in our minds.

DeRenne and I made our way across the rotunda, avoiding the mother and her children, now staring at the holographic compass star. We entered an empty room in the back corner. "Daileass…my ancestor," I mumbled, dropping into the polished stone recliner.

The lights in the room dimmed, and the auto voice said, "Daileass assisted the thirteen American Colonies to establish a democratic…"

"Know that already," I grumbled, crooking an arm behind my head.

"Phrase your question so that the information you are requesting is more specific and direct," DeRenne said, sounding preoccupied, her thoughts like mine light years away from here.

"Okay. I guess what I really want to ask is…How? How could someone leave their life on Arden? Well, leave their life anywhere in the Universe, according to Nazca, to mentor a planet. And don't give me the, 'It is an honor to serve The Accordance' line either. These people sacrificed their lives, displaced their families. Benjamin…I mean Daileass had children that never even knew the truth about their lineage. Is that really fair?"

"Lighten the room," DeRenne requested.

"Sorry," I said, in a little girl voice.

"Emily, you ask a valid question. However, you are asking a rational explanation for something that cannot easily be explained rationally. I want to give you my views first, and then show you." She scooted into the dip in the recliner, assuming the teacher pose, and waving a hand. "First, no one is ever forced. They choose to go. Candidates are put through a strict screening process before granted permission to mentor a planet. They are asked the tough questions; the ones concerning spouses, children, and extended family."

"The Accordance discourages mentors from becoming personally involved with humans on the worlds they guide. Let's face facts, humans are just that, human. You never really know who you are going to fall for until you actually fall. Does that conveniently happen on your home world or on a different planet?" She swung her foot out, and poked me in the side. "An excellent example is sitting next to me in this very room."

I gave her a sideway glance.

"Anyway," she continued, grinning. "There are certainly situations where a mentor becomes overly involved and then fakes their own death to minimize the pain of separation. Others immerse themselves into a planet's society, and never look back. Some, however, play both sides. As you now know, nothing interesting is ever completely one-sided."

"Huh?" I mumbled, giving her another sideways glance

"Show Emily the route she traveled from Earth to Arden," DeRenne instructed, sliding back down into the seat.

The room darkened, "Emily, unpracticed in intergalactic water travel was swept up by the current, journeying at an accelerated velocity along a relatively direct path between Earth and Arden," the mechanical voice whirred. A map of the Universe materialized all around, obscuring the ceiling and the floor, showing a somewhat straight red line between Earth and Arden. “This in turn skewed time. As a result, six weeks on Arden correlates to a passage of two hours of Earth time.”

I remembered Lachlan’s comment, ‘your time is limited’, and did the math. I’d been on Arden for almost two weeks of their time, which meant…only four more stinking weeks! I panicked. I wanted to stay and see how the relationship played out with Lachlan but I had no idea when he’d return from this mission. And the waiting with no end in sight was maddening.

“There are other options,” the monotone voice droned. How creepy; it was almost as if the room read my mind. “If a traveler varies their route to avoid massive planets and black holes, time balances between the departure and arrival worlds.” The image dissolved, re-forming to a view of the Universe showing a second gently curving red line between Arden and Earth.

“So, if I travel a different route back to Earth, that might buy me some more time here on Arden?” I speculated aloud.

“Since your initial trip was so direct, I am not sure,” DeRenne said. “With some calculations, you might be able to manipulate the time discrepancies. Or perhaps, you could journey back to Earth, balance the time, and return to Arden. I think the process might be a little more complicated than I make it sound.”

“Good to know,” I muttered.

“Lachlan and Shaw, well Lachlan mostly, have traveled some pretty creative paths these last few trips trying to cheat the time game,” she said. “Shaw says he is getting space sick with all the crazy twists and turns.”

"Really?" It came out higher than my normal speaking voice, again.

"You are pretending, right?" she asked.

"Seriously, how would I know any of this?"

"True," she sighed. "You fit in so well around here that sometimes I forget that you are not from Arden." I accepted her backhanded compliment. "Lachlan calculates the routes to ensure as little time as possible passes on Arden while they are away. Not that Shaw is sad."

My head was reeling. I'd suspected, hoped, but never ever dreamed. If Lachlan is fiddling around with the routes and time discrepancy that means he wants to spend more time with me. Doesn't it?

"Emily! Emily!" DeRenne said, snapping her fingers to get my attention.

"Yeah, I know." A long silence ensued in which I attempted to process this new information.

"Show us the routes Daileass traveled," DeRenne said, sensing my bewilderment.

The image blurred, shifting to an expansive view, showing about forty different routes between Earth and Arden. Talk about your superhighway! "Daileass benefited from the two most common forms of travel popular during the time period, ships and horses, either of which could take several weeks or even months to complete the journey," the mechanical voice dinned. "He took advantage of these discrepancies and traveled back to Arden. No one on Earth ever suspected he was gone in the first place, assuming that he was still somewhere in transit.

The Seren would monitor the situation, and alert him if necessary."

"You're saying that when Benjamin Franklin was supposedly voyaging across the Atlantic Ocean, he was in fact, here on Arden?" I shook my head, dumbfounded.

"Although complicated, it is possible to travel so that the time works to your advantage. I know this seems horrifying to you. Daileass understood that one day his descendants would know the truth. In your case," she said, and I heard the muted laughter in her voice, "sooner than later."

"Well, from everything I've read about Benjamin Franklin, he certainly was an odd man, disappearing for long periods of time, and then suddenly reappearing with some newfangled invention. Who else from The Accordance mentored Earth?"

The room revealed various members of The Accordance, and their contributions such as Aristotle, Guttenberg, Galileo, Newton, and Mozart. As Earth's society became more sophisticated, their assistance began to blend more into background roles: the Wright brothers' financial backer, Alexander Fleming's lab assistant guiding his discovery of antibiotics, Rosalind Franklin's X-ray photographs contributing to Watson and Crick deciphering the structure of the double helix.

I felt sure that Einstein was from another planet. As it turns out he came by his genius honestly. He was identified early on, contacted by The Accordance, and had visited Arden on more than one occasion. "Albert, whose name means *bright nobility*, would return to Earth," DeRenne said. "He would rearrange the wording and diagrams in his theories so his contemporaries could understand them."

"How do you even know that?" I asked, sort of stunned.

"Tutors," she moaned.

After another hour of random searching, I slid out from the stone recliner. The lights in the room brightened although my head still swirled. "Do you want to shop in the village?" I asked, wishing she would stay for the evening.

"Absolutely," she answered quickly.

Wandering aimlessly through the shops and the artisan's marketplace, talking about anything except what was really on our minds, we spent the late afternoon in a numbed state of denial. Before the inevitable darkness rolled in, we found ourselves back at Paden and Ccri's house. "In the kitchen, girls," Ccri called out.

"Thought we'd hang out here for a while," I said with little enthusiasm.

"Oh. I see. The guys must be off-world," Ccri surmised, guessing the reason for our long faces. She scooted her chair from the kitchen table, stood up, and patted the folds in her skirt. "Then I shall prepare some tea."

DeRenne and I walked along the front hallway. We heard Ccri humming, and smiled at each other, grateful to have someone needlessly fuss over us. Once inside my room, we flung ourselves across the canopy bed and let out long lonely teenage girl sighs. I handed DeRenne the round, lime green pillow. "When are you leaving?" I asked, wedging the pillow with the tangerine piping underneath my arm.

"Not until the morning," DeRenne said, angling her body kitty-cornered across the foot of the bed, tucking the pillow behind her head.

"Have you always lived on Arden?" I asked to keep the conversation going and myself preoccupied.

"My family mentored a planet when I was younger, although I do not remember much." I laughed. "What is so funny?" DeRenne asked, flipping over onto her back, staring at the gauzy fabric draped across the canopy.

"What you just said reminds me that all of this is just so outrageous that sometimes I think I must be dreaming."

"And, your favorite part is …"

"Everything—the colors, the pace, the unexpectedness of each day. And I guess I don't have to tell you that I have feelings for your brother because you already know that." She arched her head back and rolled her eyes. I also saw a smile. "Where's Shaw's family?" I asked to distract her.

"His parents and two younger sisters are currently mentoring a planet. He visits them when he gets a chance—which is infrequent these days."

"So, he and Lachlan are childhood friends?" I asked, hoping this was a good way to get her to fill in the gaps in case I accidently said something that I learned while watching the images at The Assemblage. Plausible deniability, I think they call it.

"Yes, they were inseparable…until I came along. I had feelings for Shaw my entire life. He never acknowledged my existence until about a year ago. With a considerable amount of planning on my part, I started arranging situations where it was just the two of us. He eventually got the hint. We had to sneak around at first, very tiring, although exciting. By the way, I should thank you." She arched her head backward again, a girlish smirk on her face this time. "These last two weeks have been great with you keeping my big brother occupied."

"Glad to be of service," I said, with a quick nod.

DeRenne flipped over onto her stomach, her feet flying up in the air. "Exactly what is going on between you two?"

"No idea," I sighed. "Today, it went to a new level. Don't get me wrong, I'm not sad; just apprehensive as to what the future holds."

"If it is any solace, you should know that Lachlan is guarded with his emotions. One thing you have to watch out for is that he is overly cautious. Remember that night at supper when he said you should return to Earth."

"Gee! Thanks for bringing that up. Later that night, walking back here," I said, implying he didn't whisk me straight home, "he explained that he was concerned for my safety... hmm...something to do with Jokull." And then I remembered that night for a totally different reason; Lachlan could be soulful when you least expect it.

"This is my point," DeRenne mumbled, crunching the corner of the comforter in her fist. "You are perfectly safe on Arden. Why does he have to open his big mouth... and ruin the moment?"

"I was thinking you might have an answer to that question."

She looked me directly in the eye. "Sorry. No idea. The only thing I do know is that his face goes soft whenever he looks at you."

I thought about that for a moment. “I have to go back, to Earth, you know…my Mom.”

DeRenne stretched out a consoling arm. “Difficult choices lay ahead for us all.”

δ^+

I'd finished the day's research at The Assemblage, and shopped till I dropped. I knew they'd allow me to take only a few items back to Earth, so what was the point? Five days passed without a single word from either Lachlan or DeRenne. That's like a month in 'girl waiting to hear from her special someone' years. Traitor-time, even by Arden's standards, dragged dismally with no end in sight.

The sun skimmed large and red in the evening sky as I unlatched the door to Paden and Ccri's house. I lingered in the foyer, listening, and didn't detect a lull in the conversation coming from the open-space living area. There'd been a constant influx of guest over the lasts few nights. It seems tonight would be no different.

"Great," I huffed, "another evening of irrelevant chit-chat." Thirsty from the walk here, I made my way to the kitchen along the front hallway, deciding to sneak something back to my room for an hour of solitude before plunging into the boredom. As soon as I entered the kitchen, I stopped dead in my tracks. A thick, heavy cloak, embroidered with the Water emblem, was lying across the kitchen chair.

My heart skipped a beat.

Is he here?

I tiptoed to the door connecting the kitchen to the open-space living area. I flattened my back against the wall near the door jamb, the pulse of time suddenly invigorating. Lachlan's voice wafted through the slightly ajar door, "This is my mission."

A gleeful thrill swept through my body just like the day we found my dog at the pound.

"Lachlan, I am not sure if it is a good idea for you to remain personally involved," Paden said, sounding conflicted.

"I need to see the mission to completion," Lachlan answered without hesitation.

"Will you keep your emotions in check?" Paden said more as a statement rather than a question.

"Absolutely."

"And for DeRenne?" Paden asked.

"She is…trying," he said, and I heard the pride in his voice. "True, she is more emotional. Her oath to The Accordance is solid and steadfast. Although, I cannot deny that it is sometimes difficult for her to take orders from her big brother. Shaw's commitment to me is resolute."

I knew it! Lachlan's the one in charge. But how and more importantly…Why? Clearly, these words weren't meant for my ears. And before I overheard anything else I shouldn't hear, I stepped backward and went over to the sink to fix a cup of strong coffee, banking on a late night.

"Hi," I said, glancing over my shoulder a few minutes later when I heard Lachlan's footsteps on the flagstone floors.

"Hey you," he said, a soft buttery yellow pixelating across the fabric of his mission uniform.

Man, he looked good in that uniform. I realized that over the last few days something inside of me felt all wrong. Almost like I was standing on one foot, and seeing the world askew. Now that he was here in the kitchen beside me, the scales self-adjusted, tipping until perfectly balanced. We gazed at each other for several long moments before he said, “I was about to send a message with Nazca.”

I sighed. “When did you return?” I walked toward him, blinking rapidly to clear the haze of infatuation, and handed him a mug of steaming coffee.

“A short time ago,” he said. “I needed to discuss a few items with Paden. Do you have plans for the evening?”

“Nothing that I cannot change. What did you have in mind?”

“There is a café in the adjacent village,” he said, his lips curving into an appreciative smile.

“Works for me,” I said, my heart racing at the thought of an evening alone. “Is that what you’re wearing?”

“I will return home and change into more casual clothing, and then rendezvous with you back here,” he said, trying to hide his disappointment. “I must leave again tomorrow.”

I thought about what DeRenne had said; all the crazy twists and turns. The convoluted route he more than likely traveled to be here tonight. “Give me a few minutes,” I said. “That’s Earth minutes.”

“Dress warmly,” he called out as I dashed down the hallway.

I changed into a thickly woven, long-sleeved dress steeped in passionate hues. Grabbing the hairbrush off of the bedside table, I gathered the unruly curls and clamped them in place on the left side with the jeweled barrette. If we ended back on the mountaintop before the evening was over, I didn't want my hair blowing in my face all night long.

Running a hand down the pin-tuck pleats, I grinned at the stranger in the mirror. "Be smart," I teased, waggling a finger at the giddy girl staring back at me. "You're smitten."

Lachlan pulled the chair out from the table and stood off to the side. Under a deep purple sky, admiring the delicate shades of color layering upon one another, we walked hand-in-hand across the stone bridge to an outdoor café in the adjacent village. I kept pinching myself the entire time. I'm not even sure how I stood upright.

This café was clearly an upgrade in the romance department; candlelit tables arranged in secluded corners surrounded by feathery foliage alive with glittering Seren, glimmers from their luminescence rippling across the stonework in the courtyard. Maybe my mind was playing tricks, but a whisper of a thrill seemed to *whoosh* down through the café with each breath of wind. "Thank you," I said, sliding down into the seat feeling insanely happy.

Lachlan moved a chair from the opposite side of the table next to mine. As he sat down, I noticed a few strands from his tightly bound hair graze the nape of his neck. I surprised myself by reaching over, and tucking those stray wisps back in place. An appreciative glint crossed his eyes at my spontaneous gesture as he reached up, and folded five fingers around mine. As our entwined hands came to rest on the tabletop, I marveled at how natural all of this felt.

"May I order for us tonight?" he asked.

"Yes," I said, ogling our interlaced fingers.

A woman hovering nearby walked to the table to take our order. "Two sauté fish meals," he requested politely. She wrote down the order with a dramatic flair. "And some wine and bread beforehand."

When she left, I looked over at him. "Wine?"

"I am not sure the wine on Arden is very potent. Perhaps a sparkling fruit drink is a better choice of words. Do you remember the pomegranate juice we enjoyed at our picnic near the waterfall?" I felt the flush in my cheeks as images from our first kiss roared through my head like a wildfire. I dropped my eyes. "Emily...Emlyn," he said. "Am I moving too fast?"

"No idea what you're talking about," I mumbled.

"Is that so?" He lifted our entwined hands into the air, his tone implying that it should be obvious. "And now?"

"Maybe…" I said, arching a single eyebrow. "A girl might misread the signs, especially if that girl is unfamiliar with the rules in a world completely new to her."

I saw him open his mouth and then shut it, looking apprehensive. I couldn't tell if the delaying tactic was in hopes of unnerving me, in which case it worked, or because he couldn't decide what to say next. Anyway, his eyes narrowed as the words came out, "And how would someone from that world assure her his intentions are true?"

As usual, he subtly shifted my attention and reframed the question back onto me. I really hate it when he does that. I sighed. "Under normal circumstances, time should tell. Unfortunately, that's her one giant gray area." I glanced at him and set my gaze on his face. "At some point, she must return to her planet, in her galaxy."

"And naturally, she thinks this will simply end?" He exhaled a sharp breath, keeping a hold this time on the words I suspected he really wanted to say.

"Hopefully not," I whispered.

He shook his head almost imperceptibility. "Nor do I," he said, not nearly quick enough for me. "At this precise moment, all I can offer are the feelings I have for you."

Out of nowhere, the waitress returned with our drinks, plates, silverware, and a basket of bread. Apparently, in the space between one sentence and the next, we'd inclined our heads together. Separating, I lifted the crystal glass and took a sip; the wine robust and fruity with just a hint of alcohol.

Not brave enough to look him straight in the eye, I set the glass to the side, and arranged the plates and silverware on the tabletop to keep my hands busy and my mind occupied. In my side view, I watched Lachlan tear a chunk of bread from the loaf and put it on my plate, and then place the rest of the loaf on his plate.

"Don't they feed you when you're away on these missions?" I asked, lifting the crystal glass for another sip of liquid backbone.

"They do," he said. "I had a few other pressing matters on my mind today besides food."

I grinned at him over the rim of the glass. At least now I knew that he was thinking of me, and trying to make time. Our conversation idled in superficial until the food arrived. Lachlan picked up the oversized fork and dove right in. I ate a few obligatory bites before pushing the plate toward him. "I can order another dish if I'm still hungry." Of course, I wasn't going to eat anything else; my stomach was way too queasy with anticipation.

Lachlan polished off both plates, and looked up. "There is another meteor shower. Care to venture back to the mountaintop?"

"I would like that very much," I said, winding my way down that precarious path.

"Good." He dropped his napkin on the tabletop, leaned in, and kissed my cheek before rising from the chair, the gesture as natural as throwing on a favorite fleece. "That will have to do for now."

I watched him disappear inside the café. I realized that Lachlan was the kind of person people would notice. Not because he wanted them to but simply because they couldn't help themselves. I knew I couldn't. I smiled, running a finger down my cheek, savoring the memory of his moist lips. "Lachlan should come with a big red warning label," I thought.

A few minutes later, he walked through the door carrying a sealed package, and two bulbous flasks. I got to my feet and threw the cloak over my shoulder. Lachlan took hold of my hand as he passed, and pulled me through a side pathway leading to a small traveling pool. I detected urgency in him; a desire to reach our destination as quickly as possible. Without uttering a single word, he catapulted us into the shimmering water.

The short trip was an indistinguishable blur.

"Are we in a hurry?" I asked, stepping out from the stream on the top of the windswept mountain. Keit dominated the scene, the stately orb filling the night sky with a soft coral glow.

"I must leave earlier than anticipated," Lachlan said, pushing aside the hemlock branches, and walking over to the granite overhang.

I watched as he set the package and the flasks on the fur pelts covering the craggy granite floor. Drat! The evil time-tyrants reign ruled. He must've received a communication while he was inside of the café. The question jumped from the back of my throat before I could stop myself, "When?"

"By midnight." He knelt down, and lit the neatly arranged fire.

I noticed that neither the wood in the fire or the fur pelts were covered in frost like everything else, implying that he'd thought this through and planned ahead. I nervously chewed my lip, struggling just to think.

Here I was on the top of the world, the night air electrifying, worried that this would be our pattern; bits and pieces, here and there. It took little imagination to see the whole picture. The sound of the fire roaring to life a minute later roused me from the pity party that I was throwing at my own expense.

Lachlan stood upright and wiped his hands on a pant leg. "Let me wrap that around you," he said his tone both inviting and playful. "You will catch a chill if you are not careful."

I'm not sure what made me decide to act. With just an air of anticipation separating us, I closed the gap in three quick steps. Never fully taking his eyes off of mine, he took the cloak from my outstretched hand. Lachlan skillfully *swooshed* the velvety garment up into this night of nights, causing the folds of fabric to drape across my shoulders.

Taking longer than necessary fastening the metal clasp, two inquisitive thumbs lightly traced my collarbone through the thick fabric. "Perfect," he said, looking rather pleased with himself.

Pulling away slightly, widening his stance, Lachlan leaned forward, cupping my face between both of his hands. I put my own hands up, placing them over his hands, and arched my head back. His translucent green eyes, backlit against the intense star-shine, glistened. I knew he waited for my expression to soften with desire, and my breath to catch.

I sighed.

Lachlan leaned in, and kissed me. An honest to goodness, no doubt about it heartfelt kiss so intense that I melted into his arms without conscious thought. Keeping the back of my head captured in one hand, he reached up with his free hand and unclamped the barrette holding the curls in place. Taking his time, he ran five fingers through my unbound hair. From another time and place, I thought I heard the barrette hit the ground, and made a mental note to remember…to remember.

Okay…I had no idea what I was supposed to remember. What I did know; I was kissing the most exquisite creature in the entire Universe.

Forget the stupid barrette.

Overcome by the slow burn of desire, I stood up on tippy-toes, crushing myself into his strong chest. The unexpected movement distracted him. I took advantage of that momentary lull and gazed at his face drenched in Keitlight. "What do you see?" he asked, dipping his down head until our eyes were level. Finding my thoughts difficult to think, I opened my mouth. A pathetic little whimper gurgled out. "Is that so?" Lachlan laughed, trailing a finger down my throat.

He'd shaken his head, and made to turn away when I said in a low voice, "Listen, I just want to say that…"

Lachlan turned around, and with the gentlest of movements, lifted my chin with a finger, and murmured, "Emily. You talk too much." Then he closed his mouth over mine. Lachlan kissed me again, and nothing else in the world mattered.

When he finally released me, I stood there, legs weak, eyes more than likely dilated with desire, breathing in the cool night air, and fighting for composure. "Care to explain?"

Lachlan had a wild look about him here in the heavens. "Just making my point," he said, kneeling down next to the fire.

"Got it," I mumbled, grabbing the barrette, and making my way to the granite overhang, the entire way willing my wobbly knees not to cave.

Lachlan stoked the fire, tossing on a few more logs. I settled into the granite overhang, unfolded the paper package to find chocolates, and then opened the flasks of hot coffee, arranging each item on a small rock ledge.

"Room for me?" he asked, collapsing onto the fur pelts.

Scooting closer, Lachlan slid his hand through the thick fabric folds until he found what it was that he was looking for; my hand. As before, our fingers dovetailed perfectly, a fresh supply of adrenalin sluicing through my veins at the intensity of his touch.

"Happy?" he murmured against my cheekbone, igniting a warm feeling melting all the way down to my toes.

I took an unsteady breath but didn't answer.

"Is something wrong? Again."

"No," I whispered. "Everything's perfect. That's the problem."

There was a pause in which the wind howled, and the fire crackled in response.

He inhaled a sharp breath, "But…"

Insecurity seeped out from every pore. "Why me? There's got to be more interesting girls in the Universe; ones without the added complications that I bring to the table." I shook my head, but didn't meet the eyes I felt focused on my face. "And I don't stand a chance around you. You're so completely different from any of the boys back on Earth."

He whispered one word, "Emlyn." He'd said his special name for me twice tonight and honestly, I found it the single most alluring word I'd ever heard. With a forced determination so that there'd be no doubt, he wrapped his arm around my waist, repositioned me, and tipped my face upward with his chin. "Do you need a reason?"

I found myself assessed by cool green eyes, and as usual, I raised a bright yellow caution flag. "For this to make sense. Yes. I need a reason."

"If you insist then. I find you…refreshing…your approach to life unique."

My back stiffened. "Are you referring to the fact that I'm constantly dangling from a spider-silk here?" He opened his mouth to answer. I raised a finger to *shush* him. "That I've had to reconsider the way in which I view the world?" His eyes widened but this time he kept quiet. "That basically everything I thought to be true is turned upside down."

I blew out a flustered breath.

"That is certainly part of your appeal," he said, not doing a very good job of hiding his amusement. "Emily, in every sense of the word you did not merely dip a toe in the water. You jumped into my world feet-first, and never looked back. Any reasonable person would have crumbled by now. You decided to stay, worked hard to understand The Accordance—offered us a new perspective on Jokull."

"Any reasonable person?" I grumbled. That's all I heard.

He smiled, just a tiny twitch of lips. "And, I enjoy deciphering what you are thinking." He stayed steady, focused on my face in what might be considered a rude stare.

"How do you know what I'm thinking?"

"Your eyes," he said, brushing a fingertip across my eyelashes. "I love watching your fiery-amethyst eyes mimic the out-of-control thought process inside of your head. I find myself captivated by your endless expressions."

"You noticed that?" I knew he especially enjoyed stumping me, throwing in random tidbits about his world, catching me off-guard just for the pleasure of it.

"And now," he said, sounding both satisfied and amused. "Your eyes betray your true feelings."

I looked up to find a pair of raised eyebrows, daring me to deny. "Exactly when was the first time my eyes gave me away?"

Lachlan's tightened his grip around my waist, drawing me close to whisper in my ear, "The night I caught you trying to catch a Seren in the passageway. The whole experience was thirst-quenching."

"Thirst-quenching?"

"Absolutely thirst-quenching."

"You make me sound like a drink of water!"

"The highest form of a compliment here on Arden. Never forget that what is pleasing to one's mind varies from person to person. Your colors complement the world in which I dwell. I have seen you on an energetic level, and this essence is the truth of life. You cannot hide or shield yourself when you are in the water. This is the real you, and I like what I see."

I glanced at him sideway and wanted to huff, but didn't.

"Satisfied?" he asked.

"For now," I whispered, surprised by the little lurch in the pit of my stomach.

"May we please enjoy the rest of our limited time tonight?"

I rested my face against his shoulder, angling my chin upward, seeing that his eyes weren't cool, but warm like his voice. "Like I said, I don't stand a chance around you."

δ^-

Nazca flitted into the kitchen through the open window. I wanted her to deliver some good news and save me from another boring evening. She did. DeRenne was on Arden for the evening. She requested that I meet her in the village.

"Yes, you must join her," Ccri said. It took but five minutes for me to change clothes and bolt out of the door.

"I have no idea," DeRenne muttered as we waited in line at the artisan's marketplace to purchase some glasses her mother had ordered. "I heard a rumor that my brother managed to return for a night, something about needing to talk with Paden. Clever boy."

I attempted to rearrange the pout on my lips. "That was three days ago. I haven't heard a word since."

"Well?" Her eyes were bright.

"A quick dinner at a café and then we went back to the mountaintop," I said knowing the location implied this wasn't an ordinary evening. I lifted a hand to drop the curls so she wouldn't see too much on my face.

"I am thankful he has enough sense to treat a girl to a lovely night," she said with a nod.

"He told me that I was thirst-quenching. Is that kind of like a compliment?"

DeRenne snorted. "Coming from anyone else; probably not. Coming from Lachlan, yes, it is a compliment."

We consoled and comforted each other until way past midnight. After her departure, I nosed-dived into the deep end of the desperation pool once I fully realized just how much I'd immersed myself into his world.

To make matters worse, the constant tug-of-war inside of my mind seduced me in opposing directions. One side dangled the Lachlan carrot, toying with my emotions, enticing me to stay on Arden as long as possible to give the relationship a chance to develop. The other side waved a red flag, shouting out a warning to return to Earth before my mother noticed that I was gone. My dilemma; I wanted both sides to win. But time was racing toward an inflexible departure date.

The next day, after a morning and an afternoon with nothing constructive planned, Ccri sent me to the village to shop for a few items for supper. She recognized that I wanted to stay busy, keep myself occupied. Walking through the leafy green corridor, swinging the cloth bag back and forth, I veered off left only to have the metaphorical flying monkey swoop down and sink its poisoned claws deep into my spine.

Lachlan stood underneath the stone archway at the end of the passageway, talking to…Raffye. I shrank back into the prickly hedge, my hand flying up to suppress the primal shriek rumbling deep within my chest. How long had he been on Arden? Why didn't he let me know he was here? Why was he talking to…her?

Stop! A persistent voice insisted. There's got to be a logical explanation. In the past whenever Lachlan returns to Arden, he deals with his responsibilities first. Silly girl, you know the mission takes top priority; steer clear from the pit of second guessing. Hurry home. He will either drop by shortly or send a message with Nazca.

Okay, that did make sense to the minuscule portion of my brain still retaining some common sense. I flattened my spine against the prickly hedge and made my way back to the main passageway. Once around the corner and out of sight, I quickened my pace, a battalion of wayward thoughts marching through my head as I stomped along a less direct route to the plaza.

"Paden's household account," I barked at the holographic image, shoving a dozen apples and an onion into the cloth bag. Out in the sunlight, I felt foolish. For all I know, Raffye stopped him. She does live on Arden after all.

I sighed, and then suddenly cheered up waiting in the line at the bakery. I'd better get some extra food in case Lachlan decides to stay for supper. And then perhaps afterward; a trip back to the mountaintop. "Four loaves of bread," I said to the baker's pudgy wife.

My heart now light as a feather, I blew around the backside of the house and tossed the cloth bag on the kitchen counter. "Emily, did you run here from the market?" Ccri asked when she saw me flushed from head-to-toe.

"Yes!" I said, skipping down the hallway.

I flung the door open and leaped into the room. He's back. I was, well…over the rainbow. About to burst open from the ballooning swell of happiness, I closed both eyes, allowing the magic to whisk me to the mountaintop.

When I finally opened my eyes, the colors in the room were somehow richer, the sound of the bubbling water delightfully sweet. I considered a bath, and then quickly dismissed the idea. What if he arrived during the next few minutes? Not wanting to waste a single second, I decided the better plan was to change clothes and fix my hair.

A short amount of time later, pacing back and forth, wringing my hands raw, glancing at the window every other second, I wish I could zipper open my stomach and free the butterflies giving me the jitters. Instead, I decided to go help Ccri prepare the food. At least it wouldn't give the impression that I was waiting around for him. Even though I was.

I unlatched the door, stepped into the hallway, and stood perfectly still, listening for the sound of Lachlan's voice. The only sounds emanating throughout the house were Ccri's pleasant humming and the unmistakable *clink* of pots and pans. I went back inside the room, promptly turned around, and then continued to the kitchen.

"Anything I can do to help?" I asked as I walked into the kitchen, looking a little harried after all of the turmoil. Ccri noticed that I'd changed clothes but she kindly refrained from commenting.

"Paden always appreciates your apple pie."

Lachlan also liked apple pie. "Not a problem." I went to the sink to wash and slice the apples.

The usual suspects gathered around the rectangular wooden table beneath the sweep of leafy trees behind the house, the weather like my mood, a bit on the frigid side. We'd finished dessert; Paden loudly scraping his fork across the glass plate to get every last morsel.

Tonight I was a terrible hostess, completely distracted the entire meal. I deluded myself into believing that Lachlan would walk around the corner any minute. The slightest breath of wind made me jump. Every shadow in my eye made me turn. Each tiny flicker of light in the trees made me think that Nazca would swoop out from the canopy to deliver the message I so desperately wanted to receive.

But he never came.

My mind roamed through the never ending maze of *would of, could of, and should of.* True, we'd only know each other for a few short weeks although his recent behavior indicated that he *would of* let me know if he'd arrived back on Arden, even for one night. Maybe I *should of* walked past him and Raffye instead of creeping through the hedges like a frightened child. I guess I *could of* asked Ccri if she knew anything because she usually had prior knowledge on these matters.

I kept going over every detail as though repetition would shed some light on this dark subject. No matter which route I traveled, every agonizing twist and turn resulted in a dead end. I was in extreme danger of *shouldofing* all over myself.

Long after everyone left for the evening, I sat outside by the fire, claiming that I wasn't sleepy in the least. Sitting alone in the misty night, I waited and waited and waited, a constellation of thoughts swirling aimlessly as Keit rose in the night sky. At one point I thought I heard something. Not sure if my imagination took a sudden left turn into crazy town, I sat still. In the silence that followed, I heard or thought I heard the faint sound of a human voice. But Lachlan, or anyone else for that matter, materialized.

Sometime after midnight, I admitted defeat and went to bed. Punching the pillow into an oddly twisted shape that mimicked the state of my insides, I threw the quilted comforter over my head. Under the cover of darkness, a blitz of ominous forebodings attacked from every direction. I tried to push them away. They didn't stop. Wayward thoughts raced through the backstreets and alleyways of my mind, playing out every possible scenario. Each one ended with me standing in front of a blinking caution light.

Blink, blink, blink; he doesn't want to be with you.

Blink, blink, blink; you were a novelty at first.

Blink, blink, blink; Lachlan has come to his senses.

"Come on," I moaned, twisting the comforter into a knotted wad, "we'd only kissed." Neither one of us had uttered those *three little words***.** There aren't any real commitments here. Sure, he dominated my thoughts every waking minute and my dreams at night. But isn't this due more to the unusual circumstances over these last few weeks than to him?

After another hour of roaming the dark corners of my mind, I had no clear answer. And then I asked myself why I feel the need to pick everything apart layer by layer?

Thirst-quenching my foot!

Morning brought no change. Not only was I completely exhausted, I was jaded to everything and everyone around me.

"Emily, what do you have planned today?" Ccri asked, cautiously.

I sat slumped in the kitchen chair, eating a late breakfast, not really seeing her. "Oh…not sure," I grumbled, pulverizing a muffin into small pieces with the fork.

"I must travel to Keit today. Care to accompany me?"

"No thanks," I said, forcing a polite southern edge to my voice. "I think I'm going to hang around the house for the day. I didn't get much sleep."

Teenage girl translation—I'm going to stay here all day and wallow in self-pity.

"Oh. I see," Ccri said. I'm pretty sure she wasn't buying any of it.

After some pretty creative finagling, I finally convinced her to leave without me. As soon as the door latched closed, I reached an all-time low and sent Nazca to scout around for Lachlan. She reported back that Lachlan was not on Arden today, and that yes, he was here yesterday, but left almost immediately.

Not immediately; he had time to talk to Raffye. That tidbit sent me reeling into a new downward spiral. I burrowed underneath the quilted comforter, curled into a pathetic heap, and tried to block out as much of Arden as possible.

Ccri found me later that afternoon in the room with the gauzy fabric covering the windows, contorted in a fetal position in the bed. "Emily," she said. "I am not sure what happened, and you do not have to tell me. I do know that brooding is never the answer. Paden and I thought, perhaps you might like to practice traveling between Arden and Keit…alone."

I folded the comforter back and lifted a hand to rub my temples. Wait! What did she say? Hadn't they warned me a thousand times not to travel alone through the water? Now they're practically handing it to me on a silver platter. I must really look pitiful. "Me on Keit and Paden on Arden," she clarified.

Her plan worked. "Sure," I said, hoping the colors would brighten my mood.

"On the next trip, linger in the water for a moment before stepping out," Paden instructed.

This was the fifth attempt. "Got it," I said.

He gave me an encouraging push into the water. A dazzling array of colors whirled through my mind at a quick clip. I hovered in the water for a moment, discerning a shimmering Ccri through the ripples. She excitedly waved me out of the water. "Well done, Emily," she said.

Paden surfaced from the water a second later, standing at the ready, awaiting further instructions. "Let us dine in the village tonight," Ccri announced. "I will go ahead. Paden, send Emily after a few final instructions." She passed us, and with a satisfied smile, vanished into the rippling waves.

"This time, practice slowing your velocity," Paden said, sounding a little like a proud father.

"Thanks for your help," I said, feeling more like my old self. Focusing on something besides the unsolvable Lachlan dilemma did wonders for my attitude.

"It has been a long time since I taught someone to travel with the water between planets," he said with a smile. "Now visualize the bottom granite step at the traveling pool in the village on Arden."

I nodded and drew in a deep breath. Overconfident, I jumped into the water feet-first. Bad move! Swept up by the surging current, arms and legs flailing in every direction, I had no idea which way to go. I attempted to right myself and kick my way back to Keit. All that seemed to accomplish was to propel me deeper into the shadowy water.

Spiraling downward, tiny little light bursts erupted behind my eyes as the weight of the water intensified to bone-crushing levels. I sensed heaving tides of nothingness, stretching dark and endless. My core body temperature plummeted as a steady stream of sinister, shapeless colors, falling through viscous oil, howled an unearthly howl inside of my head.

I thought I was a goner.

And then seemingly out of nowhere, a faint echo called out in remembrance. Paden's energetic vaporous arm reached out and jerked me back from the edge of the precipice.

"What was that?" I shrieked, surfacing from the water, and shaking uncontrollably. "Where did the threatening colors come from?" There was no other way to describe the texture of the dark inky colors or the terrifying experience.

"Emily entered the water rather swiftly," Paden said to a stern-faced Ccri. He draped a reassuring arm across my trembling shoulders. "You got caught in the undertow."

I looked at him in confusion, the sound of the water waves lapping against the bottom granite step suddenly frightening. "The what?"

"The undertow strikes a darker harmonics in us," he said. "This heavier water lacks clarity and brightness and is usually hidden by the radiant flowing waters. It is a bit scary the first time you stray into the murky current. Emily, water has two sides. One side, powerful beyond measure, forever flows toward the light. How are we to navigate these waters if they are not radiant in comparison?"

"There is another side to the water," he said, and there was an unmistakable seriousness in his tone. "Absolute darkness, void of any light whatsoever, washing everything in its path into the utter despair of midnight. You must be extremely diligent while voyaging with the water between planets and galaxies. Steer clear of the undertow. Evil is a force that will take you down under."

I shivered. At least tonight, Lachlan wouldn't haunt my dreams. I was going to be too busy rescuing myself from the undertow.

δ^-

I burrowed beneath the covers and slid back into an uneasy slumber. The brilliant flashes pursuing me in the running dream didn't stop. I finally opened an eye. Nazca hovered near my face, all bright and cheery.

"Oh," I cried out, my hand flying up to touch the silver disk.

"Lachlan is on Arden today and requests that you meet him for a late lunch," she said in her lilting voice. "Unsure of an exact time, he will send a second message."

I flipped onto my back, choking back the frustration, staring at the gauzy fabric draped across the canopy. The part of me wrecked from the internal battle over the last few days eclipsed the part of me jumping up and down from joy at the thought of seeing him again. Regardless, I knew that my answer would eventually be, *Yes*, so what was the point in putting off the inevitable? I ran a hand through my sleep-tousled hair as if that would clear the fog. "Tell Lachlan that I will join him."

Paden and Ccri were gone for the day, something about a planet close to a reveal. They would check the conditions. If everything seemed in order, I would join a group watching the process from the sidelines. Home alone, I stayed in my pajamas and padded down the front hallway to fix some breakfast.

Rummaging through the kitchen, I sliced some bread and then poured myself a giant mug of coffee.

I flicked the cloth napkin over my shoulder, reminding myself that I shouldn't put words into someone else's mouth. I carried the plate and mug into the open-space living area, wishing I'd worn socks, the frigid flagstone floors about the same temperature as my resolve. I set the plate and the mug on the side table, stoked the fire, and snuggled into the corner of the oversized sofa. I wrapped my legs in the woolen throw, suppressing the dark thoughts marinating inside of my head.

I told myself I needed to wait and hear firsthand from Lachlan about the events from a few days ago. After all, this morning he had sent a message with Nazca. This meant that he'd planned ahead and that he wanted to spend time together. Right? Still, I couldn't deny that the forebodings kept attacking, chipping away at the minuscule amount of willpower remaining.

An hour later, I decided the great outdoors was the best form of distraction. Lost in thought, still over-analyzing everything, I walked into the courtyard and followed the well-worn path to the meadow behind the house.

It was an odd sort of day on Arden; a fall-like chill in the air. The wind blowing through the trees didn't sound at all like the fall winds back on Earth, simultaneous rustling thousands of leaves that were on the verge of turning, dying, and then fluttering down to the ground.

Watching a bird remain absolutely motionless in the sky, and then suddenly fold its wings and plummet towards the fish pond with lightning speed, I tried to ignore the nagging questions. But things weren't going well. A good conclusion was nowhere in sight despite the countless hours I'd spent looking for one. Nazca found me in the meadow, sitting on the stone bench, methodically ripping the petals off of a flower, muttering to myself, "He loves me, he loves me not."

"Change of plans," she announced in a high-pitched voice this time. The last petal from the *loves me not* plucking stuck to my thumb. "Lachlan will meet you here."

"Oh." I stood up, brushed the petals off my lap, and headed back toward the house. As I rounded the corner, Lachlan stepped from the small pool of water. When he saw me, he raised a hand in greeting. The mere sight of him stirred those giddy feelings of infatuation. I felt a little peppier despite my bad mood.

"There you are! I have only the afternoon and evening free," he said, his eyes all flirty. "I am grateful that you were not off-world. I hear that you will join a group on a planet close to a reveal. So, I rearranged my plans." He firmly gripped each shoulder, bent forward, and planted a quick kiss on my forehead. "I want to go home first and change clothes. Do you mind?"

"Not at all," I said, a faint smile working its way across my sullen face.

"Off we go, then." He seized my hand, and pulled me into the water.

I didn't have time to mentally prepare for this first trip through the water after the undertow fiasco. Thankfully, he didn't notice that I clung to his arm with a vice-like grip. Maybe, he just thinks I'm glad to see him.

"Anyway," Lachlan resumed, as soon as we surfaced from the stream behind his house. All muscles tense, I felt myself lurch forward, and as usual, a pair of strong arms caught me about the waist. "Watch out you," he teased. "Now that I have you where I want you, we do not need any unnecessary accidents. Let us get a quick bite to eat. Afterwards, we can decide how to spend the afternoon."

I practically had to run to keep up with him.

"See what you can find," he said, disappearing down the sunny hallway to his side of the house. Shrugging off the remaining remnants of melancholy, I walked around the river rock fireplace into the kitchen.

"Emily," he called out a few minutes later.

"In here," I said from deep inside the pantry. "What sounds appetizing?"

"Fruit, bread, cheese; something light for now," he said, sounding in high spirits, his mood infectious.

I decided on several pieces of fruit, a wedge of cheese, and a loaf of crusty bread. I walked out from the pantry with my arms overloaded.

"Let me help," he said. Devilishly handsome, carelessly dressed in a crisp, ivory linen shirt nipped at the waist, I couldn't deny that electricity sparked across the room between us. Despite any warning to the contrary, I decided to get over my bad self and enjoy the afternoon.

"When did you return?" I asked, trying to sound casual. I wanted to find out how long he'd been on Arden today.

"A short time ago," he said, stretching out a hand. I handed him the cheese and the loaf of bread. "I needed to enter some information into the history annals and reference a few outstanding issues." He smiled about something, turned, and walked to the kitchen counter, glancing behind his shoulder for once. "You were third on my list but first in my heart."

I sighed. What's wrong with me? At this point, I shouldn't be surprised that the mission factor continues to be a major stumbling block in the dating dilemma. This is just one of the endless problems you encounter when your special someone lives on a planet, in a totally different galaxy, and travels the Universe daily. I went over to the sink to wash the fruit.

And then it happened.

My head snapped up at the exact moment the hairs on the back of my neck rose. I turned around and saw the regret written all over his face. They were contacting...him. I watched the light in his eyes dim as he raised a hand, and touched the silver disk in his ear. "Yes," he said, unable to keep the disappointment out of his voice. "I would like to finish eating lunch first." I felt the gloom settling in again. "No," Lachlan said, exhaling slowly. "I will leave from here."

He touched the silver disk again, folded both arms against his chest, and leaned back against the counter, transforming into a statue posed in a defeated position. I stood there for a moment, fidgeting with my hair before deciding to slice the fruit. I picked the wooden handled knife up and recognized it as the one from our picnic at the waterfall.

"Duty calls," I said a few minutes later, trying to sound chipper.

"Constantly," he grumbled from directly behind my right shoulder. I nearly jumped out of my skin. I didn't even hear him walk over, my thoughts were so preoccupied. That was sort of odd. I was normally sensitive to his presence, tuned into his every move. Perhaps that was the problem. Lachlan filled my senses so completely that everything else around me seemed irrelevant.

But I could no longer afford to ignore the warning signs.

Wordlessly, he added the bread and cheese to the cutting board where I'd arranged the fruit, reached over my head, and opened the cabinet door. He rummaged through the cabinet and removed a couple of bottles of juice and two small ceramic plates. "Will you carry the food?" he asked.

"Sure," I said, giving him a tentative smile.

I followed him through the glass door, down the turning and twisting walkway in the tree canopy to the outdoor eating area beneath the willow-like trees. I waited off to the side while he arranged the food and the drinks in the center of the table.

"Thanks," I said when he pulled the chair out for me.

"Emily, I am so very sorry," he said, his tone oozing like an infected wound with disappointment. "I had anticipated some free time today."

And then he walked around to the other side of the table and plopped into the empty chair on that side of the table instead of sitting in the empty chair next to mine. That single act spoke volumes. Even I couldn't deny the obvious anymore. Here we sat within hands reach of each other but it could've been a million miles apart. Eyes focused somewhere else, not really seeing me, he said in a low voice, "Perhaps this is not such a good idea."

Well, there you go. He'd ambushed me with the words I'd expected and dreaded. Lachlan was breaking up with me even though we were never officially a couple. A persistent ringing in my ears drowned out all truths except for one; the hurt was coming, and that hurt would devastate me just like my parents' divorce had.

In a mindless daze, I leaned forward and put some bread and fruit on the plate. I lifted the pear-shaped bottle, grateful that my hands weren't noticeably trembling. I would save that part for the pity party I'd be throwing at my own expense later tonight—in my room, in the dark, and it seems, all alone.

Lachlan, on the other hand, piled the food sky-high on his plate. Apparently, the sudden change in plans didn't affect his appetite. I wish I could say the same. The pieces of food on the plate were now only props used to play out this particular scene. There was no way I was going to eat anything. I'd only vomit the food right back up.

Through the strands of hair, I watched him eat a couple of chunks of fruit and a slice of cheese. Lachlan wiped his mouth with the napkin, raised his head, and the depth with which his eyes appraised me caused the breath in my lungs to freeze. He opened his mouth to say something, and then thought better of it—a dark veil shrouded his face.

My hands went clammy.

I dropped my head and started shredding the piece of bread into crumbs. I figured he was biding his time, hatching a plan to find a better way to phrase the words that would change my life forever. Honestly, he needn't bother; they hung in the air between us as though already spoken aloud. From somewhere far away, I heard the long inhale and knew it was time. I braced for the reveal before looking up.

"Emily," he said, his eyes degrading to a dark green. "I do not know what to say. I must leave again with no idea of when I will return to Arden."

These words were becoming our theme song and trust me, the novelty was wearing thin. How had I missed all of the clues leading up to this conversation? I should've done a background check on feelings before becoming overly involved in his world and in The Accordance. That mistake was my fault. I vowed right then and there that this would never happen again. I glared at him without trying to disguise my impatience. I doubt I could've been any less conspicuous if I'd set my hair on fire.

Let's get on with it already.

Lachlan propped his elbows on the table and leaned in, his eyes squinted and steady. "I have so many responsibilities," he said. "I am not sure what to say. I know that it was completely unfair of me to…"

"Make me believe there is something between us."

Lachlan's head snapped up, shock and disbelief visible on his face. "Trust me, my feelings for you are sincere," he said, and it sounded more to me like he was avoiding the real issue. "My life is complicated. Please never doubt that I have tried to arrange the time for us. I simply do not have many options."

"What is that you do on these mysterious missions?" I asked without trying to mask the sarcasm. Come on, don't I have a right to know what I'm competing against?

He stared at me, his lips pressed tightly in exasperation. "What I do; details to attend to, questions to be answered, patterns to be deciphered."

The vagueness of his response meant that he isn't going to tell me what's really going on so I guess we'll just keep it a mystery. I also couldn't deny that I longed to reach over and touch the stray wisps of his hair caught in the afternoon breeze. Instead, I squirmed uncomfortably in my seat before deciding to go ahead and drop the bomb. Under the circumstances, I figured the best plan of action was to cut to the chase.

"What about three days ago." I went for a preemptive strike so I wouldn't have to rationalize my seemingly erratic behavior. "Weren't you here on Arden?"

A perplexed look momentarily flashed his eyes. "Yes, for a very brief amount of time. Today, I anticipated having the afternoon and evening free." I didn't say a word. I gazed at him, longing for him to feel what I feel. He sat straighter in his chair. "I cannot make any promises. However, I assure you…a day does not pass that I do not think of you."

Now, he sounded annoyed that I'd questioned his intentions. It was either feast or famine with Lachlan. Is he breaking up with me or justifying his actions? Either way, I didn't know if I could give this matter any more attention. I really didn't see a way to get out the tool box and fix this predicament. My stomach muscles clenched as I pictured Lachlan leaving today and not knowing if I'd see him again. "I have no idea what to say," I mumbled.

Lachlan however, noticed the subtle shift in my attitude. His keen powers of observation never missed a beat. Slowly, almost hesitantly, he pushed aside the cutting board and swept his hand across the tabletop towards mine. I'd never seen him diffident before but I wasn't fooled. When I dropped my hands in my lap, his soulful eyes registered the rejection.

"Emily, it was not my intention to mislead you," he said. "I wanted this…to work out between us."

I nodded mutely, my eyes glistening from the tears welling in the corners. I struggled for an answer but failed to come up with one. Fumbling around for something to do, I popped a few bread crumbs into my mouth to keep from saying something that would add to the misery. The bread tasted like cardboard, the flavors weeping their way out of my life.

I slowly chewed on the unwelcome truth and swallowed the stark reality. Here we sat at the same table without really seeing each other, enduring and enduring and enduring until I couldn't tolerate it anymore. I ran my fingers through my hair, took a couple of deep breaths, and stood up from the table. I started stacking the dishes for something to do.

"Allow me," Lachlan said, cautiously getting to his feet and edging his way to my side of the table.

Those stealthy eyes, clearly aimed at me, said that he wanted to take me gently into his arms. As he rounded the table, I shied away, warning him with a glance to keep his distance. Never one to be dissuaded, he redoubled his efforts, and in a blur, closed in.

Lachlan grasped both of my wrists. He flung my limp arms up into the air, and then around his neck. In one move he managed to rearrange both of my wrists until they were trapped in his left hand. I opened my mouth to protest. Before I could get a single word out, he slipped his right arm around my waist and pulled me close. "Forgive me," he whispered. "I know that it was selfish…I simply could not help myself. Emily, Emlyn…do you have any feelings for me?"

I could feel the slight tremor of indecisiveness in his posture. An angry tectonic shift adjusted mine, the rage of a girl scorned rising to my defense. I broke free from his embrace. "Are you joking? Am I not still here on Arden? Do you remember the night you invited me to spend the day with you, DeRenne, and Shaw?"

I shook my head in disgust remembering how easily I agreed to go. "I stayed because…because…" I had to come to terms with the fact that there was no way to get around the ugly truth. "I stayed because of you," I said, unable to hide the longing in my voice.

Lachlan stepped forward. Almost in tandem, I stepped backward simultaneously establishing a protective perimeter around my bruised ego. He looked down at me soberly, the intensity of his focus prickling the skin on my forearms. "Have you lost your faith in me?" he asked.

"Maybe," I huffed, taking a giant step backward, water from the stream soaking the heels of the leather skimmers. "I keep thinking that you're hedging your bets."

Now he looked puzzled.

"Hiding something," I said in disgust. "Why can't you tell me what's going on instead of all this mystery and intrigue, disappearing and reappearing?"

The silence pressed upon me. I'd given him the perfect opportunity to come clean. He didn't take the bait. My eyes glazed over as today suddenly lost its brightness. I was suffocating. I needed…I needed to get away. My overwrought, hormone driven mind reasoned that sometimes you should stay, and sometimes you should just leave while you're ahead. No good is going to come out of hanging around here.

The muscles in both of my legs flexed as fierce determination replaced any lingering doubt. In an almost mechanized movement, I pivoted on my heel and jumped feet-first into the water, the sheer recklessness of my decision fueled by embarrassment and rejection.

"No, Emily!" Lachlan yelled from somewhere beyond the realm of good judgment.

The instant my foot touched the water a shackle cuffed my right ankle, and pulled me into the undertow. Swept along by the surging current, tumbling forward, I frantically kicked at the shackle with my left foot. Dark deafening colors shrieked an unearthly howl inside of my mind. A scream of unbearable agony; the single most frightening sound I'd ever heard.

I kicked harder.

Out of nowhere, a sidewinder riptide smacked me off balance. The sinister colors seeping into my bone marrow dragged my limp body to the edge of terror. This time, there'd be no Paden standing at the ready to rescue me.

Caught in a downward spiral, falling through the moonless, starless darkness, pulsing with billowing plumes of red, I couldn't stop the endless motion, circling the drain like the last little bit of bathwater, forever gone.

δ^-

The water tossed out me onto a concrete pad covered with a thick sheet of ice. I was wet. Wet! No one steps out from water travel wet. That fact alone threw up a big red caution flag, not to mention that I had absolutely no idea where I'd landed. I glanced over my shoulder, half expecting Lachlan to materialize. Surely, he'd jumped in after me. And come to think of it, where's Nazca?

I waited a moment. Neither of them appeared. I reached up, tucked the strands of wet hair behind my ear, and touched the silver disk, thankful that it was still attached to my earlobe. "Nazca," I said, the mist from my breath forming a cloud around my face.

I counted silently to ten. "Nazca," I said louder as if that would make a difference. She didn't dart out from the ripples. I thought about jumping back into the water and then immediately decided against it. I didn't want to get caught in the murky undertow. That was two close calls in three days.

Okay, this time, it felt more like I was being dragged along by the surging current instead of becoming a part of the cohesive forces between the spinning water molecules. The whole feel and texture was a completely different experience from when I first arrived to Arden, and way more intense than the undertow episode with Paden. What have I done? Didn't they warn me a million times on Earth and on Arden? Water Travel 101—never ever, enter the water angry or upset.

I shivered, and not from the cold.

Okay, Plan B. I stumbled and skidded over the ice sheet to a metal rail, grabbed hold, and looked around. Frozen, misty, and gray described the place in three short words. No brilliant colors, no inviting entryways, no thriving populace of villagers idling away the afternoon window shopping. I wondered if I was even in the Triangulum Galaxy or had I hurled myself to the outer edge of the Universe.

I inched along the ice sheet to a man sitting in a small, wooden shack. The tiny building looked so rickety that I thought it might implode any second. "Excuse me, sir," I said, the mist rising around my face again. He straightened his back, the expression on his face one of total shock that someone actually spoke to him. "I've made a huge mistake. I guess I was pissed, and I…" He stared at me with blank eyes. "Sorry, sorry," I said, waving a hand. "My name is Emily Harrison, and I came from Arden. Well, I'm originally from Earth, and I guess that I jumped into..." A siren started wailing. I stared at his hand on a big red button. "Hey! Why'd you do that? I'm trying to explain to you that I landed here by mistake."

"No one comes to Hidde by mistake," he said, his voice gritty.

"I did," I said, squaring both shoulders.

I heard the ice sheet behind me crack, and the distinctive creak of leather boots. I turned around. Two men, one large and burly, the other short and squat, marched toward us. The burly man reached out to grab my right arm. I jerked it out of his reach and stepped backward.

"Listen," I said. "I tried to tell this guy who for some reason felt it necessary to sound an alarm that I came here by mistake."

"No one comes here by mistake, missy," the burly man said. "We need to figure out how she got through the barrier."

Barrier? A barrier around the water? And then I remembered my research. Paden said that you could create a distortion barrier around a source of running water that would realign the electrons in the water molecules. This would stop them from spinning, and restrict water travel in that area. Never in a million years did I think someone would actually do that. "I am prepared to admit that I made a mistake coming here," I said. "I would appreciate being returned…"

"Sid, I was told there were no scheduled arrivals today," the burly man said before I could finish my sentence.

Sid's knobby hand flipped through several sheets of paper fastened together. "Nothing scheduled for today, Randolph."

Randolph? He didn't look like a Randolph. "All right, take me to your leader," I said before I could stop myself, knowing it sounded silly.

"No one sees him without an appointment, missy."

"You don't think someone slipping through your precious barrier justifies seeing the person in charge?" I said, regretting the choice of words as soon as they came out of my mouth.

"If you insist missy, we can take you to see the person in charge," Randolph said. The three men exchanged a rather interesting look. "Come with me."

All of a sudden, I found myself nestled between the two men like a prisoner being escorted to an uncertain future. I also realized that I wasn't getting anywhere standing in the cold dealing with Sid. We followed the worn-down path littered with trash, walked past a couple of nondescript storefronts filled with utilitarian merchandise: cookware, yard tools, bolts of plain fabric. A slight elderly woman, the thin lines around her lips frozen in a permanent sneer, poked her head out from the door of…a garden shop? The droopy yellow plants on the shelves looked like they hadn't seen the sunlight for months. She stared at us as we walked past, motioning with her hand for someone in the back of the store to come check out the dripping, wet girl being escorted along the path.

"Did Sid say that the name of the planet is Hidde?" I asked to make polite conversation.

"Yes, missy."

How appropriate. "Is Hidde part of the…"

"We're not part of anything," the short, squat man said rather abruptly.

Well, that made perfect sense. "Have you lived here all of your life?"

"Doesn't this look like the kind of place you'd want to get away from?" Randolph asked.

He had a point. "Oh, I'm sure when the sun is shining it's not so bad."

"The sun is shining, missy."

"But the fog," I said.

"It's always foggy on Hidde," Randolph said. He opened a door to a windowless, square structure built of corrugated metal panels. The short, squat guy stayed outside. I followed Randolph down a dimly lit hallway with bare concrete floors, leaving a trail of water behind me.

The young girl sitting at the small table didn't look much older than I did. Except for the hard look in her eyes. The severe ponytail and four ear-piercings didn't help soften the edges either. She looked me up and down like she remembered something from her past. Then the veil lifted. "What am I supposed to do with her?"

"Get her something to wear Sara," Randolph said. "I'll find out how to handle this situation."

"You could take me back to Arden," I said.

Sara's back went stiff.

"Did you say, Arden?" Randolph asked in a rather peculiar tone.

"You've heard of Arden!" I said.

"Oh, yes missy, we have," he said, sarcastically.

"Emily Harrison from Arden," I said, holding my hand out. I thought a better plan was not to complicate things by mentioning Earth this time.

Sara didn't accept my outstretched hand. "This way," she said. I followed her down an adjacent hallway, leaving a second trail of water. "Wait here," Sara said, disappearing around the corner.

For a brief moment, I thought about making a run for it. Before I could get my bearings, Sara returned holding a … gray prison suit? "Am I in trouble?" I asked.

Sara didn't answer for a moment. "My opinion counts for nothing. You can change in there." She pointed to a tall metal door, held shut by a bolt latch that looked like it'd been broken on more than one occasion. "Don't try anything funny."

I took the garment from her hand and opened the door. I found cleaning supplies. I figured it was better than standing around in wet clothes on this frozen planet. I went inside, pulled the string on the solitary light bulb, and shut the door. I waited to hear the bolt latch shut, but it didn't. For a brief moment, I thought Sara might lock me inside. I unfastened the buttons, and slipped the dress over my head, careful to gather the folds before they touched the dirty floor. I would make sure to launder the dress before I returned it to DeRenne.

No one gave me anything to dry off with so I stepped into the gray grab slightly damp, the fabric itchy like burlap. I knew I'd eventually dry; my shoes were another story. I slapped the leather skimmers against the wall a couple of times—didn't help one bit. Well, it's not like I'm going to be here for long so I decided to wait it out, and apologize to DeRenne for ruining her shoes and her dress.

I opened the door. "Hey Sara, is there somewhere I could wring the dress out, and a towel to wipe my shoes? I don't want to..." I had a bad feeling in the pit of my stomach. He stood straighter, looked like he knew that he was two, maybe three steps above everyone else on this dismal planet.

"Follow me," he said, tugging at the sleeves of his perfectly fitted uniform jacket.

"Why?" I asked.

Sara looked scared for me.

"Excuse me. That came out all wrong. I'm Emily Harrison, by the way. Have I done something wrong? No one can give me a straight answer." He didn't say a word. "What about this?" I held the wet dress up, the sound of the water droplets hitting the concrete floor, ominous.

"You!" he said in an irritated tone. Sara snapped to attention. "You take care of this."

Sara's eyes grew big as I handed her the wet mess. I kept the leather skimmers. Wet shoes were better than no shoes. "Thanks," I said.

"No, thank you," she said with a grin like she knew something that I didn't.

"Come with me," he announced, turning on his heel.

Although his demeanor creeped me out, maybe I'm finally going to talk with someone in charge. I quickly followed, slipping on the left skimmer as I went, and then the right. Once outside, we crossed the barren quad, avoiding a swirl of leaves caught in a whirlwind, to a corrugated metal building behind a tangle of untrimmed hedges. This guy didn't turn around once to check if I was following. But I didn't want to risk running. He was athletic and would easily catch me, and I still had no idea where I'd landed. At a minimum, I needed to know the name of the galaxy. I dutifully followed, pulling the scratchy gray garb tighter; the cold settling in my chest having nothing to do with the temperature.

He opened the dented metal door, and we entered a small, windowless room. The only other door in the back right-hand corner looked like it was locked. "You can wait here," he said, gesturing to a small utilitarian sofa covered in dingy fabric. "You came from Arden."

"Yes! I keep trying to explain to everyone that I came here by accident. I did something I shouldn't have." He didn't look too surprised at my admission. "If you can get a message to Paden, he's the one in charge on Arden," I added, hoping to make myself sound important. "They'll send someone to get me."

I'm pretty sure I didn't sound confident. I mean come on—I'd done the one thing they all told me not to do. Perhaps they're letting me sit it out, kind of like going to jail overnight to learn my lesson, although that's really not their style.

"I will take that," he said, pointing at my head with his trigger finger.

"The barrette?"

"No silly girl, the silver disk in your ear."

Crap. He knew its use. I peeled the disk from my earlobe and handed it to him.

"Wait here," he ordered, turning on his heel for a second time, and shutting the door behind him with a decisive *clink.*

I looked around the room; bare walls, bare floors, more gray. The muffled voices outside the door meant they'd decided to post a guard this time. I walked over to the door in the back corner. I yanked the knob but it was locked tight. I plopped down on the sofa, scooted around, and tried to find a spot where the springs weren't broken. I settled in the dip between two cushions, drew my knees to my chest, and wrapped both arms around my legs. I knew it'd be a long wait.

δ^-

I'd followed the dagger of light snaking through the bottom of the dented metal door as the sun set, and eaten two meals. At some point, I fell asleep until the howling from the undertow woke me in a grip of fear. If I had to guess, I'd been waiting about sixteen hours when the well-dressed guy who'd escorted me here, threw the door open.

"Follow me," he ordered.

"Yeah, I figured as much," I mumbled, slipping my feet into the dry leather skimmers.

Back out into the cold, the sun was now a big red ball struggling to shine through the fog. The recently built house at the end of the path looked decent from the outside. Another athletic looking guy with a scar on his left cheek, dressed in the same crisp uniform, stood outside. Two guards. Good, maybe I'm finally going to talk to the person in charge. I walked up the three short steps, and through the open door.

In the wide entrance hall, I saw Lachlan and Shaw. My heart melted. I started to run to him until I saw his face. It was the same expression I'd seen on his face the first time I stepped out from the water on Arden. Not the friendly smile or the familiar, 'Hey you'. No, he looked more serious. He looked like someone who had to make the hard decisions and deliver the unwelcome news; his eyes taking in every detail of my gray garb, unkempt hair, and general disheveled appearance.

I glanced at Shaw. He didn't say a word but his eyes jutted to the left a smidgen. I gasped, and took a giant step back. Jokull. I recognized him from the footage I'd watched at The Assemblage. The images didn't do him justice. Seeing him in person, it became abundantly clear that Jokull was gorgeous in that tragic, bad-boy kind of way. The sort of boy who if he decides to turn on the charm, even the sanest girl in the room willingly falls under the deadly allure of the beautiful snake, throwing all of her good judgment out the window without a second thought.

"As you can see, she is unharmed," Jokull said, assessing me with hawk-like eyes.

I swallowed, feeling a bit queasy.

"Emily, this is Jokull," Lachlan said, sounding proper. That's when I noticed he and Shaw were dressed in brocade, hip-length waistcoats and stiff linen shirts with high collars.

I made myself breathe slowly. "Nice to meet you," I said, even though it sounded more like a question.

"Why are we all standing in here?" Jokull said, looking pleased as if he'd just opened a gift. "Come in, and have a seat."

We followed him down the short hallway. I noticed that he had a decisive walk and that his knee-length, midnight blue coat was perfectly tailored and trimmed.

The inside of the room reminded me of Arden; roaring fire, rich carpets, inviting furniture. This place didn't fit in with the rest of the planet, and he meant for it not to. "Lachlan and

Shaw, you may sit there," Jokull said, gesturing with his hand to two chairs strategically placed in front of the massive, carved wooden desk. "Emily, you may sit there." He pointed to a small chair off to the side. I sat in the assigned seat, reluctantly.

Jokull walked behind the desk, standing still for a moment, and then lowering his six-foot frame into the leather chair, everyone in their place according to the subtext of his directions. "Lachlan, as you know, water travel to Hidde is allowed only with prior authorization."

"Now hold on just a second," I said, getting to my feet.

Shaw quickly threw his hand into the stop position, signaling me to sit down. Neither he nor Lachlan turned around. That pissed me off. I sank back into the seat not really knowing if I could play along.

"Although true, Jokull," Lachlan said, and there was something about the slightly flattened tone in his voice that I couldn't get a read on. "I am not sure if those parameters apply to someone whose planet is currently unaware of the complexities governing The Accordance."

He delivered his line perfectly, sounding rehearsed. That's it? That's his defense?

Jokull rested his elbows on the polished desktop, cracking each knuckle one by one, looking pensive. Or at least trying to look pensive; we all knew he'd already made his mind up about how this whole thing would go down. "Even though what you are saying is correct, she admitted coming from Arden. And you know, Lachlan, because you were in attendance, as were you, Shaw, that the conditions of the treaty state that no one from Arden is allowed to travel to Hidde, just as no one from Hidde is allowed to travel to Arden," Jokull said, smiling. "As mutually agreed upon."

"Emily arrived here accidently," Lachlan said. My heart sank. He'd never have had to say those words if I hadn't acted rashly.

"And how did that come to be, Emily?" Jokull asked, aiming the question at me even though he was looking directly at Shaw and Lachlan.

I needed to choose my words carefully. "I misunderstood," I said, slowly. "They'd warned me a million times. I thought that I could handle it. I guess I entered the water…hmm… unfocused."

"Interesting," Jokull said, ignoring me. "However, what is most astounding about this incident is why Arden's heir apparent is allowed to visit my humble planet at this late hour." Shaw's slight squirm of discomfort didn't go unnoticed.

Lachlan sat straighter in the chair. "I did not ask their permission. I requested an audience with you under my own recognizance." I could sense his distress even from my assigned seat in the corner.

"Fascinating," Jokull said. "I made a few inquiries myself. All information stored at The Assemblage is available to everyone, even on Hidde. I thought, perhaps, the annals might shed some light on this unique situation. And they did."

I had no idea what he was getting at—the quizzical look on his face unexpected. He reached down, and touched a spot on the desk, the familiar hologram whizzing to life.

As if one, we froze at the same instant. Scrolling through the smoky, whirring hologram was my research. They don't password protect on Arden. I just started talking, and The Assemblage automatically stored the information. Anyone could come behind me and look. The thought just never occurred to any of us that Jokull would be the one looking at the information I'd researched about Jokull. I dropped back into the chair. Here I thought I'd been helpful, but basically, I'd signed my own death warrant.

"Care to explain?" Jokull asked.

No one said a word.

"And then I asked myself why someone from a planet currently unaware of The Accordance, as you so eloquently stated Lachlan, would bother researching me in the first place?" Jokull waved a hand, indicating a gracious dismissal of the matter. "How could I possibly be interesting?"

We still sat in stunned silence.

"Then, I asked myself; is there another reason? Are we dealing with an affair of the heart instead of an affair of the state? Now that I have met Emily, she seems like a lovely young lady." As I listened and watched him talk, I noted that he had a habit of fixing his eyes on someone, appearing not to blink. If he meant to unnerve his current victim, it did the trick. "If this is so, Lachlan, then I must propose a very important question. Are you prepared to enter the arena? It is certainly fraught with peril or worse, the possibility of rejection."

"Absolutely," Lachlan answered without hesitation.

Regret yanked on my heart again.

"Now, Emily," Jokull said, bursting at the seams to get his question out. "Has our Lachlan informed you that he will assume a high-level position with The Accordance on the occasion of his twenty-fifth year?" I opened my mouth to answer but he dismissed me with a flippant wave of his hand. "And has anyone explained to you that this preordained road is paved with high expectations and unending obligations?"

Held by the intensity of the question, I had to swallow once, twice, before I could answer. Everything hinged on my choice of words; he is too perceptive for me to show my hand in any way. "There's been so much to absorb over these past few weeks that at times I found it difficult to see the forest for the trees," I said calmly, even though my insides were balled into knots.

"Well put!" Jokull said, clapping his hands in a childlike manner. The massive chair creaked as he sat back. "This has been a most rewarding visit. However, I cannot honor your request for her release. You see, there are procedures, bylaws, meetings," he recited, ticking his pointer finger back and forth like a metronome, "...all the pesky little details. No, I think Emily shall remain our guest on Hidde a little longer."

Lachlan got to his feet, and said with a short bow, "May I have a word with Emily?" Shaw stood from his chair and positioned himself next to Lachlan so there'd be no doubt whose side he'd taken.

Something evil caught the light as it moved in the depths of Jokull's eyes. It was gone in a flash but I never wanted to see it again. "Of course," he said with a sly smile. "We are not barbarians."

"In private," Lachlan quickly amended.

"Yes, by all means," Jokull said, swooping up from the chair in a swell of midnight blue. "I will take a moment to speak with Shaw."

I slowly rose from the chair and watched Lachlan's face harden as I walked toward him. I felt as bleak as the clothes I was wearing. "I can't believe, I…I'm sorry," I murmured once we stood in the entrance hall. I so wanted to unsay everything leading up to this moment.

He looked down at me with his unfathomable eyes. "*Shush*," he breathed. "No need to apologize." His tone and few short words could've been taunting, should've been taunting, but they weren't. He draped his arm around my back but did not lean in as I hoped. This felt more formal, almost like a brother comforting his sister.

My shoulders dropped.

"No," he said, tightening his grip. His embrace kept all of my emotions in check which I'm absolutely positive was his plan. Still, I couldn't help myself. I rested my forehead against the hollow in the center of his chest and inhaled deeply. I could smell the sunshine on him even in the gloom of this forgotten place.

Lachlan held me in his arms for several long minutes without speaking a word. He didn't loosen his embrace or glance down at my face. I completely forgot about everything in the Universe, and for the first time since my accidental arrival to Hidde, I believed this fairy tale could end happily.

Once my breathing returned to normal he stirred, sliding his nose across my cheek to the corner of my jaw, whispering in a voice so low that I could barely hear him, "You will recognize my signal. Keep yourself safe until then. I *will* come for you. Do you understand?"

I squeezed him with everything I had.

"Mean it," he whispered, forcefully. I constricted both arms around his waist in a vise-like grip. "Better," he muttered, resting his chin against the top of my head for a lingering second.

Pulling away slightly, gripping my shoulders in his each of his hands, he leaned down until we were eye-level. When I looked into his eyes, all resolve melted. Can I really do this? Can I hold myself together until he comes for me? The flicker in his eyes told me that he understood. They also said he didn't want to leave me either but that he didn't have a choice. I swallowed the pool of remorse in the back of my throat and nodded once to show him that I understood.

The decision made, the instructions delivered, Lachlan turned and made his way down the short hallway. I blindly followed, putting a foot exactly where he'd just placed his. Jokull and Shaw conveniently walked out from the room to meet us.

"Thank you," Lachlan said with a perfunctory bow. He was speaking calmly now but I saw something I'd never seen before—his eyes were wild with pain and regret. "I appreciate the opportunity to speak with you in person."

A long dangerous smile curved Jokull's lips as he said, "Anything for my pupils."

Lachlan and Shaw exchange a nod, and then, walk together out through the door into the fog without a backward glance. By now, I knew better than to expect one.

"Take her to the dormitory," Jokull barked to the guard at the end of the hallway. Completely ignoring me, he walked away, the tailored hem along the bottom of his midnight blue coat sailing behind him.

It seems that playtime was over for the night.

δ^+

"Well, that was enlightening," Shaw said, stepping out from the stream behind Lachlan's house on Arden, Keit sliding low along the horizon in the predawn sky.

"It seems that shining a light on others keeps you in darkness," Lachlan said, eyeing his friend sideways. "I found out what I needed; slipping onto Hidde should not be a problem. And you?"

"The man if overconfident as usual," Shaw said, tugging on the stiff collar. "This should be his undoing. Getting off Hidde though…as we both know is an entirely different problem. I will check the remaining order to determine a timeline."

Lachlan opened his mouth and got only two words out, "Shaw, I…"

Shaw stretched out a consoling hand and gripped his friend's shoulder in an unbreakable bond. "It is because when she looks at you, she sees you. The way you prefer to be seen. Not who you are supposed to be. It is a welcome change from the constant stares of expectation and the unrelenting responsibilities. I see you again now for the first time in years."

"I am the one in charge of the rescue whether or not The Accordance agrees, " Lachlan said. "You do need to involve yourself from this point forward."

"And miss out on all the fun?" Shaw said with a smile. "I think not. I would request that DeRenne stay behind. You could..."

Lachlan laughed. "I value my life too much. Besides, we both know she is more adept."

"True," Shaw said. "Once we go down this path; we can never take it back. I am willing to walk it with you. I am not sure DeRenne will choose…for the right reason. She considers Emily her friend and knows that you have feelings for her. That makes her vulnerable, twice. We have trained and prepared, practiced, I should say." Shaw paused, gathering a thought. "As we both know, plans can go awry. I need assurance from you that there is no hesitation in your heart."

"The situation is so delicate that I am taking every possible precaution to ensure everything goes as planned. I will do whatever is required to protect Emily, which brings me back to DeRenne."

"Do not give that concern a second thought," Shaw said, stepping backward. "You know I will never allow anything to happen to her."

"I do, and I am grateful for that knowledge. I must warn you that she has a mind of her own."

"Tell me about it. I get a daily reminder. What you should remember is that Jokull has only the solace of shadows while you have the bright light shining through Emily's eyes," Shaw said with a wink. "And that makes the fight worth fighting."

Lachlan stood firm, watching his friend liquefy into the shimmering ripples, grateful for the knowledge that Shaw would be there for DeRenne, no matter the circumstances. Shaw, his childhood friend, always first, always last, a constant in his life, and now, more importantly, his anchor. Lachlan grabbed the handrail and took the steps on the wooden staircase two at a time.

Once inside of his room, he changed into his mission uniform and pulled his hair back, securing the long strands with a double knot in the leather cord. Alone in the house, and not wanting to waste time walking all the way back to the stream, he evanesced—and then remembered. Lachlan solidified back into his corporal form and made his way to the open-space living area.

Standing in front of the river rock fireplace, he stared at the small wooden chest on the granite slab mantle. The last time he held the pendant in his hand was the day he removed the chain from around his father's neck. The day he carried his father's limp body to Paden and Ccri's house in the village instead of bringing him home to this house, as is customary on Arden. He did not want the memory of the mangled body, and the acrid smell of singed hair to be the last memory for his mother and his sister in the home that would suffer the loss of their husband and their father, and then survive without him.

At some point, yes, they both needed to see for themselves before the burial. Otherwise, DeRenne especially, would always convince herself that he had never died. And he needed her to believe, to help him get to the truth. She barely had time to heal from the news of Orlaith's death before plunging into those two horrible days searching for their father. The sadness in DeRenne's face was unbearable. He never wanted to see that look in her eyes again. Even if he wished for her to stay protected and sheltered on Arden, this path was taken from them.

Over the last three years, he watched his sister grow and mature. She poured herself into The Accordance, trained with him and Shaw to learn how to evanesce. Her practice obstacle courses, using thick cacti or whatever large plant she scoured from uninhabited planets across the galaxy to simulate the density and viscosity of human tissue were intense and unrelenting. They would never practice on live animals, but they also knew they needed to have some idea of how it felt to literally run someone through and obliterate them. This was the dark side of evanescing, why it is discouraged by The Accordance. He and Shaw witnessed firsthand on the planet where the reveal went so terribly wrong that there are others out there learning how to evanesce and turning themselves into weapons. They needed to prepare for every outcome.

Lachlan took a deep breath. He ran a hand across the Water emblem inlay on the top of the wooden chest before opening the lid. His birthright, he knew that one day he would use the pendant. But no one could have imagined this scenario—anticipated that he had more time. His father did not have a chance to teach him the subtleties of his position on Arden or how to maneuver the complexities in The Accordance. He would negotiate that road alone.

He removed the pendant from the chest, closed the lid, and draped the double-link gold chain around his neck. With a firm resolve, he evanesced for a second time, rematerializing a moment later in the recently discovered cavern. Lachlan felt confident that Jokull would not bother visiting the cavern tonight because he was way too busy gloating over Emily's predicament.

He wrapped his fingers around the gold-cage pendant, silver-laced swirls of watery azure from deep with the multifaceted crystal inside of the gold-cage stirring to life at his touch. The octahedron shape of the gold-cage; eight isosceles triangles, four of which meet at each apex, siphoned the energy emanating from the crystal causing the gold in the cage to vibrate at its natural frequency. These vibrating primary standing waves blended together in a series of high-pitched tones, reverberating a soft luminous light.

The Seren assigned to monitor the cavern zoomed to his side. "I will stay for a few minutes," he said to the flickering lights, threading his way around several small boulders. Lachlan studied the bell-shaped rock face, about the height and width of an average room wall that he explored after DeRenne whisked Emily back to the house the day she discovered the cavern. He smiled—the day she discovered the cavern, and the day he discovered her.

The sinking feeling he experienced that night at supper when he realized that Emily had inadvertently put herself in the middle of a very dangerous situation, threatened him once more. This time, he so did not want to be right. Ignoring the sound of the low moaning wind, Lachlan ran both hands over the deep grooves and incisions carved into the stone like a blind person finding their way. After several passes, he stepped back to contemplate the awe-inspiring intricacy in front of him.

As his focus sharpened, the crystal responded in kind, increasing in intensity, resonating ample light to illuminate the entire map wall. It was like standing inside of a thought process; an expression of a scheme, or perhaps a stream of dizzying math that created everything in the known Universe. "Perhaps it is a guide," he thought, staring again at the intricate working maps detailing a series of grid-lines crisscrossing Arden, revealing four or maybe six dynamic energy fields across the planet surface.

The overlapping grid-lines designated regions sensitive to the symmetry between the sky and terrestrial earth. What had driven them to do such a thing? Why design something to such overwhelming proportions? The first travelers had created a nonmoving entity corresponding to a living analog, revealing an astounding sense of order transferring this hidden information into a readable image.

Even more impressive, they used these inherent instructions to harness several fluid energy fields into a single convergence point. Beginning in the top right-hand corner, Lachlan used his hand to methodically trace the smooth groove back to its point of origin. Next, he traced the groove starting from the lower left-hand corner. No matter which position he started from, the grid-lines always traced back to the same convergence point.

"Thank you for your assistance," Lachlan said to the wavering lights with a short half-bow. "Stay in the cavern, but remain hidden." He watched as the small swarm darkened until barely visible.

Lachlan evanesced, and then materialized inside of the enclosure formed by the three soaring standing stones and massive capstones in the village plaza. He came to a complete stop but did not coalesce back into his solid form, staying vaporous—the sensation odd and a bit uncomfortable. At this early hour, no one was out and about. And, if anyone did see him, he would appear to them as a shadowy silhouette instead of a dimensional body.

How ironic that while the villagers of Arden slept, the world they knew was about to change, and that he was the person who would start the process. Since his father's death, he had watched them go about their daily life with no idea of what was brewing in the distant corners of the Universe. Far away yes, but make no mistake, moving closer every day.

Lachlan stared at the three immutable giants, a passive background to him for most of his life, in and of themselves of no importance. Or, so he thought. He now understood that they were markers. Like the hanging signs identifying the shops in the village, these standing stones were meant to mark something.

While in this insubstantial vaporous form, he touched the pendant with his energetic hand, the colors inside of the crystal transforming into a vibrant, whirling mass. The efficacy of this intermediate state of matter, combined with the energy emanating from the crystal, allowed him to walk straight down into the ground. The sensation was unlike anything he had ever experienced. It took him a moment to come to terms with the idea of standing inside of the solid earth and to get over the innate fear of becoming stuck.

With a calm that belied the turmoil inside, concentrating on putting one energetic foot in front of the other, the progress slow and sluggish, much like moving through thick, wet clay, Lachlan made his way underground. Here he found a steady stream of silvery water, bubbling up from an underground aqueduct. This moving current supplied water to the fountain in the center of the enclosure, and also to three diverging side streams, almost as if someone had purposely routed a watercourse. He stepped into the moving current to his right and walked upstream until he reached a second shimmering pool of water. From the distance covered, and after studying the map wall, he knew that he now stood directly beneath the solitary standing stone at the end of the passageway leading to Paden and Ccri's house.

This effervescent water, spilling up and over into the culverts running underneath the closely cropped hedges lining both sides of the passageway, converged with several side streams before disappearing back underground. The flowing water acted much the same as a beacon would; collecting and rechanneling the waters energy from this standing stone in the passageway back to the three standing stones in the village plaza.

Lachlan had a hunch, and made his way back to the center of the enclosure, ignoring the crushing weight bearing down on his shoulders. He stepped into the supply of luminescent water bubbling up from deep within the planet and arched his head upward. From this vantage point and while in this insubstantial form, he discerned that the triangular-shaped field inside of the three massive capstones on the top of each of the three standing stones was, in fact, the mouth of a dynamic wormhole—a swirling pearly-pink event horizon.

Inexplicably, the pendant hanging around his neck levitated, revealing a link between the multifaceted crystal inside of the gold-cage and this wormhole. He wrapped his vaporous hand around the pendant, twisting and turning it around. The shimmering connection passed through his incorporeal arm and his abdomen but it never severed from its link with the wormhole. Lachlan stepped backward, and as he did, the throat of the spinning vortex lengthened. A triumphant glint flashed his eyes. Perhaps, just perhaps, he could sidestep the barrier around Hidde, and bring Emily safely back to Arden through this traversable portal.

He sighed. The energy from this sigh washed through his vaporous incorporeal form in soft violet hues. What is it about her that had gotten under his skin? Why did he react so powerfully her first night on Arden at Paden and Ccri's house when she described the colors, falling in love with their splendor? Had he not carefully bottled his feelings into a singular purpose; to find his father's murderer? Working day and night, following every whisper, Shaw and DeRenne caught up in his fervor.

He did not look for a relationship, assumed that option was taken from him. Yes, at one time, something lumbered along with Raffye because it was convenient, not because it was unexpected. And is Shaw right? Does his old self stir to life, the one he had to lock away, whenever he sees himself in Emily's fiery-amethyst eyes? Her eyes. Edging from lavender to gray, her eyes were so like the wispy smoke from the wood fire on the mountaintop, revealing her ever-changing thoughts. She was a conjuror—one that he could not get a fix on but one that pulled emotions from him. His feelings for her were absurd and extraordinary and perfect. How he loved catching her off-guard, throwing in random comments about his world, watching her take it in stride just for the pleasure of. It was impossible to be with her for long without being surprised by what she said or did.

He needed her in his life.

It had been nearly four weeks since their chance meeting on the granite step at the traveling pool in the village plaza, and a little less than one hour since he left her in the hands of Jokull. She looked alert, not nearly as fragile as he expected. Not that he had any idea what to expect from her. Seeing Emily tonight, her hair as wild and uncontrolled as the look in her eyes, just about killed him. But he also knew that now is not the time to dwell on personal feelings. His desires and wishes would have to wait; there was work to be done.

More determined than ever, Lachlan made his way above ground just as the sun peeked over the horizon, a new spring in his step.

δ^{+} δ^{-}

I'd been on Hidde for three days. The second day it rained; a sleek drizzle that traveled horizontally in the wind, soaking the thin fabric of my gray garb and chilling me to the bone. The place smelled; the air pungent with a faint metallic odor. I even tasted it, almost like I carried around moldy coins underneath my tongue. For the people who lived here, the days were filled with hard work and the evenings bland with boredom. No doubt about it, the entire planet needed a window open to let the bad smell out and the sunshine in.

They let me roam around the small town. My new best friends, Randolph, Sid, and a third person no one bothered to introduce were now my constant companions. The nameless guy must've drawn the short straw because he sat outside of the dormitory each night.

On more than one occasion, I'd considered going to talk with Sara under the pretense of asking her about DeRenne's dress. That idea never materialized. After staying on Hidde for a few days I now knew that dress was the brightest piece of fabric on this dismal planet. No wonder Sara smiled when I handed it to her. Secretly, she hoped I'd be gone, and she could keep the dress. I didn't blame her but that also meant we weren't going to be friends.

I'd pieced together from eavesdropping on several conversations that Jokull pretty much assumed control of Hidde after some big dispute, and a failed reveal. He'd installed a distortion field around the planet that restricted but didn't entirely stop water travel under the guise of leading the planet in a new direction, thus the constant fog. The barrier allowed others to travel to Hidde through something that sounded like a one-way bottleneck. The distortion field also affected planetary water travel. Instead of stepping into the water and voyaging to the other side of the planet in one fell swoop, you had to take three or four legs. You'd eventually arrive at your destination, it'd just take longer.

Who would do such a thing? Obviously, someone who wants to bypass the procedures and protocols put in place by The Accordance to protect a planet's inhabitants after the reveal.

I decided to keep to myself, eyes and ears alert for Lachlan's signal. I jumped at everything; a limb cracking, paper blowing across the barren quad, a bell ringing in the distance. I constantly speculated about how he'd get around the distortion field, find me, and get us off of the planet. I had to believe. He said to stay strong, and I was trying. Our last encounter at Jokull's house was constantly on my mind. Not just the picture of Lachlan in that formal outfit although that image popped into my mind with annoying regularity. His face is what hounded me, the cold courage in it. Is this the other Lachlan I'd speculated about that day at the waterfall? And if so, is this the whole package or just the tip of the iceberg? With nothing else to occupy my mind, I kept looking for answers. Regrettably, as elusive desires have a tendency to do each evening, hope dwindled along with the setting sun.

Tonight, I decided to stay awake as late as possible so that when I finally went to bed in the rickety metal cot, I'd fall into a deep sleep. My brilliant plan worked for a few hours until the nightmares woke me in a grip of fear. I tried to fall back asleep but whenever I closed my eyes all I saw was my Mom's face and Lachlan's eyes. Unless this latest voyage messed things up, I should still be good on the crazy time discrepancy issue. If I didn't get back to Earth soon, she would notice that I was gone.

I'd disappointed everyone around me.

I threw the threadbare blanket over my head, changed positions for the hundredth time, and counted sheep to no avail. I spent several more sleepless hours worrying that my mom already found out that I was missing and was freaking out. That thought raced like danger through my blood, keeping my heart pounding away in my ears. Seriously, who can sleep with all that noise? The faint light streaming in through the window meant that it was almost morning and watching the sunrise on this horrible planet would at least add some color.

I sat on the edge of the bed, slipped my feet into the leather skimmers, pulled the blanket off of the thin mattress, and quietly made my way to the bathroom. I washed my face and rinsed my mouth. I looked in the smoky glass mirror, ran a hand through the messy mop of hair, flipping the strands first to left and then to the right, and finally twisting the mound into a bun. It's the best I could do under the circumstances. I didn't have a jacket and the blanket would do but honestly, I looked forward to a walk in the cold morning air.

I decided to use the back entrance so that I wouldn't wake anyone and pushed the door open. I'd scouted a clearing the day before that would offer a good view. I walked briskly across the sodden ground of the quad saying seemingly to no one, "I'm going to watch the sunrise." Out from the shadows came my constant companion. "Make sure you alert Randolph." I didn't bother to look but I heard the distinct *click* of someone pushing buttons. As soon as I rounded the corner, I stopped dead, a fresh surge of adrenalin sluicing through my veins. An iridescent turquoise feather, turning and fluttering, floated down through the air.

He's here. The rescue is now.

And before I could call his name, Lachlan appeared out of nowhere in a cloud of water vapor. Without uttering a single word to give me a hint of what was about to happen, Lachlan went for the nameless guy who'd followed me. I barely had time to blink. A brilliant mustard yellow color roared across his uniform a split second before he evanesced in midair, and then simultaneously reappeared fully formed directly behind where a person had stood only a moment ago. A glutinous pool of crimson oozed across the barren ground.

You could've knocked me over with that turquoise feather.

Lachlan snapped his head around, his eyes sweeping side to side. Satisfied, he bolted in my direction—the look in his eyes indicating that he had no intention of stopping once he'd reached me. After the similar experience with DeRenne down in the cavern, I bent my knees to brace for impact. Amazingly, instead of smashing directly into my body, he seized me in his arms as he screamed by. The velocity with which we were borne along was unimaginable. There was pain associated with this trip though the gaseous water vapors.

We *smacked* into the ground. I fell forward and bumped my head, the tiny little light bursts in my eyes momentarily blinding me. Incredibly, Lachlan managed to get to his feet, grab me underneath my arms, and hoist me upward. Out of nowhere, Jokull appeared suddenly and silently in a cloud of water vapor, dragging along with him a bewildered looking Sid and Randolph. Dressed as usual in head-to-toe midnight blue clothing, Jokull's body was veiled and shadowed in the dawn light making him look like some distorted bobble-head doll.

"I see your skills at evanescing have improved Lachlan," Jokull scowled in a threatening timbre. "However, you must understand that you cannot travel very far on Hidde nor rely on those pesky glittery friends of yours."

So that's why Nazca never came for me; she couldn't. But perhaps she told Lachlan where I'd landed. I felt the coolness on the back of my neck when Lachlan evanesced from behind my shoulder. I dropped to the ground like a marionette whose strings had been cut.

Randolph and Sid realized what was about to go down. They ran in opposite directions but neither one of them evanesced. I would've done the same thing if I were in their shoes. I knew I shouldn't look but I couldn't seem to turn away either. I sat on the ground and watched in utter disbelief as Lachlan's rippling incorporeal form plowed through Sid, whose body exploded into an enormous red cloud, raining blood all over me. Hot, sticky blood, Sid's blood mind you, covering my arms and my chest. I stared at the scene before me, the finality so complete that it took a moment for me to accept what my eyes told me had happened. I lifted my arms drenched in blood and opened my mouth to scream.

Lachlan coalesced back into his solid form. "Quiet Emily!" he said with such authority that I imagine no one ever dare disobey him. I shut my gaping mouth.

Randolph headed for the closest tree. Lachlan was having none of it. His eyes heated, glinted dangerously. Vanishing on the spot, he blustered through Randolph, leaving a red human silhouette hovering in midair for a fraction of a second before splashing down to the ground with a sickening *swish.* Jokull stood off to the side, not bothered in the least, almost as if he were merely refereeing a game of croquet. But their blood called out to me, causing a stark chill of terror to spread across my chest.

I managed to get to my feet with no idea of what to do or of what might be coming next. Out of nowhere, Lachlan appeared in a cloud of water vapor right in front of me and instinctively, I stepped backward. Jokull did not miss that gesture and all that it implied.

"Perhaps she no longer wants to be with now that you have revealed your true colors," Jokull smirked. That snapped me out of the funk. I reached over, grabbed Lachlan's hand, and faced Jokull head-on, not surprised at my resilience. "Even after so grand a gesture," Jokull said. "Emily still may not leave Hidde."

"I did not come to ask your permission, Jokull," Lachlan, said in an amazingly calm voice for someone who just killed three people.

"Make no mistake, word of your little rescue will get back to Arden," Jokull said.

Lachlan squeezed my hand. "I would expect nothing less."

As soon as the words were out of Lachlan's mouth, Jokull started spinning on the spot, drawing in his arms much like an ice skater does before executing a dramatic spin. I had no idea what was happening but Lachlan obviously did. He pushed me behind him, instructing in a clear voice, "Emily, hold onto something!"

All of the surrounding sounds became distant, as though we were suddenly standing far away. A short, quick updraft of air puffed out the cuff of my pants. A stillness so complete gave way to leaves scuttling across the ground, and branches *creaking* and *snapping* in the trees. The feel and texture in the sudden drop in temperature and air pressure reminded me of the precise moment right before a destructive summer afternoon thunderstorm howls down through the neighborhood.

Whomp... Whomp... Whomp

Lachlan too started spinning on the spot, drawing in his arms.

Whomp... Whomp... Whomp

With a deep oscillating whir, a geyser of water spewed up from the ground engulfing Lachlan in a brilliant whirlpool of azure. I stepped back, not fully believing what I was seeing and hearing. Lachlan had literally transformed himself into a rotating vortex of water, the consistency of hot molten glass, fueled by a continuous inflow of water rising up from the ground. I should've expected something like this. It's always about the water. Isn't it?

Movement in my side vision made me turn. In the fraction of a second that it took me to look, something midnight blue heaved past. Unspeakable horror, the kind that splits the ends of your hair curdled the blood in my veins. Jokull had morphed into a fiercely spinning storm of unimaginable fury; a screeching sound emanating from the inky vortex reminded me of the howling from the murky undertow.

I stared into the storm and felt its menace, the gyrating winds unleashing a powerful spray that pelted my hands and face with millions of tiny, stinging pinpricks. I crooked my arm over my forehead and watched the scene before me with a total sense of detachment.

At first, they lurched awkwardly, almost as if learning a new dance step, each circling vortex of water glistening in intense shades of pewter. I stood braced, looking for an opportunity to act, the winds waves from the spinning columns of water lapping fear against my chest. After a few more awkward lurches, first Jokull's, and then next Lachlan's, vortex darkened. Fiercely and furiously, they surged toward each other, a thunderous midair collision rumbling a deafening sonic boom. The rolling sound wave generated from the collision hit me and I pitched left, keeling over.

At the same instant, Lachlan flew out of his vortex in a brutal downdraft and hit the ground, tumbling head-first. Don't ask me how or why but something told me that this was the time to try and help. I crawled toward a nearby tree trunk, glancing over my shoulder to see where Lachlan was, crawling forward some more, and then glancing back again. I stumbled to my feet, and made a run for it.

"Emily! Stay where you are!" Lachlan commanded as a bright tangerine orange exploded across his uniform. Every cell in my body balked in protest but I stayed put. And the fact that I did stay put was an indication of just how serious this situation had become.

Lachlan now stood between me and Jokull, holding Jokull's rotating vortex at bay with his right hand. With a single fluid motion, Lachlan flicked his left hand up into the air in my direction. The ground below my feet heaved and pitched in a sideways motion. An inexplicable roar came out of nowhere; a high-pitched *shrill* growing louder and louder as I quickly stuck a finger inside of each ear to dull the head-splitting pain. I actually felt the deep rumbling *whoosh* intensify before I ever saw the churning column of water rise up from the ground, engulfing me in a molten spinning cocoon of blue.

I knew he did it for my protection. But trapped inside of the rotating vortex, I couldn't see or hear what was going on between Lachlan and Jokull. "No," I shouted, pounding both fists against the circulating water wall, pissed that he'd blocked me out. As hard as I pounded, there was no escape; he'd seen to that. I stepped back into the eye of the spinning whirlpool and told myself to be rational. Screaming would get me nowhere.

The deep groaning turbulence from the rotating water wall didn't drown out the thundering *crack* from subsequent midair collisions, forming a vivid scene inside of my mind. After four or five more intense sound waves, I pounded the spinning water wall with both fists again, my terror for Lachlan unbearable. On the verge of hysteria, I interlaced all ten fingers flat against my forehead and leaned in. Nose pressed flat against the cycling water, frictional resistance scorched my knuckles but at least I could see what was going on.

From what I could tell, they appeared evenly matched; neither one was able to completely submerge the other. I got the feeling they came to the same conclusion because after a few more violent midair collisions, first Jokull, and then Lachlan, resumed their normal corporeal form.

I couldn't hear what they were saying but their body language and hand gestures left no doubt that the words flying back and forth between them were anything but kind. They were two circling tigers, maintaining equal distance in a deadly dance, looking for an unseen opportunity, a split second chance to pounce. Rather swiftly, considering his stature, Jokull shifted his body weight. I wondered if this was a trick or a lure to catch Lachlan off-guard. Before I could decide, Jokull crouched low to the ground and flung both of his arms forward like someone hurling knives.

Lachlan obviously anticipated this move because he evanesced on the spot, simultaneously rematerializing right behind where Jokull crouched before he had a chance to summon the water back up from the ground. Lachlan's hand shot out lightning fast and *smacked* his former tutor on the shoulder. Jokull instantly froze in an oddly contorted pose.

Time stood still as I stared at the frozen Jokull, not really sure if it was over or not. Lachlan ran out from behind Jokull, waving a hand in my direction. The protective column of water around me plummeted straight to the ground, soaking the leather skimmers.

"Are you hurt?" Lachlan asked, his elevator eyes rapidly assessing my blood-covered body.

"Yes…yes. I'm…fine," I stammered. Honestly, what else could I say?

With a considerable amount of self-control on his part, Lachlan wrenched his eyes off of me, and back onto Jokull. "I have only partially frozen you," Lachlan said, positioning his body between the two of us for the second time.

Jokull obviously couldn't speak but the murderous look in his eyes clearly conveyed his feelings. I noticed that he wiggled his pinkie finger just a little.

"We will have another opportunity to resolve our differences," Lachlan continued, "and I still have more questions regarding the mysterious circumstance surrounding my father's death that you reported to The Accordance."

"Lachlan, let's get out of here," I whispered, walking forward, my insides tingling with unease at the sight of the melting Jokull. Even a dead bee can sting.

"In a moment," Lachlan said in a reassuring tone, his hand flying into the air, warning me to stay put. Jokull's right arm dropped to his side—he was definitely thawing.

And then the very last thing I ever expected to happen, happened.

δ^+

DeRenne appeared in a cloud of water vapor in the middle of our little party. She surveyed the scene, and the knowing expression on her face meant that she'd accurately processed and deduced what transpired over the last few minutes.

"DeRenne," Lachlan said, his tone nonchalant, on the surface. From my viewpoint, I saw a tiny glistening bead of sweat slide down his temple.

"Looks as if you boys decided to play with the big toys today," DeRenne said. "Thought I could lend a hand."

DeRenne wore the pixelating uniform and had her hair pulled back into a tight ponytail, her signature feather earrings gone. I wondered how she talked Lachlan into letting her come on this mission, not to mention Shaw.

"Before this situation goes any further, there is something of I wish to give to Jokull," she said, answering Lachlan's unspoken question, her fierce eyes so like her brother's eyes coming to rest on Jokull's face. Jokull met her stare with no visible change in his frosty expression.

I ran over to Lachlan's side and grasped his hand. Without looking or saying a single word, he pushed me behind him. His gesture and all that it implied was not missed by Jokull; his lips involuntarily twitched at the corners. I saw firsthand that Jokull considered Lachlan's feelings for me a vulnerable weakness just as Lachlan feared the day I discovered the cavern. There'd be no room for negotiations with him after this. The inevitable eventuality; I'll be sent straight back to Earth when we get out of here.

If we get out of here.

"Lachlan, know that I have this under control," DeRenne said, matching Jokull's confidence with the level gaze of a lioness. If I had to bet on a staring contest, today I'd put my money on DeRenne. "Jokull, I am going to reach into my pocket if that is acceptable to you."

He nodded once, and I wondered why he'd agreed.

DeRenne removed a small velvet bag from a pouch in her mission uniform; the fabric of her uniform pixelating a neutral taupe. She kept all her emotions in check. Too far away to see the intricate design embroidered on the velvet bag, Jokull knew exactly what it was because even he couldn't hide the softness in his eyes behind the usual sneer. Lachlan stepped sideways a fraction, meaning that he too recognized the bag. I wanted to ask but keep quiet which was hard for me.

"DeRenne," Jokull hissed, shaking his arms and legs, but somehow still trapped. "Is this some type of trick?"

"I have you know that you are referring to the most precious of all my birthday gifts," she said, her hand slipping upward to finger the braided silver, gold, and copper chain draped around her neck. "Ever."

"I want you to have the handwritten note inside," DeRenne said in a low voice. Lachlan and I exchanged an anxious glance. "No, this is not a trick." Her words rang sharp and clear in the air. She took two steps forward, placed the bag on the barren patch of ground near Jokull's feet, and then took two steps back.

A plumage of midnight blue swooped down and seized the velvety catch in its claws. Jokull's hand trembled ever so slightly as he reached back into his past, and removed a small roll of parchment secured with a piece of twine. Rather dramatically, considering the circumstances, he slid the piece of twine off of the roll, and looped the twine around his pinkie finger.

"Emily, you know that Orlaith was married to Jokull," DeRenne said, and I heard something in her voice. "What you are unaware of…is that…is that she is Paden and Ccri's daughter."

Wham! A sledgehammer hit me square in the chest. I started to drop but Lachlan caught me beneath the arm before I hit the ground. I glanced at DeRenne, and then up at Lachlan. "I'm so sorry. I cannot believe…Paden and Ccri were so kind. And this is how I repay their kindness, making them relive…" My head fell in shame as my voice trailed off.

"They never shared this vital detail with you?" Jokull asked his voice frigid with fury.

I shivered at his icy words. "No…never. They welcomed me into their home and into their lives with open arms." I'm not sure he believed me, but he at least seemed satisfied with my current dismal estimation of myself.

Jokull unrolled the piece of parchment, lifted it in the air, and read the note. In a fleeting moment, the smugness was gone, replaced by endless, bottomless regret.

"Jokull," DeRenne said in a compassionate voice. "We are going to take Emily with us, and leave. Orlaith would want you to do this. She would want you to come out from the shadows, and choose once again to stand in the light."

Jokull's upturned eyes slid first on Lachlan, next on me, and then finally on DeRenne. "Well played, DeRenne," he said, the tiniest twitch in the corners of his lips hinting at hesitation.

It happened quickly. The guard who escorted me to Jokull's house my first night on Hidde and the guard with the scar on his face who stood at the door, appeared out of nowhere in a cloud of water vapor. But, so did Shaw. I'm not sure if a looked passed between Shaw and Lachlan or maybe they knew all along this is how it would play out or maybe somehow they were in communication. Anyway, Lachlan turned, swinging his arms wide, blanketing my entire body with his.

A powerful updraft lofted us skyward into an inward twisting vortex of water vapor, centripetal acceleration pinning my arms and legs flat against the spinning water wall. As swiftly as it started, the dynamic forces inside of the vortex stopped, catapulting us across the damp ground, a *clanking* noise chiming away in both of my ears.

Lachlan leaped to his feet, grabbed me from behind, and hoisted me upright. We stood on the top of a high cliff covered in low-growing shrubs overlooking the ocean, the view shrouded by the ever present fog on Hidde.

"Hold still," Lachlan ordered, whirling me around on the spot. He dipped his right hand, almost like he was dipping his hand into a pool of water on a hot day to splash his face. A steady stream of water rose up from the ground following his hand motion, drenching my hair, face, and clothes. I was completely soaked but no longer caked in blood.

I ran a hand through my wet hair to untangle the long strands. "Thanks, I needed that."

He leaned back to appraise me. "Yes, much better. If truth be told, you covered in blood is not my favorite look."

"You killed three people," I said, shaking out both arms. Crap! My mouth has a life of its own.

Lachlan went stone still. He didn't say anything for the longest second of my life. "Were you expecting an uneventful extraction?" There was a wild look back in his eyes.

An extraction! What am I? An abscessed tooth? "Er, well…yes." I assumed no one would get killed, hurt perhaps, but not killed. Someone's father, brother, husband, uncle, son, was now dead. I'd even talked to Randolph and Sid. My rash actions literally ripped several families apart. I'd have to live with that knowledge every single day for the rest of my life.

"Emily, I told you the journey with the water is a lifetime commitment. To the death." He looked neither sorry nor guilty. "At some point, you too must choose to embrace the water of your own accord. What you need to understand right now is that Jokull used you as bait to get to me. I did not plan to kill anyone, which is why I came in the morning. Trust me, Jokull's guards are very well trained, and given the chance, they would strike, and that strike would have taken your breath away." Now he looked angry. "They would never allow me to simply walk off Hidde with you. I can assure you that Jokull is not adhering to any code of conduct. Today he revealed his weakness. I suggest you do not let him see yours."

I shut my mouth, his words bothering me more than they should because they were true.

He pointed to a jumble of rock slabs scattered here and there by the advance and retreat of glaciers over time. "I need you to go over there and take your clothes off."

δ^+

I was glad to see him, grateful that he'd rescued me, but … "Excuse me?"

"They may have placed a tracking device in the fabric," he said, mumbling under his breath something about a lack of training, and other military-speak.

"Oh." I'd never considered that.

"DeRenne thinks this is about your size," he said, pulling a pixelating uniform from a pouch in the pant leg of his uniform. "I do not think I can…I can stand…Never mind."

He held the uniform out, and I could see the wad of fabric near his hand wavering a deep scarlet. Great. This is going to be a problem. I don't know how to control the stupid pixelating fabric. Every time he comes near me it's probably going to swirl pink or some other embarrassing color.

"Hurry if you please," he said. "We need to meet Shaw and DeRenne."

"Everyone had to stop what they were doing and come save the poor little Earth girl in distress," I huffed.

"I told them not to involve themselves. You know Shaw."

"Certainty not," I said, shaking my head in disgust. "Shaw would never miss an opportunity to see me in yet another pickle."

"Pickle!?"

"Predicament," I amended.

"Why did you not say that in the first place?"

"I did say that. Why are we stopping here? Why not meet them now? Are we still on Hidde? How do you know DeRenne got out of there?"

"To cover our tracks. We are trying to meet them. Yes, we are still on Hidde. I do not know if she did, which is why we need to get moving." He had a concerned look in his eyes and tried to hide it from me. "One cannot travel very far on Hidde, so we are each taking a different route. I will explain everything, in great detail, when we are safely home on Arden."

"Yeah, you're right," I said, noting that his choice of words did include *we, home,* and *Arden*, all in the same sentence.

I flung the uniform over my shoulder before walking behind the jumble of slabs. I unzipped the itchy garb, not sorry in the least to watch it fall lifelessly to the ground, ceremoniously kicking the mound aside. Not too shocking, the fabric blended in with the craggy gray rocks. I slipped the sleek uniform on and fastened the sleeve tabs.

"Ready," I said, coming out from behind the rocks, pushing the mop of wet hair behind my shoulder.

Lachlan walked toward me. I couldn't tell if he was going to give me another stern talk or gather me in his arms. He stopped, and said with a rather pleased smile, "Now, this is a look I could get used to."

I glanced down. Not a bright pink but you could definitely see soft waves billowing across the fabric. I patted the uniform, vigorously, trying to rub away the telltale ripples.

He stifled a laugh. "The fabric does not work that way."

"Right," I said, hoping the uniform glowered a deep red. "You said we're in a hurry, so let's get going."

He held his hands out. As our fingers interlaced, a soft, buttery yellow undulated up the sleeve of his uniform. "See, it works both ways," he said, still smiling.

"Except that you can hide yours if you want," I huffed, again. "Anyway, is this going to be one of those rough rides or …" Too late. This time, we stood on the top of a plateau surrounded by orange-colored sandstone formations. Not a plant or animal in sight. "You need to work on your destinations choices. This place has nothing to offer the picky traveler."

"If the point of the journey is to hide your tracks, and go someplace where no one can find you, then it is perfect."

"Oh! I see it now. Perhaps, a little chalet on the far ridge would be nice." I rolled my eyes. "How many more?" These short jumps were hard on the body.

"Just two."

I shook both hands. "Okay. Ready."

He reached down, taking my hands into his. A quick stop near the ocean shore, and then a second stop inside of a dark cave, we materialized in the middle of a grove of widely spaced scrub pines interspersed with shards of granite rearing up from the ground. Now that I'd done several of these jumps back-to-back, I had to admire his landing skills. It does take practice and determination not to re-form inside of a tree trunk instead of landing right next to one.

My second intergalactic voyage landed me on the most desolate planet in the Universe. Bleak, hopeless, and colorless, just like my mood right before I jumped into the water.

"We are to rendezvous here. First, I want to make sure everything is in order," Lachlan said, unfastening the pouch behind his neck, pulling the enormous hood over his head. "Wait here." He pushed his way through a thicket of gnarled undergrowth, and *Poof*, like magic, he vanished, only a few quivering sticks to mark his passage. No doubt about it; the illusion is a pretty cool trick.

Feeling exposed, I went a little deeper into the forest but not so deep that he couldn't find me. I leaned against a giant tree trunk and twisted the long strands of wet hair in the breeze so they would curl. After what seemed like an eternity but in reality was probably fewer than ten minutes, three figures appeared in a cloud of water vapor at the top of the hill.

"I left her standing…" Lachlan said, sounding a little miffed.

"Here," I said, walking out from the forest, and up the hill.

"Emily," DeRenne cried out, meeting me halfway with a big hug.

"Welcome back…good to see you," Shaw teased in a friendly embrace. "Try and stay out of trouble in the future."

"Working on it," I said, grinning at him. "DeRenne, you were magnificent. Shaw, you should've seen her."

"Even though I..." Lachlan said, sounding as usual like the big brother in charge.

DeRenne fisted her hands against her hips. She had a determined look in her eye. Shaw raised his eyebrows in approval. "Lachlan, you need to accept that I am old enough to go on some of the more dangerous missions." Oh great! I'm classified as a "dangerous mission". I'll be sent home for sure. "I thought, perhaps, you might need a distraction," DeRenne continued, sounding like she needed to get her words out before he stopped her. "Emily's profiling got me thinking."

"What!" I said, taken aback.

Lachlan held his tongue but you could tell that it was hard for him. He gestured with his hand for her to continue.

"Remember that you said Jokull consider his mind the ultimate weapon, that he liked games of strategy, that deep down he truly loved Orlaith, to look for a theme." I nodded as she talked but didn't say a word. "If anything would bring him back to us for a brief moment, she was the only way. He would never have taken the bag from Lachlan or Shaw. The necklace was made for and given to me. I needed to be the one to distract him."

"The note," I gasped. "What did the note say?"

"The note was from Orlaith on the occasion of my thirteenth year. Jokull used his surreptitious jewelry-making skills to fashion the necklace," she said, and we could all hear the disgust in her voice. "Orlaith sewed, and embroidered the bag as her gift. The note read:

"dearest derennE/
on the occasion of your thirteenth year, my ardent wish is that one day, you too will find the love of your life, and experience the happiness I founD/
foreveR/
orlaitH/"

DeRenne swung her head toward Shaw and smiled. Shaw's eyes flickered over to Lachlan, who nodded once in approval. "I thought if we got into a bind, we might need something to entice him back to Orlaith and to his life on Arden," she said, flipping the long ponytail over her shoulder. "Yes, it was a risk. Still, I wanted to try."

"Jokull was right about one thing, sis," Lachlan said, and I could just hear that official tone in his voice. "Your idea was well played even though you disobeyed my orders."

"Tread lightly," Shaw muttered under his breath.

DeRenne opened her mouth to let him have it, again.

Lachlan threw both hands up in exasperation. "I am not going to deny that it worked because it did. It also put me in an awkward position. If something went wrong…"

"Which it did not," DeRenne stated, kicking out her left foot.

"True," he said with calculated intent. "If it had, who would I save first, you or Emily?"

We both turned to glare at him. "He is going to have such a big head after this," DeRenne said. "Lachlan, you know that I can take care of myself."

"Guess that leaves me," I said, giving him a quick wink.

"Got your hands full there," Lachlan said to Shaw as he walked past DeRenne, yanking her ponytail.

"And you do not?" Shaw said, throwing me a sympathetic look, following Lachlan.

The two friends walked behind an enormous tree trunk, reappearing a moment later, dragging a six-foot long, cylindrical-shaped bark container, lashed with leather ties. Shaw unwound the bindings and then tipped the container sideways. A dozen or so flat metal strips *clanged* and *banged* across the needle-strewn ground.

"Guys," I said, and even I heard the urgency in my voice. "As you know, Jokull's created a distortion field around the planet that blocks travelers from coming and going at will. That's why it's so foggy around here."

"And here I thought the fog added a little ambiance to our experience on Hidde," Shaw grumbled, contemplating the metal strips.

"Thanks to you, Emily," Lachlan said, kneeling down on the ground next to the jumbled pile. "I may have found one chance to get us off of this planet."

"What?" I gasped, shocked yet again.

"Like DeRenne, your profiling research got me thinking about all of the nights that Jokull spent at The Assemblage. I had a hunch, and returned to Arden—the day you saw me." I winced because he was referring to the day I started down the dark path. "Counting on his overconfidence, I wondered if I could also access his files, and extrapolate some detailed information. I thought it better to search in person so as not to unnecessarily alert The Accordance by accessing the information remotely. Jokull assumed that no one was on to him, and did not bother blocking his research. And he was right, until you came along." Lachlan looked up and smiled, letting me off the hook for my rash behavior. "Jokull had amassed a huge amount of data. I spent the next day sifting through his mindset and located the initial schematics for the distortion field. I found the one loophole of his invention; pure metals thwart the restrictive property of the magnetic field, opening a narrow doorway for water travel."

"True to form, leaving a backdoor open for his quick escape," Shaw said through gritted teeth. "Always such a kind and thoughtful man."

"Unfortunately, I did not have enough time to methodically investigate the entire plan," Lachlan said, looking perturbed, "in theory, his loophole should work and..."

"And turn the tables on His Royal Behindness?" Shaw said with a low sweeping half-bow. "Sounds like a majestic plan to me." We all burst out laughing at his antics, relieving some of the stress we all secretly harbored.

"DeRenne," Lachlan said, giving his sister an official nod. "You said you wanted to assist with the more dangerous missions."

I frowned. I still didn't like being classified as a "dangerous mission".

"Welcome to my world with your brother," Shaw said, kneeling down on the ground next to Lachlan. He started sorting the gold, silver, and copper metal strips into three piles.

"How does it work?" I asked, completely baffled as to how a bunch of metal strips would magically whisk up back to Arden.

"And come to think of it, how'd you get past his travel restrictions, and land on this horrible planet in the first place?"

"Slipping onto the planet through the barrier is not the issue," Lachlan said. "Getting off of the planet is an entirely different problem. According to Jokull's research, pure elemental metals, forged and folded at extremely high temperatures, and then rapidly cooled to absolute zero in the presence of an active superconductor magnet, realign... *blah,blah,blah...*the field surrounding the altered metal now acts as an enhanced conduit because of these intrinsic chemical changes. It is how he opens a window to leave Hidde. With his permission, of course."

Okay. Whatever. I understood about half of what Lachlan said. I was way too distracted by the staggering amount of precious metal on the ground at my feet. "Where did you get the money to pay for all of this?"

"Emily, you must remember that we do not use money the way you are accustomed," DeRenne said. "Thousands of uninhabited planets in this galaxy alone could supply the raw materials. The question you should ask these two is the how, and more importantly, the where. To manufacture these types of metal strips with such a unique magnetic signature at short notice is almost impossible."

"Thanks for the clarification," I said, sharply.

DeRenne, insistently tapping her left foot against the needle-strewn ground, Shaw and Lachlan met our scowls with innocent looks. "Where, Lachlan?" DeRenne grilled.

"The how and the where is of no importance, sis," Lachlan said, his eyes staring somewhere else. "The *will it work* is what is of concern right now."

"I knew it—Black Market," DeRenne said, shaking her head in disapproval. "That is what you two were doing off-world."

Great. Just one more reason for Lachlan to get in hot water with The Accordance. He'd been forced to delve into the illicit dealings of a shady underworld. My head was reeling.

"Time was short. There were not many options," Shaw said, not an inkling of guilt on his face.

Lachlan rocked back on his knees. "Emily, I did some research. Daileass is descended from the Water lineage."

DeRenne reached for my hand, grinning. In a silly girl-kind-of-way, that information validated the connection we already felt in our hearts. I squeezed her hand and smiled back.

"Shaw's lineage is Fire. His emblem is interlocking silver and copper squares," Lachlan continued. "We need to arrange these longer strips into the three interlocking triangles of the Water emblem, and then place the interlocking squares of the Fire emblem on the top of the converging point of the three triangles." Lachlan's eyes degraded to dark green as he ordered his thoughts. "The next issue to resolve is where we each should stand. I considered placing Emily inside of the third triangle since that is her lineage. This places Shaw on the top of the interlocking squares as he should." Shaw accepted Lachlan's acknowledgment with a nod. "That also places him on the top of the converging point of the triangles. Perhaps, this is where Emily should stand since she is the least experienced traveler."

They each directed their attention to me. I knew right away that I had to make a decision— a decision where the odds were stacked against us, coupled with a high degree of failure. If ever I needed courage for the day, that day is today. "I can do this," I exhaled.

Lachlan looked relieved and pleased.

We each grabbed a handful of metal strips, arranging the gold, silver, and copper interlocking triangles across the ground. Next, we centered the interlocking silver and copper squares on the top of the converging point of the three triangles. A series of sharp metallic, *dings*, reverberated through the air as we all worked in silence.

"Emily, what metal feels right to you?" DeRenne asked once we'd finished.

What an odd question. On Earth, I would've immediately answered gold. Gold is a safe and familiar choice. However, if truth be told, Arden and the metal copper are more embedded in my psyche. The funny way my heart goes pitter-patter whenever I glimpse Arden's symbol pounded into the copper circle in the top right-hand corner of the hanging signs identifying the shops in the village. To get the fruit, and I really wanted this particular piece of fruit, sometimes you have to go out on a limb. "Copper," I answered, and noted that I felt no regret.

"I will take silver then," DeRenne announced. I wasn't that surprised by her choice since silver is a metal that she and Shaw share in common.

"Everyone have their stone?" Lachlan asked, getting to his feet and wiping his hands on a pant leg.

Shaw and DeRenne each patted a different pocket on their uniform. Daileass' stone was on the bedside table at Paden and Ccri's house. Thank goodness, I didn't have the stone with me or it, along with DeRenne's dress, would be lost on this miserable planet forever. "I'm sorry, mine is on Arden."

"Not to worry," Lachlan said, unfastening a small flap pocket in his sleeve." I saw the stone on the bedside table when I evanesced inside your room to get the feather. Paden was about one second away from discovering me."

Lachlan firmly took my hand in his; Daileass' stone a solid link between us. I accepted DeRenne's waiting hand, and she securely gripped Shaw's hand. With a collective sigh of relief, the four of us stepped into our one chance to travel safely back to Arden.

Lachlan reached inside the front of his uniform with his free hand and pulled out a gold-cage pendant attached to a double-link gold chain. For a brief moment, we all were transfixed by the mesmerizing colors inside of the milky blue crystal. "I am pleased you have Father's pendant," DeRenne said. "It is the right time."

Lachlan acknowledged DeRenne's words with a slight smile, and said, "I need for each of you to visualize the three standing stones in the village plaza."

"Ah, drawing energy from the stones," Shaw remarked, sounding impressed.

"Yes, much thought and time went into choosing that sacred location," he said. "As it turns out, this crystal and those standing stones are connected by a traversable wormhole. I am not exactly sure what a water stone has to do with any of this.

The first travelers reference a stone several times in their design. I do not want to take any chances."

Watching Lachlan's heated eyes cool as he spoke, I thought his plan was crazy enough that it just might work. "As a precaution, I placed more of these gold, silver, and copper metallic strips on the top of each of the three capstones. The triangular field framed by the three capstones is our arrival destination." He hesitated, choosing his words carefully, "No one has ever…"

"I believe it will," I said with absolute faith.

"As do I," DeRenne's voice crisp.

"You have never let me down before." Shaw's assurance was irrefutable.

"I will evanesce first, taking Emily with me," Lachlan said, tugging on my hand. A soft pink blushed across my wavering uniform. I didn't care. I wanted him to know how I felt. "DeRenne, you evanesce after Emily dissipates. Shaw, hold tight until you receive my signal."

"As you wish," Shaw said with a slight bow to Lachlan, an encouraging nod to me, and an adoring smile to DeRenne.

"Shall we," Lachlan said, and it wasn't a question.

Eyes closed, I visualized the three soaring standing stones and their massive capstones in the village plaza, and now our way home. I saw myself leaning against the rock face of the pinnacle standing stone the day I waited for Lachlan. The unforgettable day he took me to the waterfall for a picnic lunch. The memory of that day replayed with such accuracy that I saw myself or rather I saw the goofy grin on my face, vibrant images…Whoa! Wait! Hold up!

It was as if a giant rubber band recoiled and *snapped*, hurtling us headlong at breakneck speed through what could only be described as a series of narrower and narrower tubes, forcing our molecules to align in a single continuous strand. Linked to one another in a perfect chain, bound by our mutual desire to return to Arden but still tethered to Hidde, our molecular strand swayed precariously in the cosmic winds.

Lachlan's *'All clear'* vibrated along the molecular strand through me, onto DeRenne, and then finally to Shaw. Amazingly, he and Shaw managed to simultaneously tighten their stance at either end of the strand. I sensed Shaw's decision to let go, and once he did, the molecular strand ricocheted violently, whipping and snapping like a live electrical wire. It took the four of us concentrating in concert to keep the strand from becoming tangled. There were no pleasing colors associated with the voyage, only intense bursts of red and blue coherent light, and a persistent low-frequency buzz adding to the confusion. *'Hold tight'* sparked along the full-length of the molecular strand.

Determined not to be the one to break the chain, fixating on the gleaming triangular field inside of the three capstones back on Arden, I mustered all of my strength to keep myself and my friends linked. And just when I thought things couldn't get any worse, an updraft lifted our strand into a dense rotating vortex.

The gravitational tidal forces surrounding the mouth of the spinning wormhole congealed our molecules into a thick viscous liquid, and we poured like cold molasses into the wormhole. The shear rate was unimaginable as our strand careened across the event horizon at the speed of light. Flailing dangerously in all directions from the vertical rotation of the column, frictional resistance burned like a flash-fire through our tightly packed molecules each time the strand bounced off of the sides of the cycling mass.

If I could have screamed, I would have. But without a body, there was no mouth to produce a sound. In an exquisitely timed coordination, our four individual thoughts and our mutual desire to reach Arden harmonized into a fifth ringing chord, blending into a unified overtone in the center of the wormhole. This stopped the strand from flailing against the inner sheath. And then, something seized. Energy momentum from the rotating vortex sent us spiraling inward and upward, and then soaring up into the air with a steady stream of water shooting out from the fountain in the center of the enclosure, kind of like riding a wave to shore.

"I have you," Lachlan said triumphantly, hoisting me onto the capstone next to him. Keeping one arm securely wrapped around my waist, he reached out to help DeRenne. She, in turn, yanked on Shaw who vaulted upward with a huge grin on his face. Leave it to Shaw to find the fun in any precarious situation.

Standing side-by-side on the top of the capstone, Lachlan reached around in front of me and grabbed Shaw's free hand. "Thank you," he said. "You have seen me safely through more predicaments than I care to remember."

"As always," Shaw said with a satisfied smile.

I eyed the crowd forming on the plaza below. "How are we going to get down?" I asked, knowing they would never evanesce in public now that I knew its other use.

"Not to worry," Lachlan said, jumping over to the adjacent capstone. He picked up a coil of rope, and then looped and tied the rope around the rectangular stone. Easily, almost gracefully, he rappelled down the rough-hewn rock face into the center of the enclosure. Feet firmly planted on the ground, he arched his neck upward, and yelled, "Next."

I knew that he meant me. Shaw would never get down until DeRenne was safely deposited on the ground. "Be right there!" I hopped over to the adjacent capstone, leaned down, and gripped the rope. I was thankful the fibers were soft so that I wouldn't add a rope burn to the long list of embarrassing moments on Arden.

"Do not look down," Lachlan shouted through his cupped hands.

"Yeah! Yeah!" I mumbled. "Thanks for sharing."

I reminded myself that the key element here is trust. It's powerful stuff. In reality, this was my second intergalactic voyage to Arden, and what a difference a few weeks makes; the look and feel of the village now familiar and safe. I inhaled a deep breath and leaned out over the edge of the soaring stone, grateful for the sleek uniform instead of a cumbersome long dress. Trying not to over-think what it was I was doing, I dropped a couple of inches, stopped, exhaled, and then started again.

"Welcome back," Lachlan said as his hands gripped my waist. I landed on the ground with a soft *thud.*

I pivoted around on my feet until I faced him. "Thank you," I murmured.

"My pleasure," he said, a funny set to his lips. It took him a moment before he looked away this time.

"Do not mind me," DeRenne said, jabbing Lachlan in the side on the way down, winking at me.

Shaw hopped down next, stood upright, and then patted himself down making sure everything was in its proper place. "I am going to add to my short list of things to never to do again, escaping off of a planet surrounded by a distortion field. I think my eyebrows were scorched off."

We all cracked up laughing. The kind of laugh you only allow yourself to laugh once you realize you're truly out of danger.

δ^+

I turned around before stepping onto the stone stoop at Paden and Ccri's house. "Will I see you later tonight?" Lachlan didn't answer but smiled. I looked down; the fabric of my uniform pixelating aquamarine. "Oops," I said, rubbing the fabric with my hands. Hopefully, the cloth didn't reveal too much. A girl has got her pride after all.

"I wish," Lachlan said, still smiling. "However…"

"I'm sure you will have to explain everything. In great detail." I reached over and squeezed his hand. "I don't know what came over me. It was foolish. Everyone warned me not to…"

Lachlan slipped his arms around my waist and drew me slowly close. I sighed and draped my arms over his shoulders. My nose fitted comfortably into the small hollow in the center of his chest as he rested his chin on the top of my head. I allowed myself a moment to forget the regret. "Emily, you have got to stop blaming yourself." I could feel his chin moving against the top of my head. "You entered the water…hmm…unfocused. It is a common mistake, one that we all have made at some point."

I arched my head upward and blinked. "Yeah, but did your unfocused trip through the water result in your friends risking their lives? And, has anyone ever had to kill someone to rescue you?" He opened his mouth to say something but I laid a finger to his lips to *shush* him. "Never mind! Don't answer that question. Better not be seen with me in public. I've got to be number one on Arden's 'Top Ten Most Wanted List'."

He sighed this time but I could also see that his eyes were warm. "Emily, from where I am standing, I can see a little farther down the road. Let me assure you, these things have a tendency to take on a life of their own. Something was bound to happen sooner or later. This is what Jokull wanted; an excuse."

"Nice try. You're not going to shoulder the blame for my rash actions," I said, squaring my shoulders. "And DeRenne's in a heap of trouble too."

"DeRenne can take care of herself. I know that now." And then completely in character, he went all soulful. I saw the glint in his eyes dim. "Emily, after the last few days, I must pose a question."

The pause went on forever.

"Why me?" he asked.

I made an impertinent noise in the back of my throat. "Seriously, I'm not even going to dignify that question with an answer."

"You better decide on an answer. I will keep asking you until you do."

I met his gaze but didn't answer.

He released his embrace. I figured that he was going to shake a little sense into me. But once again, I couldn't have been more wrong. Lachlan ran his hands down my arms, taking both of my hands into his. "I do not want to leave," he said, gently kissing my scorched knuckles.

"Nooooooo," I moaned as he stepped backward.

"I must."

"I know but I don't have to like it," I said, keeping the regret at bay. Too late, he saw the shift in my posture.

Lachlan let go of my left hand, reached over, and gently tipped my chin up with his finger. "Emily Harrison," he said, annunciating each syllable. "This has got to stop."

"Do you even have a last name?" I asked to distract his attention away from me.

"We do not use a surname as you are accustomed. My full name is, Lachlan Belean Elgin," he said with a formal bow.

I arched a single eyebrow. "And?"

He grinned. "Belean means *arrow* and Elgin means *white.*"

"A white arrow from the land of endless lakes," I said, eyes widening.

He chuckled. "I can honestly say that I have never heard my name phrased quite that way. What I do know; you are number one on my, 'I Want You List'."

I laughed this time. "It's the 'Top Ten Most Wanted List'."

"I believe that is what I just said." He took another tiny step backward and made to turn away.

"Noooooo," I moaned louder. There was a hopeful expression on my face until a brilliant light danced toward us, landing on Lachlan's shoulder.

"Hey, can I get one of those silver ear thingies again?"

His eyes narrowed. "I venture to say they are not in a giving mood."

"You're probably right," I said, frowning.

"I want to stay," he said, only our fingertips touching.

All I could do is nod. I understood but I didn't like it. *And snap!* just like that, he disappeared around the corner. That was twice today but I knew there'd be a lot more of this in my future.

I went inside to face Paden and Ccri. An hour later, I felt more like myself after eating a bowl of stew and sipping two mugs of hot, strong tea. I think we were on the third rehash of the assorted details. I sat on the tufted and tasseled chair, wrapped in the woolen throw with some type of ointment slathered across my knuckles, glistening in the firelight.

"Certainty you would, Emily," Paden said, looking especially stern. "Armed with the perspective of hindsight we would all choose to fight our battles differently. The question you must ask yourself is, 'Did I make the best decision at the time with the information at hand?'" He leaned forward. "And I am here to tell you that your answer to this question must always be, 'Yes, I did!' Any other response is unacceptable. Learn from your mistakes, and move on. This is the true litmus test of life."

I rearranged the woolen throw, trying not to think about how much pain and worry I'd caused them.

"I have watched you grow in your understanding and comprehension of The Accordance during your time on Arden," Ccri said, glancing at Paden. "Undoubtedly, I would have preferred that you skipped the part where you experienced firsthand why we adhere to such a strict set of tested procedures."

There was a pause in the conversation. I knew I had to say one more time, "People died because of me and…and… Orlaith."

I heard the remorse in her voice even before Ccri said the words aloud. "Often when we fight for what we believe in, loss of life is the price that must be paid," she said, fiddling with the folds in her skirt, not really seeing me. "Knowing Lachlan, I am sure he handled the situation with minimal casualties. We are grateful to him for your safe return."

'Were you expecting an uneventful extraction?' he'd asked me. You bet I did. Everything I'd experienced since landing in this fantasy world was so outrageous that I often wondered if I was an avatar in a gaming universe. But, this was no game; there were deadly consequences for your actions.

A Seren flitted into the room through an open window for the third time. Paden got to his feet. "I do not think I can stall them any longer."

My stomach dropped. He and Lachlan were going to have to take the fall for me.

"Perhaps a warm bath," Ccri suggested after Paden left.

I looked her straight in the eye. "How? How will I ever be able to step into the water again?"

"You put your mind to it," she said.

I sat on the rock ledge, mustering the courage to slip into the warm swirling water for two reasons. First, I knew that from now on whenever I put a pinkie toe into the water, I need to be crystal clear about what I'm doing. I never ever wanted to end up on Hidde or any place like it again. Ever. Second, this was Orlaith's room. That put a whole new spin on things. How brave of Paden and Ccri to let me stay in the first place.

'Emily dear, it has been a pleasure to have someone in the house,' Ccri had said. 'Orlaith had not lived here for several years. First, she was away at Coalescence, and then she and Jokull lived in a house in the village.'

Still, it'd be difficult to sink into the same swirling water, stare at the same flower-strewn rock wall, and not feel something. I stood up, dropped the towel on the ledge, and slid down into the water, making sure to keep a body part unsubmerged at all times. No point in taking any chances.

After the bath, I slipped on the newly laundered, lace-collared nightgown and robe that Ccri had kindly arranged across the foot rail of the canopy bed. The weather would turn cool tonight. After the last few days, I very much wanted to stay warm. Okay, that was a big fat lie. I wanted Lachlan to stop by but I didn't want it to look like I was waiting for him.

Paden and Ccri had gone to bed immediately after Paden returned. I basically had the place to myself. I sat in the courtyard connected to my room. The temperature dropped so I went back inside and tip-toed down the hallway to the open-space living area. I threw a couple more logs on the fire, snuggled into the corner of the sofa, and covered my legs with the woolen throw. I didn't want to, and I really tried not to, but at some point, I must've nodded off.

I dreamed the most delicious dream, something to do with vanilla, sea foam, and feather pillows. From somewhere dreamy, I thought I heard someone saying my name. Lachlan was watching me intently when I opened my eyes. "Hey you," he said in a low voice. "Nazca informed me you were sleeping in here by the fire. I did not know if that meant you were waiting for me."

I smiled. So, he still had her checking on me. "I tried. I really tried. The firelight, the quiet, it was too much."

He wore a sable colored tunic, his slightly damp hair falling across his shoulder. I combed a hand through my sleep-tousled hair, causing the long strands to *swoosh* across my cheek, and scooted into a sitting position in the sofa corner. I tucked my legs and lifted the woolen throw.

Intrigued, he raised a brow, settling comfortably into the space I'd just made for him, resting his arm on the sofa back. With the most natural of movements, his fingertips lazily found the lace seamed around the collar of the nightgown.

The butterflies in my stomach took notice.

"How bad was it?" I asked, pleased that my voice sounded so steady, so mild, while my heart pounded so fiercely in my chest.

"Not too surprising. We knew that Jokull would try something foolish at some point."

"It's so much more complicated than I ever realized. I guess that's the one thing my little excursion to Hidde showed me."

Lachlan leaned his head against the sofa back, a faraway look in his eyes. "You have no idea."

"I'm in your debt, you know," I whispered. He tilted his head sideways. "For saving my life."

"If I am not mistaken, I believe there is some type of reward involved."

I sighed. "Is that customary on Arden?"

"Why, yes," he said with a sly smile.

"And exactly what type of reward are we talking about?" I asked, sitting upright and running a hand across his shoulder.

His eyes closed. "Let me think about that for a moment."

Maybe it was the firelight, maybe it was the fact that he did save my life today, or maybe it was just because I'd always wanted to do this. Anyway, deciding to be brave for once, I leaned in and slid a finger down his cheek, rough with stubble, yet still amazingly soft to the touch. I took my time, running my hand across his face, memorizing every curve, every dimple, and every furrow. "I think I know what type of reward I desire," he whispered, opening his eyes.

Lachlan tucked his hair behind his ears, reached over, and gathered the bodice of the linen robe in each of his hands. With a deliberate intent, he pulled me closer to him. I sensed his powerful drive with every fiber of my being. Sliding his nose across my bare shoulder bone, and then up into the crook of my neck, Lachlan lowered his head. I saw his eyes deepen until his lips found mine.

I poured myself into this kiss. He kissed me back with such fierce intensity that I swear I felt Arden spinning on its axis, whirling us through the galaxy at the speed of light. That is until he loosened his embrace, a little.

I felt the change in the air like an impending thunderstorm. Now that I had him in my arms, I wanted this moment to last forever. "We need to talk," he said, his soft lips moving against mine.

I'd been braced to hear those words but it was a blow nonetheless. I plucked the question from the irrational section of my brain. "You're sending me back to Earth?" Unfortunately, he nodded. "Not even one more day?"

"We leave again tomorrow," he said with that official edge he gets. "I went through all of the arguments but your presence here on Arden violates the treaty. Earth is so protected that even Jokull would never risk confronting the full force of The Accordance. I could not justify you staying. It is a good place for you until these issues are resolved."

"So, basically, you're saying that I'll be out of everyone's hair."

"For some reason," he said in a low but determined voice, "you still seem unclear about my feelings for you."

"I know that I bring a lot of complications to the table."

"Or a breath of fresh air…depending on your perspective," he said, lifting a finger to trace my pouty mouth. "Regardless, the decision is final."

I blew out a flustered breath, "That's it, then?"

He shook his head slightly. "Are you giving up on us? After all the paths we traveled together these past few weeks, not to mention today."

I arched my neck to meet his unrelenting gaze. "Do I have a choice?"

"Emily, there is nothing but choices in front of us. We have time to take all of the wrong turns, and then make them right." He pulled away slightly, appraising my face. "Do you not agree?"

I could tell this time that he expected an answer. I deliberated for a moment. My answer—I hugged him tight and buried my face into his shoulder.

δ^+

Pulling on the denim cut-offs and the tank-top after weeks of wearing only long dresses was shocking. Several generations of ingrained southern manners meant that I felt compelled to straighten the room in order to leave a good final impression. I'd folded and arranged DeRenne's clothes into neat piles across the crisply made bed. I leaned down, grabbed the leather skimmers, stirring to life a myriad of memories, and felt very sad. Everything around is really so beautiful. Why didn't I take the time to notice before now instead of always trying to figure out the next step? Why do we wait until it's time to leave to notice the small things around us only when they're about to slip through our fingers?

I remembered how confused I felt those first few hours standing in this very room; doubly so after learning that there are those on Earth who are aware of intergalactic water travel and The Accordance. And after my trip to Hidde, I feel even more conflicted now that I know the Universe is filled with turmoil. I sighed. It's a lot to take in.

I walked over to the rock outcrop and bubbling pool of water. I sat on the ledge and dipped a hand in the warm water, frantic thoughts racing through my mind like the sound of wind chimes on a breezy day. An English teacher once said that a story isn't any good unless one of the main characters dies. In the end, this story had more death than I ever imagined possible. Moreover, three deaths were a direct result of my time spent on Arden.

I never ever saw myself in any scenario that would come close to a single death, let alone three. And until this morning, I didn't realize that three other deaths occurred before my character even joined the story; Orlaith and her unborn child, and Lachlan and DeRenne's father.

Those deaths tipped the first domino, cascading forward a series of events that can never be put right again, culminating in the confrontation with Jokull. That single convergence blurred an already shaky line, changing everything for Arden, and putting my friends in even greater danger.

I frowned. The desolate mood following my parents' divorce and my anger at my father for turning our family upside-down threatened me again. And then I thought about the new world I'd fashioned for myself after the move to Atlanta, reluctantly, and the unreal world I discovered on here on Arden. Were I being overly objective, which I really wasn't in the mood for, I'd have to admit that Lachlan was right when he said that I didn't take things with a proper amount of seriousness. But let's face it, who in this fantasy world could?

He was wrong though when he said that I was safer back on Earth. I knew too much to look at Earth with the same old eyes, not to read a double meaning into any new political decision, or to wonder if the strange family that moved into the neighborhood is relocating for The Accordance.

What I do know now is that all of these worlds are a part of my personal story, and the perspective I've gained over these last few weeks will determine the new storyline. I can choose to live in fear or to live a better version of myself—the version everyone on Arden sees in me. There's the silver lining to my time spent here.

The muffled footsteps in the courtyard signaled my departure. I stood, walked over to the bedside table, grabbed Pop's stone, the jeweled barrette, and the twig pen Ccri gave me, shoving them into the back pocket of the denim cut-offs. I laid a hand on the door jamb and took a moment to look around the room one last time before walking outside, and closing the door behind me.

Lachlan stood in the courtyard wearing his mission uniform, the fabric pixelating a neutral taupe. He was keeping all of his emotions in check. Wish that I could say the same. "I forgot those were your Earth clothes," he said, his eyebrows rising in approval.

I tucked the tank-top into the waistband of the shorts, feeling suddenly self-conscious. His comment meant that he did remember our encounter on the granite step at the traveling pool in the village the day I arrived to Arden. "Hopefully, my flip-flops are still next to the creek back on Earth," I said to change the subject.

"Are flip-flops a type of shoe?" he asked, assessing my bare feet.

"Yes. They make a *flip-flop* sound when you walk; hence the name."

Standing there, gazing at him, knowing this is the last time I'd see him for who knows how long, I felt the lump in the back of my throat double in size. Neither of us made a move or said anything, the unspoken words flying back and forth between us arguing the same questions out to their logical conclusion. The sound of Shaw coming around the corner broke the silence. He looked like he really didn't want to be the person delivering the message. "Everyone is waiting," he said, turning around for a quick escape.

"It's not fair," I huffed.

With only a cool breeze separating us, Lachlan took two steps forward, closing the gap. "It is not over," he said, towering over me.

"But?"

"*Shush*," he exhaled, slowly. "Emily, you think too much. Forget your head, listen with your heart. Watch the clouds streaming by at a furious rate exposing all of the possibilities." He had a look in his eyes of someone who had faith in the endless possibilities. "You must choose to enjoy the ride instead of constantly stopping to see what is going wrong. If you take the time, the view is actually quite wonderful."

"It's how my brain operates," I said, justifying my impending bad mood.

Lachlan dropped his face to the level of my eyes, holding my gaze. "Have a little faith," he said, trailing a single finger down my bare right arm. He grasped my right hand, turned it palm up, and placed his hand on top of mine. When he moved his hand away, there was a small velvet drawstring pouch, mingled in hues of blue, resting in my palm. I stared in awe at the embroidered gold, silver, and copper interlocking triangles. The Water emblem—the emblem of our shared lineage.

"Open this after you return to Earth," he said in that bossy tone he gets. Before I could stall him any longer, he touched my elbow and turned me to the path leading away from the courtyard. There'd be no going back; he'd switched into the official mode.

Shaw, DeRenne, Paden, and Ccri waited for us near the small traveling pool at the back of the house. Like Lachlan, DeRenne and Shaw wore their mission uniforms implying that as soon as I left Arden, they would too.

Paden and Ccri insisted on escorting me back to Earth. In the end, I'd agreed. I would never step out from the water if Lachlan was beside me.

"I will get this started," Shaw said, giving me a quick hug. "Try not to find yourself in any predicaments while on Earth. We will not be there to save you this time."

"Yeah, yeah," I said. "Earth is such a hotbed of intergalactic turmoil."

"Ah…ah," Shaw mumbled, looking worried. "You better be careful what you wish for."

I gave him a friendly jab in the arm and tried to look confident. "I'll be fine."

After Lachlan, saying goodbye to DeRenne would be next to impossible. I told myself that I wouldn't cry but as soon as we embraced, tears welled in both of our eyes. "Thank you for being my guide, and my friend," I whispered.

"No, thank you. I was able to experience my world from your perspective. To see yourself and the ones you love in a whole new light is truly a gift. And," she managed a grin, "I so treasured having another girl around."

"Friends like you come along once in a lifetime," I said, and my voice cracked on the last word.

"I made this for you," she said. I could tell that she was also having a hard time keeping her emotions in check. She handed me a slender, tapered candle made of eight or ten different colored layers. "Sort of my specialty. I capture the scent in the wax from some of the places you visited. When you burn each layer, it should remind you of Arden."

"You have no idea, how special…" I said, taking the candle from her hand. Staring into each other's eyes for a brief moment, an understanding that only girls share passed between us. I nodded once, turned, and walked to stand between Paden and Ccri.

"We will remain in the water to ensure everything is in order," Paden said.

Nazca zoomed out from the forest canopy, hovering in the air, shimmering in the sunlight. I threw her a grateful smile. She would guide us through the various twists and turns, keeping the time discrepancy as close as possible.

"Emily, are you ready to leave?" Ccri asked in a motherly voice.

"One more second," I said, glancing over my shoulder. I wanted Lachlan to know that he should always expect a backward glance from me.

He stood firm, assuring me with his steadfast presence, a pale violet billowing across his mission uniform. A faint smile crossed my lips to let him know that I was taking a leap of faith, and betting on us.

"I'm ready," I said, confident the water would carry me home.

www.ingramcontent.com/pod-product-compliance
Lightning Source LLC
Chambersburg PA
CBHW050552260626
47157CB00002B/535

* 9 7 8 1 6 2 7 4 7 1 8 6 2 *